THE PUPPETEER

THE PUPPETEER
TIMOTHY WILLIAMS

SOHO
CRIME

Published by
Soho Press, Inc.
853 Broadway
New York, NY 10003

Library of Congress Cataloging-in-Publication Data

Williams, Timothy.
The puppeteer / Timothy Williams.

ISBN 978-1-61695-462-8
eISBN 978-1-61695-463-5
1. Police—Italy—Fiction. 2. Murder—Investigation—Fiction.
3. Corruption—Italy—Fiction. I. Title.
PR6073.I43295P87 2014
823'.914—dc23   2014019055

Printed in the United States of America

10 9 8 7 6 5 4 3 2 1

a tutti gli amici del Centomiglia

a
Gege
Emilio
Chicco
Francesco
Tito
Bruno
e le tre tettone.

Glossary

AI LAGHI: to the lakes

"AMOR, DAMMI QUEL FAZZOLETTINO": "Love, Give Me That Handkerchief," a Italian song popularized by actor-singer Yves Montand in 1963

AUTOSTRADA: highway

BORGO GENOVESE: Genovese village

BUONGIORNO: hello, good morning

CAPITANO: captain

COMMISSARIO: commissioner

CONTADINA: woman from the countryside

DIRETTO: direct, nonstop

DOTTOR: doctor

FERRAGOSTO: the 15th of August, the Feast of the Assumption of Mary

GIRO D'ITALIA: an annual Italian bicycle race

GIUDICE ISTRUTTORE: investigating judge/magistrate

GRANO DURO: durum wheat

GRAPPA: a dry, clear grape brandy

IL TEMPO: the weather, the time

ISTITUTO ZOOTECNICO: Agricultural Institute

JUVENTUS: a professional Italian soccer club based in Turin

LA TEDESCA: the German (fem.)

LASCIA O RADDOPPIA: *Leave It or Double It*, an Italian game show that aired from 1955-1959

LICEO: high school

LO SCIOCCO: the fool

LUNGOLAGO: road around a lake

MARINAIO: sailor, seaman

MATURITÀ: maturity

METROPOLITANA: subway

MONTE BALDO: a mountain in the Italian Alps that runs through the provinces of Trentino and Verona

NUCLEO POLITICO: political segment of the Carabinieri

OMERTÀ: code of silence

PALAZZO: building, palace

PALAZZO DI GIUSTIZIA: courthouse

PIAZZA: plaza

PER FAVORE: please

POLICLINICO: hospital

POPOLO D'ITALIA: The People of Italy, an Italian newspaper founded by Mussolini in 1914

PRONTO SOCCORSO: first aid

PROVINCIA PADANA: an Italian newspaper, also known as *La Padana*

QUATTRO STAGIONI: literally "four seasons," a pizza divided into four sections with different ingredients, traditionally artichokes, mozzarella, ham and olives

SCUOLA SUPERIORE: high school

SERVIZIO ESTERO: foreign service

SESTO: sixth

SEZIONE ARCHIVI: departmental archives

SIGNORA: madam, lady

SIGNORINA: miss, young lady

SINDACO FERMI: the previous mayor

SOCIETÀ SICULA PER L'ELETTRICITÀ: Sicilian electric company

STADIA: sports stadium, coliseum

TAVOLA CALDA: cafeteria

TENENTE: lieutenant

URBANISTICA: city planning

VENERABILE MAESTRO: Venerable Master

VENTIQUATTRO MAGGIO: May 24th

VIA XX SETTEMBRE: street name meaning "Road of September 20th" after the date of the Capture of Rome in 1870, the final step to Italian unification

VIALE RIMEMBRANZA: street name meaning "Avenue of Remembrance"

VITA E SORRISI: life and smiles

ZIO: uncle

1: Guerino

"AMERICA?" THE BARMAN raised his eyebrows.

"She's been there now for four months."

There was a butter dish and a couple of fresh bread rolls on the tray. Guerino placed them on the table. "On holiday?"

"She works for a pharmaceutical company." Trotti added, "In New York."

"Lucky girl."

"After thirty years of marriage, I no longer think of my wife as a girl."

The other man put his head back and laughed. "Wait till you're my age, Commissario—then everybody under fifty is an adolescent." He took the jug from the tray and poured out some coffee. He then added milk. "You're staying up at the Villa Ondina?"

"I've just arrived."

"We rarely see any of you now. The villa's been empty since Agnese's parents died. You should come and see us more often, Commissario. When you need a rest, you know that there's nowhere better than the lake." The older man looked out over the flat surface of the water. "And there's nowhere more beautiful on Garda than Gardesana."

There was no wind and the early morning mist still hovered a few meters above Lake Garda. The sun was showing over the shoulder of Monte Baldo.

Bar Centomiglia was a simple, unpretentious place. Not sophisticated—a far cry from the groomed elegance of Milan or Rome. Here there was just the smell of fresh coffee, a couple of rows of chairs that Guerino set out in the summer months, and a reassuring sameness to the décor—advertisements for vermouth and perhaps an out-of-date notice of films in the parish hall.

The orange trees were already coming into blossom.

"I've been very busy," Trotti said.

"The robbery at the Banco San Matteo?"

Trotti turned. "You know about that?"

"We get the papers here, too." He whistled under his breath. "I saw that you were in charge of enquiries. Banca San Matteo—and a man murdered."

"Nobody was murdered," Trotti said. "The manager was shot in the leg."

Guerino was leaning against the side of the table and he held the empty tray under his arm. He put his head to one side as if he expected Trotti to say more.

Trotti looked at the lake in silence.

Guerino asked, "How's Pioppi?"

"At university."

"Not married, then?"

Trotti's smile was tired. "I don't think she's interested in men."

"Except for her father." Guerino touched Trotti's shoulder. "Even when she was a little girl, she adored you."

"That was a long time ago."

"A long time ago," Guerino repeated in his mocking Roman accent and went back into the bar.

As Trotti ate his breakfast, he watched the sun climb into the sky.

From out on the lake came a mechanical beating sound. Later the mist began to lift and he saw the *Giuseppe Verdi*, the black smoke at her funnel almost vertical, working towards the shore.

There were a few cars parked here and there along the

lakeside, a double row of orange trees and the well-kept flower beds. At the jetty, the old captain—exactly as Trotti remembered him—was waiting for the steamboat to pull alongside.

A man came and sat on the same long bench as Trotti; he muttered "Buongiorno" and opened the paper, which he started to read. When Guerino appeared, the new arrival scarcely looked up as he ordered a cup of coffee.

He held the paper in front of his face and his forehead was wrinkled in concentration. He needed a shave; he did not look like a villager. He was wearing a suit that was slightly crumpled. No tie.

Guerino was whistling under his breath—an old fascist tune that he had probably learned in Abyssinia—when he brought the coffee. He placed the cup on the table; the man grunted a perfunctory thanks.

On the front page of the newspaper there was the picture of a battleship.

"War," Guerino said. "They had Kenya, the English—they had most of Africa." He tapped his chest. "I was in Kenya for four years, a prisoner of the British—and they had to throw it all away. And now they're going to war over a few wretched islands in the middle of the ocean that nobody in his right mind would even want to visit."

The man behind the newspaper glanced at Trotti. Their eyes met.

Trotti asked, "How's Donatella, Guerino?"

(Sometimes, in the first years of marriage, to escape from the oppressive atmosphere of the Villa Ondina, Trotti used to take the bicycle and cycle into the village. It was in this bar that he had first met Donatella. In those days she was blonde, with short bobbed hair and an easy friendly smile. Later—and not yet twenty years old—she married a boy from the village.)

Again the smile on Guerino's face and the Roman gesture. "Donatella? She's a very beautiful grandmother."

"Grandmother?" Trotti frowned before smiling. "Then you are a great-grandfather, Guerino?"

"Here." He took his wallet from a trouser pocket and pulled

out the photograph. "Over three kilos—and Valeria had him baptized Guerino, after me." He placed the Polaroid photograph on the table and his work-worn finger touched the pink image of a newborn baby. "She says he looks just like me."

The *Giuseppe Verdi* let out a mournful hoot as it moved towards the quay. An officer standing on the deck threw the rope to the Capitano, who caught it and looped it round a bollard. Both men spoke in dialect and the Capitano laughed. A gangplank was heaved into place and a couple of passengers stepped gingerly down towards dry land.

The woman had grey hair. The man wore a grey suit and a leather case hung from his neck—probably a camera. He held the woman's hand.

Guerino shrugged. "I'll be needing more than a couple of German tourists this year if I'm to redecorate this bar."

"The Centomiglia is all right as it is."

"A new coat of paint, some new chairs—and a new coffee machine."

"It will lose all its character."

"Tourists aren't interested in character."

A metal-green Mercedes came down the quayside towards the couple. At first, Trotti thought it was a taxi; the windows were tinted a dark grey. The exhaust pipe rattled.

Still holding the woman by the hand, the elderly German stepped backwards to avoid being run over.

The village was coming awake. The mist had vanished and a breeze had come up. In the small port the bare masts had started a rhythmic rocking movement.

"More coffee, Commissario?"

"Still, after all this time—you still call me Commissario?" Trotti shook his head as he held the photograph out for Guerino.

A young man climbed out of the passenger seat of the Mercedes.

The rear propeller of the *Giuseppe Verdi* began churning the water, the hull swung away from the land. Trotti stood up but it was too late. The German woman screamed and Trotti saw the husband turn to look at her in surprise.

The face hidden behind a red scarf. Bent knees, the clasped hands coming up slowly.

A gun, a P38.

Instinctively, Trotti threw himself to the ground. In his hand, he was still holding the photograph. The baby Guerino.

2: Mercedes

Wurlitzer jukebox.

Trotti had forgotten about it—an old, chrome-plated machine standing in the corner. He could remember Pioppi as a little girl, pestering him for coins to play her favorite songs: Bobby Solo and Fausto Leali.

His cheek was now pushed hard against the cold metal. Old cigarette stubs lay on the stone floor.

A first explosion—and plaster falling to the ground.

Another shot, then silence. The man had dropped his newspaper and was beside Trotti, behind the tipped-up table. He was crouching. One hand had gone to the waist of his trousers, to the butt of a pistol.

Third explosion.

The woman was still screaming. There was a sound of running feet.

The man did not draw the pistol. His hand was strangely bent, the palm upward. A rasping noise in his throat.

Trotti's right hand was covered with a widening circle of blood. He moved forwards and peered over the upset table. Coffee had splashed across the floor.

The *Giuseppe Verdi* had cast off and was moving south. Trotti saw the Mercedes going along the lakeside and gathering speed.

Trotti took the man's gun and he could feel no precise pain

as he climbed to his feet. He fell, got up again and placing his weight on the table, moved unsteadily forward.

Froth at her mouth, the German woman still screamed, her head thrown back. Her husband was trying to quiet her.

Trotti broke into a run.

The Mercedes had reached the end of the Lungolago. Trotti shouted. Red lights flashed as the car braked, took the corner and moved out of Trotti's line of vision.

Only one road out of Gardesana and the Mercedes would have to take it to get away.

He cut through the cobbled alley. Out of training and getting old. The alley was chill and smelled of cork and old wine. Trotti ran up the incline, leaning forwards, his breath coming with difficulty. He nearly fell when he came out into the main street.

The Mercedes was heading straight for him. Just the brief glimpse of the baker's boy coming down the hill on his bicycle. No pedestrians, a few cars parked along the via XX Settembre.

The square metallic radiator grill was bearing down on him.

Trotti jumped back into the alley and fell headlong. The side of his head hit the cobbles.

"Are you all right?"

"Look at the number plate." Trotti clambered to his feet.

"You're bleeding."

"Of course I'm bleeding." Blood ran down the front of his sweater. Trotti looked down and a long, thin string of rheum and blood poured from his mouth.

"You've been shot." The baker's boy was rooted to the spot. He stood gaping foolishly.

"Get the number."

"You've been shot," the boy repeated.

Trotti shouted, "Never seen a bleeding nose before?" He began to tremble.

"Get the Carabinieri. Hurry, damn you."

PC—Piazza. A Piacenza registration.

"Take your bike, will you, and get the Carabinieri." He took out his wallet. "Look, look—Pubblica Sicurezza. Hurry up."

A Piacenza number: Trotti had seen the two letters. But not the numbers.

The baker's boy did not move.

"Hurry!"

Without taking his eyes from Trotti, the boy scrambled on to a heavy bicycle. A few rolls of fresh bread lay scattered on the ground.

"Hurry, damn you."

The boy stood on the pedal and the bicycle moved away. Looking over his shoulder, he continued to stare at Trotti with gaping mouth.

Trotti walked back to the bar. Blood had started to drip onto his shoes.

3: Mareschini

"YOU KNEW HIM?"

The office was strangely bare; freshly painted walls, with a discreet crucifix on the far wall, a framed photograph of Pertini, filing cabinets and an immobile electric fan. On the desk, the cup of coffee was growing cold.

"Grappa, Commissario?"

Without waiting for a reply, the Captain produced a label-less bottle from a cupboard. He poured a few drops into the cup. Smiling, he said, "A northern habit." In the same voice, he repeated his question. "Did you know the victim?" He screwed the cap back on the bottle.

"No."

"You'd never seen him before?"

"I don't think so."

"You don't think so?"

In different circumstances, Trotti would have been amused by the man's slowness.

"But he spoke to you, Commissario."

"He came into the bar and he said good morning. I merely replied."

"Ah." The eyes were very dark and Trotti wondered whether the Carabiniere was as slow as he wished to appear. His name was Mareschini and he spoke with a sluggish, southern accent. A good looking man, still trim and impressive in his dark uniform.

Only a few years from retirement. The white hair was short and brushed back, the firm jaw well-shaven.

"You've looked at his documents?"

Trotti frowned. "Documents?"

"His wallet. You're a policeman, you're . . ."

"I had no time to do anything. Your men arrived almost immediately. Very efficient, I must say."

Mareschini lowered his head in acknowledgment of the compliment.

It was the first time that Trotti had spoken to Mareschini, although he had in the past seen him in the village—drinking white wine at Guerino's or walking along the Lungolago. They were all the same, the Carabinieri who ended up at Gardesana. A good quiet posting. No crime other than people tipping their garbage into the lake—or the occasional German tourist taking his motor launch beyond the speed limit. An easy job in a quiet village where the well-cut dark uniform could easily impress; a good place to live before returning to the more familiar countryside of Sicily.

"Strange that he should be murdered beside a policeman." Mareschini smiled slowly.

Trotti shrugged.

"A journalist." Mareschini looked at Trotti, waiting for his reaction. "A journalist who carried a gun. From his identity card, he would appear to be thirty-seven years old." A movement of the hands—there were dark hairs running along the edge of the pale skin. "He was thirty-seven years old. Name of Maltese." He looked up. "Mean anything to you?"

Trotti shook his head and drank the coffee.

"And you're sure he didn't speak to you?"

"Have you found the car?"

"A stolen Mercedes."

"Have you found the man's vehicle?"

The Carabiniere frowned.

"How do you think this man—Maltese—arrived in Gardesana?" Trotti said.

The policeman nodded. "We're looking into it, Commissario Trotti—but for the moment, no car has been identified."

They had let Trotti wash his hands and face, and later a matronly woman—perhaps Mareschini's wife—had cleaned the caked blood from around his nostrils. The patch of blood on his trousers had dried and turned a sticky black.

"A coincidence, then." There was irritation in Mareschini's voice.

"What?" Trotti asked.

"A coincidence that of all the people in Italy, it was beside you—an important and highly respected member of the forces of order, Commissario—that he was shot to death."

"Yes," Trotti said. "A coincidence."

Mareschini stood up, and with his hands behind his back he started pacing backwards and forwards. He kept his eyes on the door. "But perhaps you recognized the man with the gun?"

"No."

He looked up. "Can you describe him?"

"There were two men—you should ask the tourists from the boat. They were closer, they had a better view."

"Please describe the murderer, Commissario."

"Average height, dark hair—and a scarf over his face. That's all I can remember. I saw the gun—the glint of the sunlight and then the woman began to scream." He raised his shoulders. "I tried to protect myself."

"Of course. And how did Maltese react?"

A brief smile. "I didn't look. I didn't imagine that it was him they were aiming at."

Mareschini frowned. "I see." He rubbed his chin and then came to a halt by the window.

The Carabinieri barracks were new and had been well designed, nestling into the olive groves of the lakeside hills. Through the open window, Trotti saw the descending layers of the rooftops, all a dull terracotta. Beyond them, a hydrofoil was cutting through the water, coming south, leaving a wide, white wake across the lake. Like a wound.

"You believe the assassin was aiming for you, Commissario?"

"I have been fired at before, Capitano. I didn't stop to ask any questions—at my age, I no longer care to know the answers.

I merely dropped to the ground . . . and gave myself a bloody nose."

"The assassin was aiming for you?"

Trotti repressed a sigh. "I don't know who he was aiming for, but the man, Maltese, was killed with two bullets. One of them must have touched his heart, I think. A professional job, Capitano." Trotti paused, then added, "He died in my arms."

"Ah!" Mareschini turned his back on the window and leaned against the sill, the trace of a smile on his lips.

An unimaginative provincial policeman who had probably never seen anything more distressing than a car accident and who was now trying to prove his professionalism. Trying to appear brisk and efficient.

Trotti could feel the dry blood on his trousers.

"And before he died, did this man say anything?"

"Capitano Mareschini, you've told me that the Nucleo Investigativo will soon be here from Brescia. I've already signed a written statement for you—these are questions that you've already asked me. You know the answers. I'm beginning to think that you doubt what I've already told you."

"Commissario, please." An apologetic movement of the pale hands, and the thin smile. "Please remember that you're an eyewitness to a killing. A particularly bloody killing—not at all the sort of thing that we're used to in this little backwater. It's my duty . . ."

"The Nucleo Investigativo will be here any minute."

Mareschini nodded. He took a packet of cigarettes from his tunic pocket and offered it to Trotti, who shook his head. Mareschini carefully lit a cigarette and inhaled the first mouthful of smoke before speaking. "You're a policeman, Commissario."

Trotti finished the coffee.

"You're a policeman and I'm sure you know what it's like to have a feeling, a sensation that you can't quite identify but which your experience tells you is important. Something you should take into consideration."

Trotti's nod was scarcely perceptible.

"Can I ask you again, Commissario?"

"What?"

"Did Maltese say anything to you? You said he wasn't dead when you got back to the bar. You held him. You see, I've an impression"—again the shrug—"I've this impression that you're withholding something."

Three bullets. The first had hit the wall. The second had gone through the man's shoulder. The last had got into his chest, probably the heart. Trotti had seen the blood spurting, spreading further and further across the stones of the terrace. He had seen the face grow pale, he had felt the skin grow cold.

"I'm certain that in your rich experience, you've already worked with the Carabinieri. Admittedly here, this is only a small barracks. Not the big city, but . . ." He rubbed his chin thoughtfully, his eyes squinted in the blue tobacco smoke.

"I've signed my statement. I don't think I have anything else to add."

The hydrofoil had lost its speed and was settling down into the blue lake water. In a few seconds it would be alongside the jetty, opposite the Centomiglia.

In a quiet voice, Trotti said, "I arrived just as Guerino brought him a glass of water. He was thirsty—he said he was thirsty but the water ran over his face, he couldn't drink. We were waiting for the ambulance—people were pushing to see. The German woman was still screaming. And I held him in my arms."

"Did he say anything?"

"He was afraid of dying—I could see it in his eyes and he gripped my arm. But before he could say anything, the grip weakened." Trotti looked up at Mareschini and shrugged.

4: Villa Ondina

Trotti shivered.

Night was falling and the electric lamp, in the form of a glass flame, cast its wan light over the War Memorial.

"Goodnight," Trotti said as he climbed out of the Alfa Romeo. The driver did not reply—perhaps he did not like the Pubblica Sicurezza. Before Trotti had closed the door, the car started on a tight turn, and with the gentle rumble of the exhaust pipe, it disappeared into the via XX Settembre.

The wind had dropped. In the small lakeside port, the boats at anchor scarcely moved; no creaking of hull against hull, the masts were silent. So, too, was the lake, fast losing its somber color as a thin mist rose from the surface.

The Bar Centomiglia was closed. A neon light had been left on and cast a bluish glow over the tables and chairs and over the large stain on the stone slab near the wall.

Rope had been tied from chair to chair to prevent access. Guerino had taken in the tablecloths and the bar looked empty. Trotti wondered why Guerino had not washed the bloodstain away.

A sole Carabiniere stood there. He was smoking and his rifle was slung from his shoulder. From under the peaked cap, his eyes followed Trotti.

The Opel was where he had left it in the morning. Trotti unlocked it—his head ached from too much coffee, and the back of his throat was sore—and turned on the engine.

A slight deflection of the barrel and it would have been his blood smeared across the ground.

He drove to the Villa Ondina. The Opel ran silently along the viale Rimembranza, while the head beams moved along the smooth tarmac between the cypress trees. He drove past Mussolini's villa, now hidden behind a copse of trees.

A day wasted and then Mareschini had said, "Can you stay in Gardesana for couple of days?" With a sly smile, he had rubbed at his chin and, not even looking at Trotti, had added, "Nucleo Investigativo seem to have been held up in Brescia. They'll be here tomorrow."

At the Villa Ondina, Trotti climbed out and pushed open the iron gates. The stiffness of his bloodstained trousers pulled against the hairs on his legs. He took the Opel down the gravel drive and parked in front of the main door. The plastic Madonna was alight. The door was unlocked and he let himself in.

Trotti turned on all the lights.

The interior, still warm from a day of spring sunshine, smelled of floor polish and moth balls, and Trotti realized it was his first visit to the Villa Ondina since the previous summer. He turned on the television to give himself company.

Signora Baccoli—the contadina—had made supper for him. In the kitchen he lifted the inverted dish and smiled. Ham, melon, salad and gnocchi, which needed heating. Suddenly he felt very hungry.

The Villa Ondina had belonged to Agnese's father, who had made a fortune in pharmaceutical products for cattle. An unsmiling man, he had died ten years earlier. His wife, equally unsmiling and a devout Catholic in her last years, had waited seven years before following him to the family grave in Brescia.

Trotti undressed. His clothes were stiff with blood. He put them all in a plastic bag and tied the bag with a piece of string.

(Trotti had recognized the photograph.)

He could hear the mumble of the immersion heater. Signora Baccoli had turned it on.

(A coincidence, perhaps, that Maltese had a photograph of

the girl in his pocket. The same photograph that Trotti had seen in the Questura.)

Trotti shaved and then showered, letting the scalding water run against his skin until he began to feel the heat penetrate his body and the coldness within him.

The shower was still running, and the water was still hot, when the telephone rang. He had forgotten to take a towel and, in his haste, pulled the cover from the bed the contadina had prepared for him. He left a trail of wet prints down the marble stairs. "Where've you been?"

"Who's speaking?" Trotti asked and immediately regretted his own stupidity.

"Where've you been?" Repressed anger in her voice. "I've been trying to get through for the last twenty-four hours." Agnese's voice—her anger—was as clear as if she were phoning from the village.

"Where're you phoning from?"

"You tell me you'll be at the Villa and then you keep me waiting. Twenty-four hours, Piero." A slight echo along the line—or between the telephone and the satellite somewhere over the Atlantic. "You are really very inconsiderate at times."

"I was in the village."

Agnese laughed one of her unpleasant, mocking laughs. "With one of your women friends?"

"I was at the Carabinieri barracks."

"What on earth for?"

"It's not important."

"Of course not, Piero. After all, I'm just a silly woman. Why should you have to tell your wife what you've been doing? But that's the way it's always been, hasn't it?"

Trotti did not reply.

"Piero?"

"Did you get my letter?" he asked.

"Perhaps. I can't remember."

Not even the decency to lie.

Without stopping to catch her breath, Agnese went on, "I imagine you're enjoying yourself."

"I needed a rest."

"You never needed a rest when your wife wanted you to go to the Lake."

"Is your American company paying for this phone call?"

There was a silence during which he could hear her breathing.

"You've got a nerve, Piero."

"Is that what you phoned to tell me?"

"I need my diplomas." Her voice was brisk. "It's now two weeks since I asked you for them."

"I'll send them."

"Now, Piero, now."

"I've already got them out."

"I need them immediately—my university degree and my specialization diplomas. The Americans are in a hurry and you can't be bothered . . ."

"I'll post them on Monday."

"I'd ask Pioppi to do it for me—she's more reliable than you. But like you, she doesn't answer the telephone."

"Perhaps she's with the Nonna. She's working hard for her exam next week."

"Well, will you phone her and tell her to post them? I can't keep on wasting time and money on these phone calls."

"When do you think you'll be coming back, Agnese?"

Her brisk, efficient businesswoman voice. "Pack them properly. At Bertini's in via Stradella you can buy a plastic roll container. I don't want them arriving here in a thousand little pieces. Don't forget, Piero."

He did not reply.

"Well, can you do that—can you do something for your wife?"

"Pioppi's still not eating."

"She's got Nonna—and she's got you."

"She's refusing to eat."

"I know you can look after her. Listen, I'm going to hang up. I kiss you, Piero, and I kiss Pioppi. And remember, buy the container at Bertini's. Send everything airmail and registered post—I don't trust the Italian postal services." A sudden click and the receiver went dead.

The bedsheet was damp. Trotti shivered and set the phone down. But even when he got upstairs, found a towel and rubbed himself down, his hand was still shaking.

Half past seven—it was now dark outside and in Pearl River, New York, she was just back from lunch—lunch with her wealthy, American colleagues. Well-dressed men with tiepins and an impressive casualness about their easy wealth, their business accounts and their sleek, American cars.

He was cold.

Trotti found an old sweater in a cupboard. He put it on, along with a pair of corduroy trousers that smelled of moth balls.

The phone rang again.

"Sorry to bother you, Commissario. Pintini of the Brescia Nucleo Investigativo has just contacted me, saying he'll be here tomorrow with a team of investigators."

"What time?"

"I'm sorry to inconvenience you." There was no apology in Mareschini's voice. "I can send a car to pick you up at eight."

"I have my own car."

Mareschini hesitated; then his satisfaction won over his professionalism. "There's been a bit of difficulty with the prints."

"Prints?"

"After the photographs, the body was sent to the morgue in Salò. Routine prints were taken and checked on the computer." He added sententiously, "The Carabinieri central computers."

"And?"

"They were identified."

"Maltese had a criminal record?"

"I know nothing about Maltese—but the prints belong to a certain Ramoverde—Giovanni Ramoverde."

Trotti said nothing.

"Does that name mean anything to you?"

Still Trotti was silent.

"Giovanni Ramoverde was arrested in 1972 at the University of Milan."

"Arrested for what?"

"Rioting—impeding the forces of law in the course of their

duty. A suspended sentence." A humorless laugh. "You're sure you don't know the name, Commissario Trotti?"

Trotti did not reply.

"Then I'll see you here in the morning, Commissario?"

Trotti put the receiver down. Immediately, he picked it up again.

He dialed his home number. The distant telephone rang eight times.

Trotti went into the kitchen and without bothering to use a knife and fork, he hurriedly devoured the ham and melon. He ate some of the cold gnocchi.

He tried phoning Pioppi again. Then he turned out all the lights, turned off the television and left the Villa Ondina.

He climbed into the Opel.

5: Pavesi

THE LAKE, SILVER beneath the moon, was hidden by long sections of tunnel. Then the road opened out. The mountains fell behind. The silhouette of the cypress trees. The smell of the orange groves, the gentle hiss of the tires along the fast road. And in the distance, like another, distant country, the twinkling lights on the far side of the lake.

Trotti found a packet of Charms in the glove box, unwrapped one of the sweets and placed it in his mouth. Aniseed.

He skirted Salò, where already the corpse was cold in the hospital morgue; he took the Brescia road, turning right at the intersection with the Verona highway, and soon the lake was behind him, a silver reflection in his driving mirror, and then lost to sight behind the dark foothills. He drove past the marble quarries hacked into the hills. He felt that he was returning to Italy, leaving the lake behind him and coming back to the ugly, industrial plain. He glanced in the mirror. Nothing. He had the feeling that he was being followed.

Later, the head beams caught the sign post *Ai laghi* and he turned on to the main Milan/Venice highway. There was a smell of malt in the air; above the brewery on the outskirts of Brescia, white vapor poured from the stacks into the night sky.

The man was reluctant to take his money, reluctant to take his eyes from a small television set that he had installed in the toll booth. Without even glancing at Trotti he handed him the ticket and the Opel surged forward onto the autostrada. Eighty, ninety kilometers an hour, Trotti picked up speed.

From time to time, there were lights in his rear mirror. No car overtook him.

He turned on the radio.

The autostrada was empty. A few articulated trucks traveling ponderously towards Milan, and on the other side of the barrier there was the occasional set of yellow headlights—French trucks or perhaps tourists heading for an early holiday on the Adriatic.

La Forza del Destino. The radio crackled but it did not matter because Trotti knew the music. He had once taken Agnese to see it at the Verona arena. She was pregnant with Pioppi and she had fallen asleep on his shoulder. The moment came back to him with a brief, intense feeling of happiness. It was only a few days later that Dottor Belluno was found murdered.

1960—Trotti smiled to himself. He could still remember the dress that Agnese was wearing that night. He was still smiling and his fingers were following the rhythm of Verdi's music when he pulled into a service station just beyond the Bergamo exit.

The music had become an incomprehensible sound and he switched it off. PAVESI stood in bright neon letters, spanning the concrete bridge of the autostrada. He suddenly felt tired, all the fatigue of the last weeks coming back. He turned off the ignition, climbed out of the car.

Away from the lake, the air still held the chill of winter.

No other vehicle entered the car park.

"A strong coffee, please."

A bright bar, full of shadowless light, red and black plastic. The girl behind the counter nodded. She was wearing a uniform, with a cap on her bleached hair. She did not smile. The rims of her eyes were red as if she had been crying.

The bar was empty except for a couple of tourists—lovers, perhaps, who were quarrelling at a corner table. Two motorcycle helmets stood on the table beside the empty glasses. The boy wore heavy leather boots.

At the counter, Trotti took a cake from the revolving stand;

English plum cake in a hermetically sealed packet that advertised Mundial 82.

He sat down and waited for the girl to bring his coffee. His eyes felt gritty and he stared out at the passing traffic beyond the window. *La Forza del Destino*—the overture ran through his head and he could see in his own reflection on the glass the familiar, enigmatic smile of Ramoverde.

It had been on the day of the verdict and Ramoverde had come down the steps of the Palazzo di Giustizia supported on one side by his wife and on the other by his son. He had an angular face that the long trial had made weary. Before stepping into the waiting car he had looked up and seen Trotti. He had raised his hand in an almost imperceptible salute and the lips—until then devoid of any emotion—had broken into a thin smile of victory.

The same face.

Trotti drank the coffee after having emptied three spoonfuls of sugar into the small cup. Then he stood up, brushed away the crumbs of the plum cake, paid the girl and went out to the antiseptic lavatory. He felt less tired.

Outside, the air seemed to have grown colder. He pulled the old jacket about his shoulders and pulled up the collar. Then climbing into the car, he turned on the heater.

Mist had already formed on the windscreen.

"Turn right."

Something cold pushed against the back of Trotti's head.

6: Sardi

"WHAT D'YOU WANT?"

Trotti wondered how he had failed to notice the smell—bitter sweat, old tobacco and rancid wine.

"Keep your eyes on the road." The slow, slurring accent of a Sardinian peasant.

"What d'you want from me?"

The man struck him; a blow to the back of the head that surprised Trotti more than it hurt him.

"Drive—and keep quiet."

He did as he was told.

The lights of the autostrada fell behind and the car went along the narrow country road. The flat fields were empty. One or two hamlets, a church, a large farmyard with tractors naked beneath the sodium lamps, and then the countryside. Clouds had come up, and sometimes the moon revealed the lines of poplar trees.

"Turn here!"

"What d'you want?" His eyes had started to water.

"Turn here."

The headlights moved and held the image of an unsurfaced country road. Trotti drove slowly and the car bumped across the uneven surface.

"Leave the lights on and turn off the engine."

Trotti obeyed.

"Now get out."

The man slid from the backseat and as he moved, Trotti caught sight of the gun. It glinted.

Trotti got out of the car and the man hit him, fist across the face, then in the groin. Trotti fell to the ground.

Wurlitzer, Centomiglia, Fausto Leali.

A dream—a bad dream that was repeating itself.

"Stand up."

Trotti rolled on to his side, then collapsed again onto the ground.

"I said stand up."

He leaned against the wheel; it was covered with white mud. Hand on the hood, Trotti pulled himself into a half-standing position, his weight lying across the front of the car.

"Bastard!"

He had not seen the other man, he did not know whether he had been in the back of the Opel as well. He kicked Trotti in the ankle and he fell sideways.

(In the last ten years he had only once been back to the school at Padua where the Englishman with the broken nose gave lessons in self-defense and unarmed combat.)

Trotti tried to concentrate. Mucus and saliva poured from his nose and mixed with the salty taste of blood in his mouth.

The second man smelled of warm stables. He knelt down and took Trotti by the lapels. Behind the mask—a balaclava pulled down clumsily over his head—the eyes glinted with stupidity and pleasure. "Where's the money?"

Trotti managed to ignore the pain and there was a clearheadedness about his thinking. But before he could reply the man struck him hard, the harshness of his hand and the rings ripping at Trotti's cheek.

"Where's the money, you bastard? If you want to stay alive, tell me where the money is."

Trotti knew that they were going to kill him. He remembered the words of the Englishman—"Survival is a state of mind. It is the desire to stay alive and the determination to find the right way to do so"—and he knew he had little time to think.

"The money belongs to us. We're not going to allow a little

shit like you to get away without paying." They were standing over him and Trotti wondered why they bothered to wear masks. Sardinians, shepherds from Nuoro province. One kicked him in the ribs; then the other pulled him to his feet.

The Englishman had said, "There is a point beyond which the brain no longer cares." It had been in the gymnasium near the city walls. "It will send its message telling you that death is preferable. Don't allow it; only your brain can save you."

Mud, blood, the white loam wet against the palms of his hands. The smell of sheep and sweat. The smaller man took Trotti's arm and twisted it back until his nose was hard against the hood. The metal was warm.

Only his brain could save him, but he was tired, old and weak. The man released his hold and Trotti turned, and his lifted knee made sharp contact with the Sardinian's groin.

Commissario Trotti, fifty-five years old and now going bald, bunched his fist and struck out at the second Sardinian. He missed, but in stepping back, the taller man stumbled and fell.

Mud under his foot and his breath coming in short, painful gasps, Trotti started to run.

7: Lab coat

"Commissario?"

He was wearing an anorak and he had shaved away his mustache; he looked plumper than when Trotti had last seen him.

"Commissario?"

If Magagna had not been wearing his American sunglasses, Trotti would have had difficulty recognizing him.

"Well?"

He had been sitting on a steel chair; he now stood up and emptied the contents of his pockets onto the bed. "I bought you this." Half a dozen packets of boiled sweets.

"A rich man."

"One of the advantages of working in the Pubblica Sicurezza—easy money and fast promotion."

Trotti smiled; then he winced in pain as they shook hands. "Unwrap one of those sweets for me."

"What flavor?"

"Eighteen months in Milan and you've forgotten that rhubarb has always been my favorite?"

Magagna took one of the packets, removed the wrapping and placed the sweet in Trotti's mouth. "Looks as if you've been in a fight."

"I walked into a door."

"Violent doors here in Piacenza."

"You can't be too careful."

"In Piacenza?" Magagna was from Pescara and considered anywhere else insignificant. The smile vanished. "Who did it, Commissario?"

Trotti's jaw ached and as he moved his head, there was a sharp pain in his neck. "I'm trying to remember."

"They clearly didn't like you."

Trotti clicked the sweet against his teeth. "How did you know I was here?"

"The Piacenza police find a naked man staggering across the road bridge at six clock in the morning—you think that's the sort of thing that goes unnoticed?"

"Six o'clock? And what's the time now?"

"I was driving up from Bologna when I heard. After all these years, I felt that you were worth the detour."

"What time is it?"

"You've been under sedation for fourteen hours—they thought you had a concussion."

"The time, Magagna?"

The other man looked at his watch and Trotti noticed that it was an expensive Swiss affair in rolled gold. "Half past midnight."

"Christ . . . and Pioppi?"

The white door opened and a nurse entered. A middle-aged woman with grey hair and a harsh, narrow face. She wore a silver crucifix in the lapel of her spotless laboratory coat. "You're not supposed to have visitors." She placed her hand on the back of Magagna's chair. "With liquid that could well be spinal fluid coming out of my mouth I'd make sure I was getting some rest instead of getting myself excited." She spoke in a flat monotone.

"Pubblica Sicurezza," Magagna said lamely and fumbled with his card.

The lips pulled tight, as if activated by a purse string. She turned on her heel and left the room in silence.

8: Spirals

"I DIDN'T KNOW you were short-sighted, Magagna."

"You think the Sardinians wanted money?"

The road was almost empty. Magagna drove, his face partially lit by the green light of the fascia board. He had put on a different pair of glasses: the same tear-drop frame, but the lenses were of clear glass.

Trotti nodded. "And that's why they took me and beat me up. They seemed to think Maltese had given me some money."

"Ramoverde," Magagna said, without looking at Trotti, and the name hung in the silence of the car. Magagna was smoking and the world seemed to be caught up in the white spirals of smoke that rose towards the upholstered roof of the Lancia.

"You ought to give up smoking, Magagna."

"And ruin my teeth on sweets?"

Trotti ran his tongue along the edge of the chipped tooth. "That's what your friend Leonardelli always told me—he said that I would die of diabetes."

"If you don't get murdered first." Magagna smiled to himself, then added, "He's in Washington."

"Who?"

"Your friend."

"What friend?" Trotti turned in surprise.

"Leonardelli."

"He was never a friend of mine."

"You got on well enough."

Trotti asked, "What's he doing in Washington?"

"At the Embassy. He's there to liaise with the FBI."

Trotti laughed.

"He's working with the US narcotics bureau."

"Leonardelli doesn't know the first thing about narcotics."

"Perhaps not—but he earns twice the salary in America."

Trotti did not reply but he was suddenly aware how pleased he was to have Magagna beside him again. He had missed him over the last eighteen months. He had missed Magagna's common sense. And his humor.

Meanwhile, the long rows of plane trees sped past like fleeing giants. To the left Trotti could sense the presence of the river and once or twice he imagined he caught the reflection of light through the trees. From time to time the head beams lit up a billboard—VANIZZA, the same familiar advertisement that had become as much a part of Italian life as Fiat or Olivetti. Vanizza, Trotti thought, and allowed himself a bruised smile. Perhaps he was lucky to have got away with sore ribs, a broken tooth and spinal fluid at the back of his throat. They had kidnapped Vanizza for more than a month and the amount of the ransom was never made public.

"I'll have to get my tooth capped," Trotti said.

"Who were they, Commissario?"

"Never saw their faces."

"But they spoke to you?"

"You know the smell of wool when it's wet? That's what they smelled of. Sardinian shepherds." Under his breath, he added, "Animals."

"Lucky not to have been sodomized."

"They were going to kill me."

"Why didn't they?"

"I must have escaped." Trotti shrugged. "When the police found me, I was naked—naked as the day I was born."

"With a few obvious additions."

"They took everything—the old clothes I was wearing—but they must have been looking for money. They took my wallet."

"And that's when they realized you were a policeman. They got scared and that saved your life." Magagna stubbed out his cigarette into the ashtray; the interior of the car was filled with an acrid smell of tobacco ash. "You're a lucky man."

"Concussion isn't my idea of luck."

"But he never spoke to you?"

Trotti said, "Who?"

"Ramoverde."

"The man in the bar? The name on the identity card was Maltese."

"But he didn't speak to you?"

"There was blood everywhere."

"Did you have time to search him?"

"You're heartless. Magagna."

"What did you find in his pockets?"

"Five hundred thousand lire."

"A lot of money to carry around."

"Not enough for somebody to get killed for."

"Tell that to Maltese."

Magagna corrected him, "Ramoverde."

"For heaven's sake," Trotti said, suddenly losing his temper, "I don't know what his name was. I saw his identity card—Giovanni Maltese, a journalist with the *Popolo d'Italia*."

"But you knew Ramoverde?"

"Mareschini told me that the fingerprints were those of Giovanni Ramoverde." Trotti shrugged.

"Losing spinal fluid can't be good for the memory." Magagna repeated his question, with the same flat intonation, "You knew Ramoverde?"

"I knew Douglas Ramoverde."

It was as if he had made a confession and Magagna seemed to lose interest in the conversation. He drove in silence, his face emotionless in the light of the fascia board.

"Twenty-two years ago, Magagna. Perhaps Maltese was the son—it's possible—but how was I going to recognize the son after all these years?" Trotti fumbled for another sweet in the packet. "You remember the Ramoverde affair?"

"Who doesn't?"

"Twenty-two years ago—you were still at your mother's breast."

Magagna gave a thin smile and lit another cigarette in the dashboard lighter. "We studied the whole business at Grosseto—an object lesson in how not to draw up a case."

Trotti bit his lip and waited before answering. "It wasn't our fault and it certainly wasn't mine. There wasn't a valid case against Ramoverde but the investigating magistrate panicked. Twice—Ramoverde was arrested twice." He shrugged. "There was a lot of pressure—and a lot of publicity."

"For nearly two years?"

Trotti did not reply but fell into a reverie. Images were returning that took him by surprise. The Villa Laura. A warm November afternoon, the trees almost bare and beneath his feet the rustle of dead leaves. And the investigating judge—Dell'Orto, small and waspish with an old-fashioned pince-nez—getting angry with the flashing bulbs of the photographers.

"There was a photo," Trotti said.

Magagna showed no sign of having heard.

"There was a photograph in Maltese's wallet—and I took it." He glanced at Magagna. "The photograph of a girl—probably his girlfriend."

"Manipulating the evidence, Commissario?"

"I needed to be sure."

"Sure of what?"

Trotti looked at him, suspecting a hint of sarcasm in his voice. "I needed to be sure that Maltese was the intended victim—and not me."

"Nobody knew you were in Gardesana."

"That's what I thought. I could have been followed. I left home at five o'clock in the morning and never once had the feeling I was being followed."

Magagna gave a thin smile without looking at Trotti. "Who'd want to kill you?"

"Two Sardinian shepherds came pretty close to doing just that. Listen, Magagna, I'm grateful to you—I'm grateful that you came to the hospital and I'm grateful to you for bringing me home." Trotti paused. "But I'm going to need more help."

"I'm busy."

"Take time off."

"Impossible."

"Why?"

"Because I've got other things to do—like Ragusa, for instance."

"Ragusa can wait for a couple of days."

"We're controlling the telephone and all communications of the biggest dealer in narcotics and you tell me Ragusa can wait a day or two."

"Where the hell did you buy these sweets, Magagna? They don't last more than a minute."

"Because you chew them. Because you're greedy."

Trotti was genuinely surprised. "What's wrong, Magagna? You're being very aggressive."

"Listen, I don't work for you anymore. I'm in Milan and I've got my career to think about and I can't be at your beck and call—you don't seem to realize that."

"Nobody ever made you go to Milan."

"I got married, Commissario—or perhaps you don't remember. It was you who said that the Questura was no place for a married man. You said that—I didn't want to leave."

"It was your choice."

"And now I've got other work to do. Ragusa is a big fish—he's been let out of prison because of his health and is now staying in a private clinic in Monza. It's an opportunity for us to break in on the Yugoslav circuit—and it's an opportunity for me to get promotion."

"You'd have had a promotion with me."

The long silence was awkward. Magagna smoked nervously and Trotti noticed the shadows around his eyes.

"I'm not going to be very mobile for the next few days— I'll go over the Ramoverde cuttings. And I have to stay in my little provincial city. But you're forty kilometers up the road in Milan—it's easy for you to go to the *Popolo d'Italia*."

"The Carabinieri will have been there ever since Maltese was shot."

Trotti replied sharply, "Don't talk to me about the Carabinieri—I don't want to know what they're doing and I don't care. But I want you to get to the paper. Find out what Maltese was working on. See if you can locate the girlfriend before the Carabinieri get to her."

"How am I going to set about finding her? Milan is a big place—and you haven't got the photograph."

Trotti did not reply. He did not speak again until they had reached the Po.

"Washington?"

"Leonardelli?" Magagna laughed. "He's always had powerful friends."

"A bastard."

Magagna skirted the sleeping provincial town—the towers were lit up and pointing towards the sky. He turned into via Milano.

There were no lights on in the house.

Magagna got out, opened the door for Trotti and helped him climb out of the car. Trotti had the impression of being an oversize baby—or a war cripple.

"You'll go to the *Popolo d'Italia* for me, won't you?"

Magagna rang the bell on the gate. "I don't work for you anymore."

"You still owe me a couple of favors."

A light came on in the kitchen.

"Well?"

Magagna did not reply.

"Finding the girl should be a challenge for you."

Magagna frowned.

"I recognized the photograph," Trotti said softly. "I don't like coincidences and it was a big coincidence. The girl in the picture—your friend Lia Guerra. The same photograph that we have in the Questura."

9: Belluno

ON THE AFTERNOON of 2nd August 1960, the postman rang the bell at the Villa Laura. He had *Il Tempo*, several bills and a registered letter to deliver. The bell echoed emptily within the villa and there was no reply. The Fiat 600, however, was parked on the drive.

"The professor has gone to the sea. He's taken the train and he forgot to inform the post office," the postman muttered under his breath and left.

He returned at the same time the following day. Still no reply to the bell. He cautiously stepped around the villa. At the back of the house, he discovered that one of the window blinds had not been properly closed but was stuck a little way from the sill.

Behind it, the window was open. There was a black mark on the sill.

The postman contacted the police and, later that same day, two men arrived on bicycles and saw that the black smear on the sill was in fact dried blood. The Pretore was summoned and in his presence, the two officers of the Pubblica Sicurezza made their way through the window into the Villa Laura.

A building of the late nineteenth century, it had thick walls to protect it in winter from the chill of the nearby Po and in summer from the stifling heat that would lie like a plague across the plain. Despite the heat outside—it was one of the hottest summers in living memory—the interior of the house was chill.

The floor was of marble and there were three flights of stairs leading to the second floor.

Belluno's body was on the first flight. He wore a cotton singlet and lay with his head pointing downstairs. A pair of underpants had been stuffed into his mouth and suspenders—of the old-fashioned, pre-war type—had been pulled tight about his neck. The battered head lay in a pool of blood; the tongue lolled.

At the top of the flight of stairs, one of the policemen found Belluno's shattered dentures; he also found another corpse.

Eva Bardizza had been wearing pajamas when she died. Like Belluno, her body was covered with lesions; she sat, part immersed, in a bath of blood and water.

The length of the stairway, along the walls, by the window frames, along the doors, even in the bathroom, there were broad smears of blood that had dried and turned black.

Ismaele Belluno was sixty-nine years old at the time of his death.

Born in Laterza, he had moved north after the Great War and had founded a political club in Piacenza. It was in the same city that he had met his wife—a woman of solid middle-class background—and had launched a small publishing firm. Politically, Belluno was a disciple to Mazzini; aesthetically, he admired d'Annunzio.

With the rise of Mussolini, Belluno had moved away from politics and had started specializing in textbooks. Well-written and intelligent, they were nonetheless flattering towards the regime and towards the person of the Duce. Understandably they won favor with the Ministry of Education.

Belluno became a rich man. He bought an apartment in Piacenza. He also bought Villa Laura—possibly because it was nearer to Milan—and then in 1933, he bought another house on the Ligurian coast, near San Remo, which he called La Ca' degli Ulivi—the House of Olives; it nestled between the olive groves and had a splendid view of the Mediterranean.

His wife died in 1952 after a long illness. By this time, both his children were married. He went to live at Villa Laura, where a housekeeper, Signorina Fava, looked after him until her marriage in 1957. A few months later, answering an advertisement in the local press, Eva Bardizza became the new housekeeper. She had once worked in a factory and then as a maid in Turin before returning to her native city and the job at the Villa Laura. Intelligent, slim, with blue eyes, she could drive and cook. For Belluno, she soon became more than a mere housekeeper.

At the time of her death, she was not yet twenty-eight years old.

10: Padana

Provincia Pavese, 8th August, 1960

The dual murder at the Villa Laura continues to be a pole of interest not only in the city and the province but throughout the Peninsula, despite the more pleasurable activities that the continuing good weather offers to our compatriots.

The officers of the Questura, under the leadership of Commissario Bagnante, and in regular liaison with the investigating judge, Dottor Giacomo Dell'Orto, continue in their ceaseless quest for clues that will help them identify the heartless assassin of Prof. Belluno and his young housekeeper, Eva Bardizza.

Three aspects of the nature of the crime have already made themselves evident to the investigators:

1. *The amazing cunning of the assassin who managed to enter the Villa Laura, cruelly murder the two inhabitants and then leave without the slightest trace or clue to his identity.*

2. *The thorough intimacy of the assassin concerning his whereabouts. At one point he must have turned off the main electricity supply, even though the switch is to be found under the stairs in a small recess hidden from the superficial glance.*

3. *The cynical determination of the assassin to accomplish his foul deed.*

The forensic medical officer has studied both corpses and in a signed statement states his conviction that while the unfortunate Belluno died as a result of the blows he received to the head, the young woman came to her untimely end in the bath where she was drowned. The officer goes on to say that both victims were battered with more than one blunt object. A heavy onyx paperweight has been identified and the blood traces belong to the victims.

It has also been revealed that the investigators found no signs of struggle in Belluno's bedroom. On the other hand, violence occurred in Bardizza's bedroom, where ample bloodstains were left on the wall, the floor and along the frame of the large window that gives on to the garden. Also on the window, the investigators have identified the fingerprints in blood of the poor woman.

Furthermore, it was discovered late Tuesday night that a certain Sig.na Scabini of Borgo Genovese (Pv), twenty-three years old and a primary-school teacher, has informed the investigating officers that on the night of the murder (1st—2nd August) she was awoken from her sleep by a scream; she has stated that the scream occurred just after three o'clock in the morning. Sig.na Scabini lives with her parents on the edge of Borgo Genovese. Their house is 300 meters from the scene of the crime.

11: Douglas Ramoverde

"PAPA, YOU SHOULD be sleeping."

Trotti turned. "You're up early."

"I'm going to Mass." Pioppi wore a nightdress that hung loosely from her shoulders, revealing the angularity of her thin body. Her neck was narrow, the tendons taut, the skin pulled tight against the bones of her neck and chest. "Would you like some coffee?"

There were several folders open on the bed: pages of sloping handwriting that had turned from blue to mauve with the passing of time. There were also old newspaper cuttings.

Pioppi sat down beside her father. "What on earth was that hideous jacket you were wearing last night?"

"I borrowed it."

"You could have borrowed something a bit less scruffy." Her hand went to his forehead. "Your bruises are going down. How do you feel?"

"Better."

"Last night, I scarcely recognized you—you were like some monster out of a film."

"Thank you, Pioppi."

She picked up one of the cuttings. "Ramoverde." She frowned. "Why are you going through all these dusty folders?"

"Let's have breakfast, Pioppi." His hand touched hers.

"Who's that?" She pointed at a picture of Ramoverde.

"Are there any croissants?"

She shook her head. "I can make some toast." She nodded towards the photograph. "He's got small eyes." She turned to her father. "Who is he?"

"An old friend."

"An old friend in handcuffs!" She laughed—almost gaily—and stood up. "Be ready in five minutes." She went out of his bedroom and later he heard the sound of saucepans and plates coming from the kitchen.

Trotti looked at the photograph.

A friend?

At the time, Ramoverde was not even forty-two years old, but the picture showed him as tired. He looked straight at the camera and the reporter's flashing bulb. Beside him, head down, a police officer was accompanying him to the waiting car. Ramoverde's hands were handcuffed.

Small eyes, a lopsided face that revealed no emotion and hair that was fast thinning. Yet despite the flashbulb, despite the humiliation of the handcuffs, despite the fatigue in the eyes, there was something attractive about Douglas Ramoverde. He could have been a film star.

His mother was a rich Argentinian from Buenos Aires who died a few months after bringing her only child into the world in 1918. Ramoverde's childhood had been spent partly in South America, partly in Milan where he later went to university. Douglas Ramoverde gave up his studies in 1941 to marry Signorina Belluno. For a year he was posted to the military hospital in Piacenza and it was not until after the war, in 1946, that he finally acquired his degree in medicine. By then, his son was two years old.

Trotti looked up.

The same son was now dead, lying in the morgue in Salò.

On his father's side, Douglas Ramoverde had an uncle, a member of parliament and a major shareholder in the Società Sicula per l'Elettricità, who helped him find a well-paid job in his company.

Ramoverde was sent to Palermo but within three months,

the uncle had denounced his nephew to the police, accusing him of embezzlement. Soon afterwards, Ramoverde returned to Piacenza.

He found work in the municipal hospital but was suspended in 1952 following various accusations. Perhaps it was his good looks that had got him into trouble. It was rumored that Douglas Ramoverde had been carrying out abortions—and making a lot of money for himself.

It was in 1952 that Douglas Ramoverde set up his dental practice. He had no qualification in dentistry, his clientele was limited to old ladies who succumbed to his matinée-idol good looks, and had it not been for the financial help from his father-in-law, Ramoverde would have found it difficult to maintain the standard of living which he enjoyed—a Fiat 1100, an apartment and a surgery at 700,000 lire per year, a maid, weekends at the Villa Laura, long summer holidays at San Remo.

"Papa!" Pioppi called from the kitchen.

The muscles had become stiff. It hurt Trotti just to stand up and put on his dressing gown. Walking slowly, one hand using the wall as a support, he made his way to the kitchen.

The air was thick with the smell of fresh coffee.

"I phoned on Friday night, Pioppi, but you didn't answer."

"I was with the Nonna." She poured coffee into two cups.

"Your mother phoned from America."

"Two sugars, Papa?"

"She wanted her diplomas."

A distracted laugh. "I sent them off years ago."

Trotti lowered himself on to the chair. "You never told me."

"You're hardly ever at home."

"You should have let me know. You know how your mother gets angry."

"She likes getting angry with you—it makes her think she's still a young woman in love. Toast?"

The clock on the refrigerator ticked noisily. It was not yet six o'clock and Trotti watched his daughter as she took the toasted bread from the oven and placed it on a plate. She looked very thin.

"Did you tell anybody I was going to the lake?"

"The lake?" She frowned. "Why should I tell anybody?"

"You and the Nonna were the only people who knew I was going to Gardesana."

"Well?"

Trotti shrugged. "Perhaps it was me they were aiming at."

She sat down and took his hand. "Papa," she said and her eyes reminded him of the little girl she had once been. She shook her head.

"A coincidence, then."

"Look after yourself, Papa. You take risks." She shook her head again, this time more violently. "You mustn't, do you understand. I don't want to lose you."

"You're having breakfast with me?"

"A cup of coffee—I'm not hungry."

"You must eat."

When she shook her head this time, it was like a willful child. Her hair, once dark and glowing like her mother's, seemed to have lost its gloss. "I can't concentrate when I eat."

"Concentrate on what, Pioppi? You'll die of starvation."

"I've got my exam on Wednesday."

"Be reasonable. You've already sat your urbanistica exam once and the professor wanted to give you twenty-six. Twenty-six out of thirty, Pioppi—it's a good mark. Nothing to be ashamed of. When I was at the university, I was pleased to get twenty-six—I don't think I got it more than twice in all my university career. But you—you turn twenty-six down?"

"I want thirty." She folded her arms.

"What on earth is wrong? Why d'you work like this? You're young and you should be enjoying yourself—yes, Pioppi, you should be enjoying life, going dancing, having boyfriends. Like your mother when she was your age. But apart from Mass, you spend all your time at the university or here with the Nonna. You don't enjoy yourself. You just study—and you starve."

She had filled her cup with a few centimeters of black coffee.

"Pioppi, my daughter, I love you. But please, can't you see that you are being unreasonable? You're obsessive."

"I'm obsessive because I am like my—" Her mouth snapped shut.

She stood up and left the kitchen.

The toast lay untouched on the plate.

12: Two-tone

ON THE NIGHT of 21st July, 1960—just ten days before the assassination of Belluno and the young housekeeper—a group of friends, carried away by the Olympic fever which now gripped Italy, held a bet.

Francesco Barbieri maintained that he could run the eight kilometers from the bar in which the friends were—Bar Città di Genova—to the point downstream where the Po met its confluent.

The record over this distance had been set the previous night by a certain Matteo Bianco, alias Lo sciocc. Consequently, just after midnight and accompanied by a convoy of bicycles, Vespas and two cars, the slightly inebriated contestant set off into the night along the track that followed the banks of the Po. When the runner and his entourage reached a place known as the Zona Spagnola—it had once been the site of stables at the time of the Spanish occupation—they came abreast of a motorcar, partially hidden behind the trees. Later in sworn statements, several people categorically identified the vehicle as a two-tone Fiat 1100. All the witnesses agreed that they had seen the car's registration, and had recognized the letters PC.

Nobody, however, could recall the precise registration number. The Zona Spagnola was about five minutes' brisk walk through woodland from the Villa Laura. In the normal course of events, passersby would not normally be walking along the secluded path at such a time of night, and the person or persons wanting to approach the Villa Laura without being observed would be well advised to leave any vehicle at the Zona Spagnola. Police investigation soon revealed that a two-tone Fiat 1100 was the property of Douglas Ramoverde, the victim's son-in-law. The car's registration was PC 23478. On 16th August—a fortnight after the discovery of the two bodies—Signora Peliti appeared before the investigating judge Dell'Orto. In her sworn statement she said that on the night of 1st August, she had been to visit her aunt at Argine Ticinese. On the return journey, despite the late hour, she decided to take a short cut. She cycled along the path beside the Po and at two thirty, the dynamo light caught the reflection of a car bumper. The vehicle had been left at Zona Spagnola. Signora Peliti stated that she recognized the car as a Fiat, but she could not name the model. She was not certain of the color of the car but as to the registration, she was convinced that it had been a Piacenza plate.

The following day, Douglas Ramoverde was arrested.

13: Dell'Orto

"YOU DON'T BELIEVE, Brigadiere, that there's sufficient evidence?"

Behind the pince-nez, the old face rarely smiled. Dell'Orto seemed to be smiling now; webs of wrinkles formed at the corner of the eyes and the colorless lips.

"I have no opinion, Signor Giudice." Trotti had been in the police long enough to know how to conceal his opinions.

"You believe, no doubt—like your colleague, Commissario Bagnante—that I'm bowing before public pressure. Is that not correct?"

"There are good reasons for suspecting Ramoverde, Signor Giudice."

"But in your opinion such evidence is merely circumstantial—is that not so?"

For a man with such power, for a man who would never have to pay for a meal in a restaurant or go short of parmesan cheese or Christmas cake, knowing as he did that these things and many others would be provided for him by people eager to find his favor, Judge Dell'Orto was strangely humble. Everyone who came into contact with him was aware of his power, but never did he flaunt it. Austere, perhaps, but in his way he was like the dead publisher, Belluno. Both men were outsiders—Belluno from Puglia, Dell'Orto from Tuscany—and both had built themselves a position in Lombardy. It was rumored that Dell'Orto was a freemason; it was certain that he held an outdated respect for Mazzini, for a different, almost archaic idea of Italy. His republicanism had remained untainted throughout the Mussolini years.

But Italy was changing.

The war was over and the country was entering a new era—as the Olympic Games in Rome clearly showed. A new, modern Italy. The wounds of the partisan war had begun to heal. The Italy of August 1960 was an Italy of hope. The papers spoke of the Italian miracle; there were autostradas and the bomb craters of Milan and Genoa had disappeared. In their place, new blocks of flats had gone up—architecture that was the envy of the rest of the world. Italians now owned their own cars and husbands bought washing machines—made in Italy—for their wives. There were Vespas and Lambrettas. The new generation of women were going out to work, leaving the fields for the factories. More money in the house and the insidious invasion of new television sets.

"Merely circumstantial, Brigadiere?" Dell'Orto pulled at the loose belt of his trousers. He wore clothes that belonged to a different era, trousers that crumpled over his shoelaces. "But of course, I respect your opinion."

Trotti shrugged. "There's very little evidence."

The old man's thin finger pointed into the air. "Many years, Brigadiere, many years I have been dealing with criminals. By and large, not nice people—sometimes amusing, often pathetic and nearly always"—his finger underlined his words—"nearly always cunning." He sat back in his chair, waiting for Trotti's reply.

Trotti looked at the older man.

"One lesson I have learned over the years: *motive*. Always look for a motive." A speck of saliva had formed at the edge of his mouth. "They are cunning, Trotti, very cunning—but they can never hide their motive."

"I'm not sure that Ramoverde had a good reason for killing his father-in-law."

Dell'Orto clapped his hands, as if amused. But he was no longer smiling and the freckled, dark skin of his forehead creased. "He was afraid that the old man would change his will—and this time he would get nothing at all."

"He had already been cut out of most of the will."

"Belluno got on well with his two daughters—and in particular, with Matilde Ramoverde. In the two previous wills, he had bequeathed virtually everything to her and to her younger sister. Then quite suddenly, last year he changed his mind. Obviously, Ramoverde was frightened he'd change it again—this time cutting Ramoverde's wife out completely." The judge pulled at the shiny bowtie underneath the wing-collar. "Human beings are rational—even in their irrationality. Remember that, Trotti, and you won't go wrong. Belluno felt he had good reason for cutting the daughters out for good—no Villa, no money, no nothing. As our French friends say, *cherchez la femme*!"

It was Trotti's turn to frown.

"A woman, Trotti, a woman and the old fool had fallen in love." He stopped suddenly, eyes bright behind the pince-nez. "Love perhaps is not the right word, it is something too young, too juvenile for Belluno. Let us say he was infatuated with the girl—infatuated with his housekeeper. He probably saw himself Pygmalion and he hoped to transform this rustic girl into something more sophisticated." Again the smile behind the glasses—an old, cynical smile.

Trotti nodded.

The judge coughed and gave a brief glance to the dusty office, the piles of faded dossiers held together with ribbon or pieces of string.

"Forty years between the old man and Bardizza, and like a fool, he must have thought he was in love." The eyes shone. "But his daughter saw the relationship for what it really was. Women are cynical in a way that you and I will never understand. Never. Brigadiere, I have been married now for over thirty-one years and my own dear wife is a woman whom I cherish like life itself. I have shared my bed with her, she has given me four wonderful children. But there are moments, even at the end of a road that we have been sharing now for so long, when I understand my dear Genoveffa about as much as I understand the mystery of life itself." He lowered his voice. "Women see things we never see; they give life and they can understand its cruelties and its envies in a way that is denied to us. We are men, we intellectual-ize, we give names to things so that we can deal with them. But women don't need names, they don't need words. And Matilde Ramoverde, the old man's daughter, she understood that Eva Bardizza was intent on one thing. She wanted the Villa Laura, and the house in Piacenza and the villa in San Remo. She wanted everything she could get her hands on. And she saw that the old man was a willing fool whom she could manipulate." Again he held up his finger, but his smile was without humor. "A cunning, very pretty little peasant girl—she had found the gold pot at the end of the rainbow—and she wanted all the gold."

"I don't feel that there is any conclusive proof that we can bring against Ramoverde."

"Ramoverde allowed himself to be manipulated by his wife. It was his wife who got him to slap Bardizza. It happened at San Remo and Ramoverde doesn't deny it. How could he, when the old man wrote long and tedious letters to all his friends and colleagues denouncing his son-in-law—the same son-in-law whom he'd always got on so well with—as a heart-less monster? No doubt Ramoverde was irritated—scared, even—by the airs that Bardizza put on, strutting about the Villa Laura as if she already owned it—when Ramoverde and his wife had naturally assumed it was theirs by right." He lowered his hands on to the cluttered desktop. "The motive, Trotti—the motive is there."

"But there were other people who had reasons to hate Belluno."

"Who, for example?"

"A young woman. There had been other men in her life. A slighted lover, perhaps or a . . ."

"A *crime passionel*!" He used the French expression.

Trotti paused, feeling uncomfortable. "Somebody, perhaps, who was jealous to see that Bardizza was intending to live with the old man."

"A crime of passion. But they didn't sleep in the same bed," the judge said.

"They didn't sleep in the same bed but they slept in the same house. And how was an outsider to know what exactly went on within the walls of the Villa Laura?"

"The murderer knew the villa well—well enough to find his way around and not leave any clues, not even a fingerprint. Somebody who cleaned up after his dirty work. Somebody who knew exactly what the relationship between the old man and his housekeeper was."

Trotti was silent.

"Piero Trotti, you're young and you're ambitious. But don't allow yourself to be carried away. Look for the motive. Can't you see that no one else had any reason to want to kill the old man?" It was as if Dell'Orto had convinced himself. "Tell me, Trotti, have you talked to Ramoverde?"

Trotti nodded.

"And?"

"He seems a pleasant man. Shy, perhaps."

Dell'Orto smiled. "A shy man with a fairly turbulent past." He set the pince-nez higher on his nose and turned towards the pile of dusty documents.

Outside, beyond the judge's grubby office, the sky was blue and cloudless. Agnese and Pioppi were up on the lake, probably swimming in the cool water or perhaps taking tea on the terrace at the Villa Ondina.

The hottest August on record.

The old Judge appeared to have forgotten about Trotti. Trotti stood up and mumbled a courteous "Buongiorno."

"Remember, Brigadiere, remember what the French say— *cherchez la femme.*"

14: Monster

Vita e sorrisi, 2nd September 1960

"WE SAW THE MONSTER OF VILLA LAURA"

Within a few days, Italy will return to work after the two-month hiatus of a summer that has given us much to be proud of in the stadia of Rome. But the Olympic Games are now over, the first clouds can be seen in the late August sky and soon the nation must return to the office and to the factory.

For some people, work has never stopped, even during the canicular heat of the Ferragosto. While others were crowding into the Olympic City or on to the hot beaches, Vilma and Giacomo Forti (both thirty-seven years old) have been diligently selling petrol and oil from their AGIP concession in the via Klepero (Piacenza). "Not everybody can take a holiday and we have been working to satisfy the demand of the local population as well as the tourists coming down from Northern Europe."

About one thing, Giacomo Forti is certain. "On the afternoon of August second, a two-tone Fiat 1100 drew into the forecourt. The driver—a tall man wearing dark sunglasses—insisted that I wash his car immediately. He appeared nervous and obviously in a hurry. When I informed him that I would not be able to carry out the job before the following morning, he got rather agitated. Eventually he agreed to pay me a bonus of three thousand lire in addition to the standard rate for tourist vehicles. Understandably, the financial agreement met with my approval."

"We have seen the monster of the Villa Laura," says Vilma, originally from the Valcamonica (Prov. of Brescia). Holding her delightful young son Andrea to her breast (photo opposite), she informed our special correspondent that the driver of the Fiat 1100 wore sunglasses and, despite the summer heat, a suit and a borsalino hat. He was, she states, of above average height.

"My husband was very busy and it was with my sister that I cleaned the car. Above the passenger seat, both on the inside and the outside of the vehicle, there were clearly defined black traces. My sister has trained as a nurse and she recognized the traces as dried blood." The proprietress gives a shrug and a smile. "We have informed the Questura of this discovery in the light of what has already been stated in the local and national press."

A phone call placed by our special correspondent to the Questura has met with the reply "No comment." Commissario Bagnante was not available.

The dentist of Piacenza remains silent. His lawyer, Avv. Michele (photo, bottom left) maintains that his client is totally extraneous to the events, real or imagined by the Forti couple. Meanwhile, Dott. Ramoverde observes absolute silence in his cell.

Gazette della Svizzera, 10th September 1960

Milan, from our special envoy: Ismaele Belluno was a retired publisher. He had made his fortune in textbooks, and for many years led a peaceful, uneventful life. His two daughters had grown up, married and had raised families.

In his will, the father had bequeathed everything to his two daughters, to be shared fairly between them. Then his wife died and in 1958 he employed a young woman to be the housekeeper of the three villas that he owned. Clearly things took a turn for the worse when Belluno, now in his late sixties, announced his intention to marry the young woman, Eva Bardizza, nearly forty years his junior.

That there was conflict between the father and his son-in-law, there can be no doubt. On one occasion, the old man was reported to have taken to his bed when Sig. Ramoverde, husband of Matilde Belluno, slapped the young housekeeper for alleged insolence. A few days later after this incident, Belluno summoned his lawyer and made drastic changes in his will; it is believed that he intended to bequeath everything—or nearly everything—to his future wife. Among other things, the Belluno fortune included a sumptuous villa in the city of Piacenza and Villa Laura ninety kilometers away, near Borgo Genovese and the confluence of the Po and the Ticino rivers. A third house in the hills above San Remo is famous throughout Italy for its beautiful gardens.

On 3rd August, Belluno was found murdered in the Villa Laura near Borgo Genovese. He had been battered to death with a blunt instrument and the walls of the building were smeared with his blood. Also murdered was his young wife-to-be; she had been battered and, according to the forensic scientists, drowned in a bath of cold water. As to the assassin, he left no clues concerning his identity; cold-bloodedly he wiped the walls and floors of any trace of fingerprints. The coolness with which the assassin behaved has led the local police to believe that the murderer knew the house—and his victims—intimately.

Three weeks after the dual slaying, the investigating judge arrested Douglas Ramoverde, Belluno's son-in-law. However, Dr. Ramoverde, a dentist from Piacenza, has an alibi and he has stuck to it consistently. After spending the weekend on the Ligurian coast at the Villa Ca' degli Ulivi, where his wife, Matilde, and his seventeen-year-old son were passing the month of August, Ramoverde maintains that he took his car, a Fiat 1100, and leaving the Villa Ca' degli Ulivi at twenty-three hours on the night of the first of August, drove straight back to Piacenza. Unfortunately, he can find no witness to corroborate his version of the facts. Furthermore, from a close analysis of the vehicle's odometer and Ramoverde's own logbook—he noted down when and where he bought petrol—it would appear that instead of driving the 250 kilometers to Piacenza, he in fact covered 285 kilometers on the night of the murder. It is thus quite possible that Ramoverde took a detour north to the River Po and the Villa Laura. One thing is certain: he was within a radius of eighty kilometers of the Villa Laura on the fateful night of 1st August.

But the most damaging piece of evidence against the son-in-law is the testimony of several local inhabitants who have sworn to seeing a two-tone Fiat 1100 identical to Ramoverde's hidden not more than 200 meters from the Villa Laura both on the night of the murder and on previous evenings. Ramoverde has claimed that such a sighting can only be a coincidence. However, on the afternoon following the murder a man wearing sunglasses paid a garage owner in Piacenza to clean his two-tone Fiat 1100. In cleaning it, the garage owner recognized dry traces of blood.

Douglas Ramoverde has been arrested and awaits trial; such things take a very long time in Italy and it is possible that many months will go by before the alleged assassin goes on trial. In the meantime, by the very bloodiness of its nature, the murder remains a burning subject of conversation for our neighbors beyond the Alps.

15: Questura

THE TAXI DRIVER helped him into the building. Then Trotti leaned against the wall, waiting until the elevator arrived. His ribs still hurt and awkwardly he stepped inside, recognizing the familiar smell of garlic. The hammer and sickle were still there, engraved into the soft surface of the corrugated metal.

The elevator stopped on the third floor and Trotti stepped out.

"Ah, Commissario!" Gino lifted his head. Behind the thick lenses, his sightless eyes seemed to recognize Trotti. "So good to see you." It was Gino's joke. "I thought you were still on holiday."

"Where's Pisanelli?"

The old man shrugged, "Probably taking time off to visit his nurse friend." Gino smiled. "Commissario, you were young once."

"And I knew what it was like to be poor and have no work."

"You are hard on the young generation." Gino shrugged. "Pisanelli may seem a little sleepy, a little absent-minded. But he's got the makings of a good policeman. And the determination."

Beneath Gino's desk, Principessa stirred and yawned to reveal bright teeth and a pink tongue. The watery eyes glanced at Trotti without interest and then closed again. Gino laughed and at that moment Trotti realized that Gino was getting old. His face was pale and looked tired.

"Being a policeman is a full-time job. If he wants to have

women, he's in the wrong profession." Trotti turned and, walking slowly, went down the familiar corridor. There were scattered packets of sugar around the foot of the coffee machine. Probably the cleaning women had gone on strike again. Spilled sugar caught under the soles of his shoes. Trotti leaned on the door handle and entered his office.

Very untidy.

The files that he had carefully stacked and catalogued a couple of weeks earlier were now in a state of collapse; on the desk there were sheets of typewritten paper and the half circles of spilled coffee. The air was stuffy.

Trotti took off his jacket slowly and then hobbled over to the window. Traffic in Strada Nuova. The morning mist was clearing and the terracotta tiles of the old city were beginning to take on their summer glow. At last, spring had arrived after a long cold winter and a wet April. Within a few days the hot weather would be back, and the still, windless air would hang over the Po valley.

He let the desk take his weight and sat down. Then he picked up the phone. "Gino?"

The voices came simultaneously over the line and through the wooden partition in the wall. "Commissario?"

"You'd better put me through to the Questura in Piacenza."

Gino laughed. "They've been phoning for the last two days."

"And what did you say?"

"Commissario, I'm paid to know nothing."

"Thanks, Gino." Trotti put the phone down and riffled through the top drawer of the desk. He had finished the bottle of grappa before going up to the Lake. Apart from a few sticky sweet wrappers, a few isolated grains of sugar and an old, crumpled football coupon, the drawer was empty.

The red light began to wink.

"Questura, Piacenza."

"Trotti, Commissario Trotti here."

"Well?" The voice was unhelpful.

"The Questore—if he's available and not too busy."

A series of muffled clicks.

Trotti waited, the phone against his ear, while he looked through the other drawers. Empty.

"Ah, you decided you couldn't make more use of our hospitality, Commissario?"

"Signor Questore, I felt I had abused your kindness long enough."

"And that's why you borrowed an entire suit from the changing rooms of the hospital?"

"I needed to get back home."

"Of course, Commissario Trotti."

There followed a long silence.

"I assume, Commissario, that there's a purpose to this phone call—or perhaps you merely wished to inform me of your state of health."

"Alive," Trotti replied. "Thanks largely to the efficiency of your Pronto Soccorso." He coughed.

"And what can I do for you? What can I do that your colleagues can't do for you?"

"I should like to know whether my car's been located yet."

"This isn't a lost property office."

Before Trotti could reply, the line seemed to go dead—not even the sound of a hand over the mouthpiece.

"Seventy-five Opel—registration PV 13379, color mustard yellow?" The Questore's voice.

"You've found it?"

"No—but I'll let you know as soon as we have."

"Thank you very much," Trotti replied, "and I'll send you the suit of clothes immediately."

"Most obliged—unless you feel that you still need them. The gardener at the hospital has been complaining and their speedy return would be appreciated, not least by the gardener himself."

Trotti thought the Questore was going to hang up and removed the hand-piece from his ear.

"Trotti, have you heard from the Nucleo Investigativo?"

"No—I don't think so."

"But you know that the money has been identified."

"What money?"

"The money that was found on your friend Maltese—it's been identified."

Trotti felt a coldness in his stomach. "Where does it come from?"

"I think you'd better contact Gardesana. I have the impression that Capitano Mareschini is most anxious to hear from you."

Without another word, the Questore hung up.

Trotti muttered under his breath; angrily his finger hit the button of the telephone. "Gino, put me through to the Carabinieri in Gardesana."

"Gardesana?"

"Gardesana del Garda—in the province of Brescia. I'm in a hurry."

He put the phone down and stared at it testily. Then he got up and, using the desk as support, went to his jacket to see if there were any sweets in the pockets. He was still looking when the red console started blinking.

"Capitano Mareschini?" Trotti leaned his weight against the edge of the table.

"Speaking."

"Trotti here."

"Ah!"

"I must apologize for Friday night—I'm afraid I got called back to the city—family matters. And then outside Bergamo—perhaps you've heard?—I was attacked by two men."

"We still await your visit, Commissario. I believe that the Nucleo Investigativo have certain questions—important questions—that they need to ask you."

"Of course. I've only just come in to the Questura—I've been in bed. But I'll phone the NI in Brescia."

"Do that." A long silence. "I look forward to seeing you in Gardesana, Commissario." The voice was cold and the Sicilian accent was more noticeable over the telephone line.

"Capitano Mareschini, I've been in touch with Piacenza. I gather that the money on Maltese . . ."

"Money?"

"I believe it's been identified."

"Possibly." The voice was flat.

"Identified as . . . ?" Trotti let the question hang but there was no reply. Outside in the corridor somebody walked past the office. Trotti recognized Pisanelli's voice and felt an irrational sense of irritation.

"Would you know in what way it has been identified?"

"No."

"I see."

After a while Mareschini added unhelpfully, "You must contact NI in Brescia."

"I really think we should cooperate, Capitano Mareschini. As officers of the Carabinieri and the PS . . ."

"Precisely. Are there any other questions, Commissario?"

"No, Capitano."

"Buongiorno, Commissario."

Angrily Trotti cut the line, pressed the button and told Gino to put him through to the Nucleo Investigativo in Brescia. "And tell Pisanelli I want him in here fast."

Trotti waited.

Almost immediately the console began blinking. He picked up the receiver. Click and then a single tone. It continued ringing for over a minute; then somebody answered.

"Carabinieri?"

The voice sounded faintly surprised. "Yes."

"Put me through to NI."

"Why?"

"Commissario Trotti phoning. Please hurry."

"Nucleo Investigativo?"

"It's about the murder of Maltese at Gardesana."

"Yes?"

"Please hurry. Give me the investigating officer. This is Trotti of the Pubblica Sicurezza."

"I'm afraid the investigating officer has gone to lunch."

"Lunch, Signorina? But it's not even ten o'clock."

"Please hold the line."

There was a knock on the door and Trotti looked up to see Pisanelli enter the office. He was wearing his leather jacket that was considerably the worse for wear—he had not changed it or had it cleaned in four years. A sheepish grin. Pisanelli seemed to be getting balder by the day. He nodded deferentially and sat down on the canvas armchair.

A man's voice. "Hello."

"Commissario Trotti here."

"When can you come in, Commissario?"

"Come in for what?"

"You were a witness to the Gardesana killing."

"I made a full statement at the Carabinieri barracks."

"Other questions that need answering. Can you come in today?"

"Whom am I speaking to?"

"When you arrive at the desk, just ask for Nucleo Investigativo."

"I believe the money that was in Maltese's wallet has been identified."

"A report has been sent out to all Commands."

"What money, exactly?"

"I'm not in a position to give information over the telephone. Come in and see us today. I think I can give you an appointment."

In a neutral voice, Trotti said, "I'll see what I can do." He put the receiver down.

Pisanelli was leaning back in the chair, studying his fingernails.

Trotti looked at him for a moment. In a soft voice he said, "If you haven't got anything better to do than your manicure, Pisanelli, go over the road and get some coffee. Real coffee. Pisanelli—nothing from that machine in the corridor. And a couple of packets of sweets." He ran his tongue along the jagged edge of the broken tooth.

"You look a bit battered, Commissario."

Trotti picked up the phone. "Last call, Gino. This time the Carabinieri. Here, in the city. See if you can get me Spadano at Caserma Bixio." In the same breath he said to Pisanelli, "You needn't worry about my health. Get some coffee—and worry about your prospects with the Pubblica Sicurezza."

"Spadano called this morning, Commissario."

"What?"

"Spadano called this morning," Pisanelli repeated.

"Called who?"

"He wanted to speak to you." Pisanelli smiled foolishly. "I was here so I took the message."

Trotti put the receiver down slowly.

Pisanelli looked at his nails. "It was about the money."

"For Christ's sake, Pisanelli—what did Spadano say?"

"Look—I took the call down." He pointed to a scrawled note that had got partially hidden beneath the blotter on Trotti's cluttered table. "Maltese."

"What about it?"

"The numbers correspond with the stolen money—the money taken at the time of the hold-up."

"Hold-up? What hold-up?"

"Here." Pisanelli nodded his domed head. "In the city. At the Banca San Matteo."

The light was blinking.

Trotti picked up the phone. "Yes."

"Capitano Spadano."

16: Banco Milanese

"NOTHING ON THE girl?"

Magagna had been smoking and over the telephone line his voice rasped in Trotti's ear. "Sentenced and then reprieved. But for the moment, I've got nothing on her. I've put out a trace. Let's hope the Carabinieri don't associate Lia Guerra with the Maltese killing." He paused. "What happened to the photograph?"

"I took it."

Magagna clicked his tongue in mock disapproval. "Where is it now?"

"No idea."

"What d'you mean, no idea?"

"It was a photograph that we had on file here and it was a chance in a million that I should recognize her—you know, that photo where half her face is covered with a handkerchief and she's about to hurl something—probably at the Celere or at the fascist forces of repression. I recognized it—and I took it."

"Then where is it, Commissario?"

"In the glove box of my car."

"And where's your car?"

"I wish I knew."

Magagna gave him an unsympathetic laugh that crackled over the line. Trotti took a sweet from the packet that Pisanelli had brought him. "Let me know when you get something on her, Magagna."

"I should be working on Ragusa."

"You'll have plenty of time to do that."

There was a moment's hesitation, then Magagna said, "I've had better luck with Maltese."

"He was Ramoverde's son?"

"He was in Argentina—after the Villa Laura affair, the entire family emigrated to South America."

"The Ramoverde family?"

"Of course." A slight pause. "After a short return to Italy, he got a job with *Popolo d'Italia*. He was their correspondent for Latin America. And apparently he was pretty good stuff. He wrote articles on the Dirty War, Videla and all the rest. He even managed to make the front page of the *Popolo*."

"Where did you get this information from?"

"Then he got the sack. 1980, just about the time the *Popolo d'Italia* changed owners. The paper was bought up by a big consortium called Stampital. This same consortium is supposed to have certain interests in South America, particularly Chile and Argentina. Which would explain why Maltese suddenly found himself without a job."

"What's your source of information on this, Magagna?"

"Look, you ask me to do you a favor." Magagna sounded peeved. "And I've done it. This isn't my field; you know that Ragusa is in Monza and that's where I should be, instead of doing all this running around for you." He paused, caught his breath. "This isn't classified information. You could have got it from Finanza."

Trotti sucked at his sweet while at the same time he folded and refolded the cellophane wrapping. The telephone was propped between his head and shoulder. "Go on, Magagna."

"Maltese left Argentina, spent some time in the States and then returned to Milan."

"When did he get back?"

"Have you heard of Novara?" Magagna asked.

"A journalist?"

"You've heard of the Banco Milanese?"

"Of course."

"Banco Milanese Holding is a conglomerate. BMH has interests in Liechtenstein, in the Bahamas and in South America. In Peru alone, there are six Banco Milanese agencies. And through Stampital, it is also supposed to have a ruling interest in the *Popolo d'Italia*."

"Go on."

"The Banco Milanese is a highly respected Catholic bank—and now it's under inspection from the Banca d'Italia for irregularities. There have even been rumors that the Banco Milanese is on the verge of collapse. The Director, Bastia, is expected to resign at any moment. A lot of wealthy families—people who for generations have trusted in the Banco Milanese as a reliable and respectable bank—are suddenly going to find themselves a lot less wealthy."

"What's all this got to do with the journalist Novara?"

"Novara used to be a partisan and a communist during the war. Now he's an agent provocateur. They used him at Fiat in Turin to set up bogus trade unions—to undermine the real trade unions that were getting too pushy for the management's liking. That and then a series of smear campaigns."

"Smear campaigns?"

"There are always good people who get left by the wayside—and who understandably feel bitter. Novara has developed a way of cashing in on their bitterness. He gets them to supply him with information—perhaps even with compromising documents—and then he publishes a broadsheet. Distributed free of charge—he sends it to bank managers and judges and lawyers and anybody else who might be interested in the facts that he's revealing. Highly unnerving. And sometimes very damaging. The final stage of blackmail."

"And Maltese?"

"Don't rush me."

"I don't see the connection with Maltese."

"He was furious with his newspaper, the *Popolo d'Italia*—or at least with the new, subservient management. He wanted revenge. More important, from Novara's point of view, Maltese possessed the kind of information that could be very damaging."

"What did he know? He'd been living in Argentina?"

"Precisely."

"Well?"

"Banco Milanese de l'América del Sur."

Trotti asked irritably, "What?"

"As a journalist—when the *Popolo d'Italia* was still a respected newspaper—he had done some work on the holdings in the Southern Hemisphere."

"Where?"

"In Argentina, Chile and Peru—and even in Nicaragua where the bank was selling arms to the Sandinista rebels."

"So what? Italy sells arms to everybody."

"But not every bank—not every national and highly respected bank, particularly with a strong Catholic foundation—is now threatened with bankruptcy."

Trotti could imagine Magagna smiling.

"There are a lot of people who have reason to regret that Maltese was ever fired. He was a good journalist, from what I gather. But with a change in management of the *Popolo d'Italia* and with considerable financial interests at stake, the Banco Milanese could not afford be on bad terms with the military men in Buenos Aires and Santiago. And in Argentina, the Generals were hardly likely to do business with people who owned a newspaper unfavorable to their régimes. So Maltese was fired."

"Buenos Aires could have expelled him."

"Maltese, in fact, did a lot of his work out of Brazil, where he felt safer. Even so, several attempts were apparently made on his life."

"In Italy he was safe."

"Until he fell in with Novara—and Novara pulled off his coup."

"You mean the Night of the Tazebao?"

"You heard about it, Commissario?" Surprise in his voice which Magagna did not try to hide. "And you know what Tazebao means?"

"Something to do with political posters." Trotti shrugged modestly. "I sometimes glance at the papers."

"Then there's no need for me to explain what happened?"

"Remind me."

"Overnight the posters went up all over Milan—plastered on every available wall. So that by the time Bastia, the director of the Banco Milanese, arrived for work—the offices are near the Scala—the damage had already been done. Of course, he tried to rip the posters down, but people had seen them and read them. One or two important people had even found copies in their morning post. They'd seen the accusations."

"What accusations?"

"A Catholic bank selling arms to South America—to both communists and reactionaries; of illegally exporting currency to Switzerland, in the face of all exchange-control laws." Magagna laughed. "There was even the secret number of Bastia's private account in Switzerland. Bastia's and his wife's. The posters on the walls also accused Banco Milanese of subsidizing fascist regimes in Central America—and of investing in the cocaine trade. A highly respected Italian bank, with close Vatican ties, was accused of being involved in the production and sale of contraceptives. But perhaps most damaging of all was the simple question on the poster. Why had the prestigious *Popolo d'Italia* never mentioned, never made the slightest reference to the illegal traffickings of the effective owner?" Magagna paused. "Nobody was fooled about the source of information—just as nobody for a moment ever suspected anyone other than Novara as instigator. Maltese had helped him spill the beans. It was as if Maltese had signed his own death warrant." Then Magagna added, "That was in January. From then until last Friday, nobody saw him—nobody, not even his old friends among the journalists. Maltese went into hiding. He was scared because he knew that his life was in danger."

17: Pergola

BANCA SAN MATTEO had once been a convent. The low ceiling of crossed arches was now white, but in places there were the remnants of a mural—cherubim and saints—forming irregular clouds of pastel color against the whitewash.

Trotti walked slowly, leaning on Pisanelli's supportive arm.

They reached the Foreign Exchange desk—SERVIZIO ESTERO—and a tall man looked up from his typewriter. Pisanelli lifted the folding board in the counter.

The bank clerk had the hangdog look of a cartoon animal. His eyes quickly returned to the keyboard.

Trotti said, "Knock."

Pisanelli did as he was told. He tapped on the walnut door then, without waiting for a reply, turned the handle. Trotti stepped past him.

It did not look like a bank manager's office. It could have been a modern living room out of the pages of *Casa Italia* or *Vogue*. A low table, a rug, leather armchairs and tubular bookcases. Books that were leather-bound, neat and untouched. On the desk a telephone that appeared unhindered by wires.

A plain wooden crucifix was attached to the wall.

"A pleasant surprise." Pergola was smoking. He stubbed out the cigarette and came towards Trotti. "Always a pleasure to see you, Commissario." He held out his hand.

Pergola limped.

A well-dressed man, he wore a grey suit with a waistcoat that emphasized the narrowness of his body. The white shirt was new and spotless; the wine-dark tie had been knotted expertly. The bank manager was a small man with sloping shoulders and short hair. He wore discreet cologne. The grey eyes registered the bruising on Trotti's face. "Please be seated." He gestured to the armchairs. "But I thought you were on holiday, Commissario. I thought the Pubblica Sicurezza . . ."

On one wall there was a long mural photograph. It showed the city—the river, the old houses along the banks of the Po and, rising above the rooftops, the familiar dome of the cathedral.

The photograph must have been taken in Borgo Genovese.

Pisanelli helped Trotti to sit down.

Pergola smiled. "I see that I am not alone in being temporarily handicapped." His smile was sympathetic.

Trotti said, "The result of a misunderstanding," and shrugged.

"Can I offer you something to drink? Or perhaps, Commissario . . ." He turned to a walnut cabinet. He took small steps, hesitating to put his weight on his left leg. He opened the cabinet and took out a tin. "English boiled sweets." He gave Trotti a large smile. "I think I know your vice, Commissario. Smith Kendon Travel Sweets."

Trotti took one of the sweets. "One of my vices."

Pergola carefully pulled at the crease of his trousers before sitting down on an armchair facing Trotti.

"How's your knee, Signor Pergola?"

"I'm lucky still to have a knee. A few centimeters lower and I would have lost it." The bland smile remained in place. "So what brings you here, Commissario? I really wasn't expecting to see you so soon." He allowed just a hint of firmness into his voice. "Can I assume that there have been developments in your enquiries?"

"Signor Pergola, you know that I'm no longer involved. The dossier is now in the capable hands of the Guardia di Finanza."

Pergola nodded. His face was small and calm but the eyes were restless, moving from Trotti to Pisanelli and back. A shy but intelligent man. "The Guardia di Finanza," he repeated, as if he had never heard the words before.

"I think, Signor Pergola—despite the administrative reorganization—I think that we can help each other. There are some things that I should like to ask you." Trotti allowed the boiled sweet to click against his teeth. "I'm not convinced that you've always been frank with me."

The ground glass window let in the white morning light and the sound of traffic along the Corso. In the office there was silence. Then Pergola gave an awkward laugh. "I'm afraid I forgot to offer a drink to your friend."

"Brigadiere Pisanelli is my assistant."

Almost imperceptibly, Pisanelli shook his head. Although he was nearly bald, at the back of Pisanelli's head the hair was long and it brushed against the collar of his suede jacket.

Another long silence while Pergola's eyes moved from Trotti to Pisanelli and then back to Trotti. The fingers of one hand tapped against the crease of his trousers.

"We've recovered five hundred thousand lire of the money that was stolen." Trotti watched for the reaction in the man's eyes: there was nothing.

"Five hundred thousand—I suppose it's a start. Congratulations."

"You can congratulate the Carabinieri."

"Is there any chance that the rest of the money—the rest of the hundred million will be found in this way?"

"What I still don't understand," Trotti said, "is why the robbers should take the money and then still feel the need to put a couple of bullets into your legs." He paused. "A way of behaving that's more reminiscent of terrorists than of professional bank robbers."

"That's an enigma that perhaps the Guardia di Finanza will be able to resolve."

For an instant, Trotti's eyes blazed. "I think you should have told me more about your bank—and who it's owned by."

"Commissario, have you ever met with anything other than our most sincere desire to cooperate? Nothing, I repeat nothing, has been deliberately kept from you and you have always—"

"Of course, of course. But there may have been an element of suppression."

"An ugly word."

"Ten and a half per cent of the shares in the Banca San Matteo are in the hands of a Liechtenstein consortium."

"Dienstinvest." He nodded. "That is the information which you can find in the annual report."

"You would have helped me a great deal—me and my colleagues of the Guardia di Finanza—if you had revealed that Dienstinvest of Vaduz was in turn controlled by the Banco Milanese."

A light laugh, but the eyes continued their rapid movement. "It's hard for me to know what you know and what you don't know."

"Tell me everything and I have merely to pick and choose."

"I've always acted in good faith. And so, I'm sure, has the staff of the Banca San Matteo. I can assure that there's been no . . ." He made an open gesture. "As for a connection between Banco Milanese and Dienstinvest—that really doesn't concern us here. On the other hand, if you feel that in some underhand way this bank is concerned with Banco Milanese, I can assure you you're making a mistake. The very nature of Banco Milanese . . ." He shrugged. "Things are very critical."

"Precisely. Then you know that the Banco Milanese has been the target of several attacks in the press and even in Parliament? You know that it's been the object of inspection by the Banca d'Italia?"

"I know what I read in the paper."

"*Popolo d'Italia*, Signor Pergola?"

For an instant the banker did not speak. "I know that Banco Milanese is run by a very strange man. I can assure you I've never met him. Signor Bastia and I do not orbit in the same circles. I can also assure you that between the Banca San Matteo and Banco Milanese . . ."

Trotti asked, "It's quite possible, isn't it, that the unfortunate attack of which you were the victim, is connected with the Banco Milanese?"

"Absurd." He laughed.

"Isn't it possible that the two bullets removed from your leg were a warning, Signor Pergola?"

"It's quite true that Dienstinvest controls an important percentage of this bank's shares. But to maintain—as you seem to be doing—that because of Dienstinvest, the Banco Milanese is exerting direct or indirect control upon us—this is quite absurd. Quite absurd."

"Who owns Dienstinvest?"

"A list of investors is something that Dienstinvest will readily supply you with. You have their address in Vaduz." He leaned back in the armchair and folded his arms. "There are always transactions going on between banks—between all banks. The contrary would be strange, I think you'd agree."

Trotti held up his hand. "These are matters that the Guardia di Finanza will be able to look into at length, and with the necessary competence."

"Neither the Guardia di Finanza nor anybody else will find any impropriety in the running of the Banca San Matteo." The same bland smile. The eyes had ceased to move dartingly; they now showed amusement. "I can't help wondering—I trust you don't mind my saying so—why you bother about these things now that another police force is dealing with the enquiry."

"You haven't asked me where the five hundred thousand lire was found."

"Another sweet, Commissario?"

"Does the name Maltese mean anything to you?"

"Maltese?"

"He was once a journalist with the *Popolo d'Italia*."

"Ah." A look of understanding. "He was, I believe, one of the gentlemen involved in the . . ."

"The Night of the Tazebao." Trotti nodded. "Precisely."

"Please don't associate this bank with what happened in Milan."

"Of course not." It was Trotti's turn to smile; as his lips moved, the bruised skin hurt him. "I am simply trying to reach the truth. When a highly respected bank manager—a son of this city, an alumnus of our university—is shot in the leg in broad daylight—the only robbery this city has known in fifteen years—and when one million lire disappear, it's only normal that, as an officer of the Pubblica Sicurezza, I ask a few questions."

An almost imperceptible nod.

"And although—like you, Signor Pergola—I've limitless faith in the efficiency and devotion and probity of the Guardia di Finanza, I can't help worrying."

"I'm sure there are other things for you to worry over."

"Many."

The two men looked at each other in silence.

"Just one more question, Signor Pergola."

"Please ask as many questions as you wish."

"You've heard of Ramoverde?"

A pause while he frowned. "That was many years ago."

"Did you know, Signor Pergola, that the journalist Maltese— the man on whose corpse the five hundred thousand lire were found—did you know that he was Ramoverde's son—and that last Friday, he was murdered at Gardesana? In my presence?"

"Really?" Pergola said in a casual tone, but both Trotti and Pisanelli noticed that for an instant the small bank manager in the neat, expensive suit had turned pale.

18: Baldassare

A PORTER APPROACHED them. Trotti produced his identity card.

"You are looking for somebody in the university?"

"Signorina Guerra?"

"Nobody here with that name."

"She's the daughter of the city architect."

The porter lifted his peaked cap with its brass escutcheon and he scratched at the receding hairline. "Signorina Guerra?"

"I think she teaches history."

More scratching and then a look of enlightenment. "History of literature, you mean."

"Perhaps."

"But she's no longer Signorina Guerra—she's been married for three years now. Signora Baldassare." He nodded. "You mean Signora Baldassarre."

"Where is she?"

"This way, please."

They followed the long porticoes. The small porter walked briskly, the iron tips of his shoes echoing on the stone slabs.

Storia della letteratura moderna was on the first floor, facing the university library across the quadrangle. They went through a door and Trotti found himself in a corridor, long, dark and chill. The office was halfway down, hidden between two large bookcases. The porter knocked on the door.

"Signora Baldassare, visitors for you."

Trotti and Pisanelli entered the room.

The walls were covered with bookcases, there was an old carpet on the floor and a ladder stood in one corner.

"Two gentlemen from the Questura," the porter said huskily before closing the door. His metallic footfalls grew gradually fainter down the corridor.

The woman sitting behind a desk—not the main mahogany desk in the center of the room, but a small, humbler one pushed into one corner, almost hidden had it not been for the light cast by the table lamp—stood up. The same light partially lit her face.

She came towards them. "Commissario Trotti, I believe."

"You recognize me?"

"I was at my sister's trial. So were you." She held out her hand and Trotti shook it.

"It's about your sister, Signora Baldassare."

No reaction.

She had large eyes—very dark brown in the feeble light—and they looked at him without emotion, waiting for an explanation. There was something prim about her. She stood with her feet together. Sensible brown shoes and a brown cardigan. Her hair was pulled away from her forehead. Her complexion was clear but pale.

"I'd like to know where she is."

"I don't think I can help you, Commissario."

"Lia Guerra is your sister?"

"I hardly ever see her."

Pisanelli took a notebook from his jacket pocket.

"We're not close." Then, as an afterthought, she added, "Lia ought never to have gotten involved in politics."

"Is she still political?"

Signora Baldassare shrugged. "In a small town like this, people don't forget." She leaned her weight against the small desk. The light was behind her and Trotti could not make out her features. Older than he had at first imagined—thirty-five, perhaps thirty-seven. Her arms were crossed as if to protect herself from any form of contact. "What Lia has done has made life very difficult for me."

"She still lives here in the city?"

"I have my life to lead—and because of my sister they think—I don't know—they think that I belong to the Red Brigades or that I'm a feminist or a lesbian."

"Signora, I have got to find her."

"Why?"

"I have to talk to her."

"My sister is ten years younger than me. She was born at a time when life started to get a bit easier for my parents. Mama always said that she was going to spoil Lia." A hurried laugh—or perhaps a repressed snort. "One of the few promises that Mama ever kept. It was as if Mama could never forgive me—she was pregnant with me when she got married. Mama who had great pretensions of becoming a politician. And she had to give it all up because I came along. But Lia—that was different. Lia was the perfect daughter—so pretty, so intelligent."

"Your mother . . ."

"My mother's dead." There was no emotion in her voice. "She didn't live to see her little Lia pass before the judges and be accused of plotting against the State. Mama was spared that."

"Can you tell me where she is?"

"The best clothes for Lia. I had to make to do with what there was with the clothes from my cousins—uncomfortable clothes that were worn and smelly. But our Lia was the princess. She had everything that money could buy. And a lot more as well."

Outside there was the sound of footfalls along the cloisters.

Pisanelli said, "We believe that your sister went to live in Milan."

The woman shrugged. "Perhaps."

Trotti asked, "What would she do in Milan?"

"Mother gave her everything—and then was surprised when she discovered that her little baby, her fourteen-year-old daughter, was going to bed with men twice her age."

"Is she living with a man now?"

"How would I know? And anyway, I couldn't care less." She

turned away from them and moved, like a moth attracted by the light, towards the opaque glass of the window. She had a small, trim body that the dowdy clothes could not hide. "Has she murdered her lover?"

"A man called Maltese was murdered in a bar. I think that perhaps he knew her." Trotti added, "He died in my arms."

She stood with her back to Trotti and Pisanelli.

"There was a photograph of your sister in his wallet."

She turned her head slightly. "There's not much that I can do about that."

"You can help me," Trotti said. "If I can talk to her, it might help me find out who murdered Maltese."

"I really don't see how I can help. I heard that she'd gone to Milan. I gave her some money—but that was eighteen months ago. As she hasn't been in touch with me—not even to ask for more money—I must assume that she has found money—or somebody to supply her with it."

"Perhaps she's got a job."

Signora Baldassare turned to face them, face taut, lips slightly trembling. "I'm very sorry. I can't help you."

Steps outside. The door opened. The porter put his head round the side of the door. "Commissario Trotti?"

"Yes?"

"A Dottor Magagna for you on the phone?"

19: Senigallia

THE TRAIN STOPPED and Trotti looked up from the dusty pages that he held open on his knees. He looked out of the window. The backs of humdrum houses, minute gardens and, wedged between two brick walls, a bowling alley where two old men were throwing bocce balls across the dusty ground.

Then the train started to move again and a few minutes later, it pulled into the grey light of the station. Magagna was on the platform. He looked up through his sunglasses and smiled as he caught sight of Trotti. Magagna helped him climb down from the train.

"Whatever made you shave off your mustache?" Trotti asked.

On the grey-green locomotive, a speeding tortoise had been painted on to the high casing. The animal appeared to be running in the wrong direction, as if it were in a hurry to return to Genoa.

"That was my wife's idea."

"And you do everything your wife tells you?"

Magagna took Trotti's case. "How're you feeling, Commissario?"

"The ribs hurt—but the bruises are going down."

"The car's outside."

Trotti had to lean against the handrail of the descending escalator.

At the bottom, Magagna guided him through the entrance

hall. Milan Central Station had once been imposing, a paean to fascism, to Mussolini's new Italy. Now it was tawdry. The city's flotsam—addicts, abandoned old women, alcoholics in their stained and shabby clothes—were already lying out on the cold stone benches.

The stench of ancient urine.

They stepped out into the sun.

There were normal plates on the 124 standing in the taxi line. Magagna opened the door and helped Trotti to climb in; as he did so, a taxi driver swore at him. The man was silenced by the brief flash of Magagna's identity card. The man shrugged and spat in the gutter.

"Where else am I supposed to park in this goddamn city?"

"If you had any sense, you'd never have left the Questura to come and live in Milan in the first place." Trotti winced as he got into the passenger seat.

It was a police car. It smelled of old oil, old sweat and old vomit. In places the upholstery had been ripped. A microphone was attached to the dashboard, a picture of Amanda Lear stuck to the inside of the windscreen. Magagna got behind the wheel and, taking the microphone, spoke into it.

Trotti looked out of the window. The exterior of the station was splattered with pigeon droppings.

May in Milan. The trees had already pushed out the green buds into the air and the petrol fumes.

"Near Senigallia," Magagna said, and turning on the engine started to drive. They went down via Buenos Aires and then turned left on to one of the ring roads.

"How did you manage to find her?"

"Nobody knows about the photograph, Commissario?"

Trotti shook his head. "Unless, of course, it has been found in the Opel."

"You realize that you could be getting me into trouble?"

"Have I ever gotten you into trouble before?" Before Magagna had time to reply, Trotti asked, "Where did you find her?"

"Milan is off limits for you—and you know it. You haven't got anything to worry about. Your career is behind you. But if it's discovered that I have been helping an out-of-city officer in making enquiries without the Questor's permission . . ." He turned to look at Trotti. "My career could go up in smoke."

"Maltese died in my arms."

"Your feelings of guilt or responsibility have got nothing to do with me." He braked at traffic lights and for a moment the high gothic spires of the Duomo were visible above the rooftops. Then the lights changed and Magagna took a left turn. "Your guilt won't get me a promotion."

"If you have any doubts about helping me, Magagna, turn round and take me back to the station." He added, "And light up a cigarette—perhaps that will help you relax."

Magagna lit a cigarette but he did not relax.

A few minutes later they were at Porta Ticinese. Magagna bumped the Fiat up onto the sidewalk. A tram went clattering past. The afternoon passengers took no notice of the two police officers.

They got out of the car and walked along the street. To the right there was an open space where sparse grass and bushes tried to grow beneath the detritus of the city and a vast billboard, a billboard advertising blue jeans—"*If you love me, follow me.*"

The sun had come out.

"You want something to drink first, Commissario?" Magagna had stopped in front of a bar, where the smell of coffee and hot bread wafted out onto the sidewalk.

"I want to see her and then get the six o'clock train back home."

Magagna said nothing; he merely nudged at his glasses.

The shop was down a side turning. A row of old buildings that had once been on the edge of the city. Some were in a state of advanced decay but others had been recently restored and repainted and the shop fronts had been modernized.

"You can buy anything here—a flea market." Magagna smiled. "Jeans, American clothes, antique furniture—and whisky taken from the TIR trucks. All part of our submerged economy."

Trotti laughed. "Submerged economy."

GRAFFITI—the neon letters blinked bravely in the sunlight. "This is where she works."

Without bothering to look at the shop front, with its display of sweaters and shirts, Trotti entered the premises. A bell rang.

"Can I help you?"

There was a lot of piping—quite pointless and painted a vivid red—and a lot of mirrors. Overhead lights were directed down on the racks of secondhand clothes. The carpet was of coarse jute. A smell of incense hung in the air and piles of neatly ironed shirts and slacks had been placed along the shelves. The shelves formed a checkered motif; behind them more mirrors.

"Can I help you?" the woman repeated. She was middle-aged and smoked a cigarette that drooped from lips as red as the piping.

Moving sideways, she came down the three steps and smiled at Trotti. The eyes were less welcoming.

"I would like to talk to Signorina Guerra."

She took the cigarette from her mouth and placed her hand on her thigh. "I know of nobody with that name." There were traces of lipstick on the large teeth.

Magagna said, "The girl who works for you."

The woman looked at Trotti in silence.

Magagna showed her his card.

"I'll get her for you." The woman turned and moved away on her gold high heels. There was the design of a horse's head on her jean pocket. The tightness of her jeans did not suit the matronly hips.

Magagna raised his sunglasses and winked at Trotti.

"Signori?"

The girl came down the three steps and Trotti saw how much she had changed. She recognized Trotti and her face fell. "What the hell do you want?" she asked, her voice low and angry.

"How are you, Signorina Guerra?"

"Go away." She glanced at Magagna. "Leave me alone and go away."

"I must ask you a few questions."

"I work here." She looked about the shop hurriedly. "I've done nothing wrong."

"That's why I needed to see you."

"What does he want?" She nodded towards Magagna.

"Signor Caiazzo works with me."

Her eyes turned back to Trotti. "Go away—you've done enough damage as it is."

Trotti held up his hand. "Perhaps we could speak. Just for a few minutes. Signorina, I merely want to ask you for your help."

The other woman was standing at the top of the flight of three stairs, a hand on her hip and her eyes squinting through the tobacco smoke.

"Alone," Trotti added.

The older woman heaved a sigh that caused her ample chest to heave. "There's a stockroom at the back." She gestured with her thumb. "Try not to steal anything."

Trotti took Lia Guerra by the arm. Magagna opened the door—painted the same deep red—and they found themselves in a dusty room little bigger than a cupboard. Lia Guerra turned on the overhead light. The naked bulb threw shadows on her hard face.

An old telephone—without a dial—was screwed to the wall.

"Well?"

"Maltese is dead."

For a fraction of a second there was no reaction. Then the face seemed to change. She caught her breath. Moisture formed at the corner of her eyes.

She had changed—in the photograph taken by the Nucleon Politico she had been wearing a handkerchief round her neck and the young face had an intense proud beauty as she pulled back her arm in the act of hurling a missile. Now she was older, the face worn and slightly waxen. The prettiness had not gone, but it was going.

"Dead, shot through the heart."

The wet eyes looked at him.

"Here."

She shook her head.

"Here," Trotti repeated, holding out the pistol that he had taken from his pocket. "The gun that Maltese was shot with."

"Why?"

"Take it."

She looked at the pistol in horror.

"Take it, feel it, have a good look at it—the gun that killed him," Trotti said and he thrust the P38 into her small hands. "The gun that murdered Maltese."

A tear ran down her cheek.

"I haven't seen him for . . ." A sob stopped her.

"And now you won't see him again."

Lia Guerra glanced at Magagna.

"Where did you meet Maltese? You were living together, weren't you?"

"Not satisfied with . . . not satisfied with having already ruined my life, you've come here to insult me and to taunt me." The eyes flared with anger. "And to soil his memory."

"You ruined your life—nobody else."

Magagna said, more softly, "Please understand, Signorina. We need your cooperation."

"I can't help you."

"I think you can," Trotti replied.

"I haven't seen him—I haven't seen Maltese for a very long time."

"Very strange." Trotti took a handkerchief from his pocket and carefully lifted the gun from her loose grasp. "You haven't seen him but your fingerprints are all over the weapon that you used to kill him." He wrapped the handkerchief round the gun and dropped it into his pocket.

The girl had visibly paled.

"What can you tell me about Maltese, Signorina Guerra?"

She hung her head.

"What do you know about Maltese? Or did he call himself Ramoverde?"

"Go away. Just go away and leave me alone."

"Tenente Caiazzo, do you have the cuffs? I don't think the young lady is going to cooperate."

She continued to hold her head down. A couple of tears fell to the dusty floor.

"Where did you meet him?"

"You think you're clever, don't you?" She looked up, tossing back her hair and she was no longer crying. "You think you know everything, don't you, Trotti? And you think you can manipulate people just as if they were animals."

Magagna produced a handkerchief and handed it to her.

"For God's sake, Trotti, what d'you want of me?"

"I want to know why Ramoverde was murdered."

"And you think I can help you?" With the handkerchief she wiped her eyes. "But I've got my life to live. I'm twenty-seven years old and I'm not going to go back to prison."

Trotti looked around the room. "So instead you sell second-hand clothes?"

"What the hell am I supposed to do? You want me to throw bombs? You want me to fire bullets into people's legs?" She gesticulated.

"Keep your voice down," Trotti said sharply and he caught hold of her wrist. The girl was wearing a checked shirt and with his other hand Trotti rolled back the sleeve.

"An expensive habit."

The arm was scarred and hard where needles had pierced the skin.

"A temporary arrest, Signorina Guerra," Trotti said. "Then you'll be sent to a center for detoxification."

She pulled her arm free, fell backwards and crumpled onto the floor. "You bastard," she muttered and she scratched at her arm.

20: Lodi

THERE WERE THREE locks and the girl fumbled with the keys, while Trotti and Magagna waited on the dusty, foul-smelling landing. The apartment was on the top floor of a building that gave onto a courtyard. Three stories below them, children were playing between the washing lines.

The housing estate was near Piazza Lodi and the sound of rumbling trains came from the shunting yards.

"My home." Lia Guerra opened the door for them.

The small room smelt of dirt. A mattress lay on the floor, the bedsheets were pushed back and had not been straightened. There was no cover to the pillow. On the floor, a lid served as an ashtray and was brimming over with burnt-out stubs.

"Did Maltese live here?"

"No." The girl sat down cross-legged on the mattress.

"Were you lovers?" Trotti asked.

"That's got nothing to do with you."

The ceiling had been painted but the plaster was beginning to flake.

A carnation placed in an old wine bottle had started to wilt. Its tight petals and its deep red color were out of place in the room.

Magagna moved carefully from the door to the sink and then to a cupboard and then back to the sink.

"Why did he have your photo?"

"I knew Maltese," she said. "Does that make us lovers? You think I must spread my legs for every man I meet?"

"There was a time when you preferred women."

The girl said nothing but her face flushed.

Magagna was at the sink. He called Trotti over. Magagna was sniffing. "Where's the lavatory?" Magagna asked the girl.

"On the landing."

"Can you smell it?" he said softly to Trotti.

"Smell what?"

"Urine—or rather uric acid. Somebody's been pissing down the sink." He looked over his shoulder at the girl. "A man's been living here. That's a man's trick—she's more likely to empty her chamber pot in the lavatory on the landing." Then Magagna moved away. He reminded Trotti of a dog following a scent.

"Signorina Guerra, where did you meet Maltese?" Trotti returned to the girl. He pulled up the only chair and sat down opposite her.

She looked up at him, was about to say something, but her voice was stifled by the rumbling of a train. The entire building shook for a few seconds.

"Where did you meet him?"

"In a bar. L'Orchidea Bianca—a bar in the Brera."

"Just like that?"

She shrugged.

"And you became lovers?"

She stood up and Magagna, who was looking through a pile of old newspapers, put down what he was looking at and followed her. The young woman approached the sink and poured herself a glass of water. She turned and leaned against the sink. "Do you enjoy bullying people, Trotti?"

"Maltese is dead—and I want to know who killed him."

"And that's why you blackmail me? That's why you get me to put my fingerprints on the murder weapon?"

"Signorina Guerra, I need your cooperation—and that is something that you can give me of your own free will. Or else I will have to force you into giving it." He paused. "What was Maltese doing in Milan?"

"I don't know."

"What did he talk to you about?"

"About things which do not concern you."

"Did he mention the name Novara to you?"

She shrugged and looked away.

"Signorina Guerra—be reasonable. You are making life difficult for me—and for yourself. Or perhaps you don't care that he was murdered?"

"I thought I was your number one suspect. I thought that was the purpose of your performance with the gun."

Magagna was looking through the cupboards—old wooden cupboards that had never been varnished. He was removing the contents and placing them in neat piles upon the floor.

"You sent me to prison once, Commissario. Isn't that enough?"

"I never forced you into being a terrorist. And you were lucky—your friend Gracchi is still inside."

"Gracchi," she repeated disdainfully.

"You once risked your life for him."

"When I was a kid," she said softly, almost talking to herself, and still not looking at Trotti. "I used to screw up my eyes and pray that my real mother would come and find me. I never wanted to believe that the woman who shared my father's bed was my real mother. I prayed, hoping that Jesus would hear me. But there is no Jesus." She looked at Trotti. "And there is no revolution. Gracchi and his ideas—he fooled me just as the priests had fooled me. The working class? The working class doesn't need me—they never did."

"Four bottles of contraband whisky," Magagna said. He placed the bottles on the floor. "And two cartons of Kent cigarettes—also contraband."

"At least Maltese did not want to win me over to some empty cause. Nor did he want to climb over me, use my body while telling me that he respected my intellect."

"You admit you lived with Maltese?"

"You're a fool, Trotti. A peasant and a fool."

"Seven disposable syringes—property of the Policlinico,

Milan." Magagna unwrapped a plastic bag. "And about five grams of a white substance—looks like chalk." He was grinning.

Guerra took no notice of him. She looked at Trotti. "It's an escape."

The cupboard doors were open. Magagna had emptied them of nearly all their contents—unwashed underclothes, scuffed shoes, one or two newspapers. The white powder, the syringes and the whisky stood to one side.

"And what is this?" Magagna had his head inside the cupboard. With both hands, he removed a thin plank of hardboard. "And what is this? And what is this?" Magagna held up a cloth-bag. He opened it and pulled out a disposable razor. "And a can of shaving cream."

The girl stared out of the window. With the light on one side of her face, she was thin but strangely beautiful. An unobtainable beauty.

"And," said Magagna, pulling out a packet, then undoing the envelope of plastic wrapping paper, "several pages of a handwritten manuscript."

21: Maturità

My father was arrested for the first time in September 1960. He spent several weeks in prison but by the second week of October, the investigating magistrate was forced—reluctantly—to admit that there was not sufficient proof against him. Papa was set free and for over a year he lived with us in Piacenza.

If the enquiring magistrates and the officers of police found my father cold, I can only say that to his family he showed a completely different nature. It was as if the tragic events at Villa Laura had caused him to call into question his entire existence.

He continued to work in his small dental surgery in via Marconi and it was possibly as a result of the publicity that the press had given him that his dental practice flourished. I do not recall ever having seen him so hard-worked. He was, I think, happy to dedicate himself to the work, for it enabled him to forget about the sword of Damocles that hung over him. As long as no culprit could be found for the murder, he knew that he remained the prime suspect. Papa worked very hard—and we were all grateful for the advantages that the money brought. Papa had always been loath to borrow—he had refused all the gifts that Grandfather Belluno had offered him when they had been on speaking terms—yet the lawyers' fees had to be met. And this was in the days before you could murder somebody and then live the rest of your life on the royalties from the newspapers.

Home life continued as normally as was possible. Mama was courageous and set us a fine example. I was still studying for my maturità at the Liceo Ippolito Nievo. Both parents were anxious about my success. They were determined that I should go to university—there was talk of Borromeo or even the Scuola Superiore at Pisa. Looking back, I must say that I think they set their standards a bit high.

Papa, who had always been for me a distant person—someone who I could speak to rarely—now became for me almost like a school companion. When he was free from the surgery we would spend hours together and we would talk about life. Did he think, perhaps, that he was going to finish out his life in some wretched prison? We would talk about life and Papa was aware of having made a great many mistakes. He regretted the early years that he had frittered away. Sometimes he spoke about Palermo and he was ashamed of himself. Above all, I think he regretted having let down those people who had made sacrifices for him. He did not want me to make the same mistakes.

Sometimes he spoke of his early years in Argentina.

Mama, too, was very good to me. And to see us at supper in the small kitchen in via Marconi—the new refrigerator, the photograph that Uncle Orazio had brought back from his audience with the Pope, the fresh smell of homemade lasagne—no one would ever have guessed that we were at the center of a drama which continued to hold the nation's attention.

I failed the maturità.

I don't know why. I suspect that I did not study hard enough. In a strange way, being the son of the dentist Ramoverde bestowed upon me a kind of mystery that I enjoyed and that I made use of. I suddenly found myself very popular among the girls of my age.

Papa was upset, even angry. I had let him down. Yet he never raised his voice or told me off. He wanted me to repeat the year. I refused. By now I was nearly nineteen and I had already decided I wanted to be journalist. I toyed with the idea of running away from home, of going to Argentina.

Perhaps Papa saw in me something of the rebel that he had

once been. I was headstrong, and though this upset him, he was in his own way proud of me.

It was Uncle Orazio who persuaded me to follow the path of reason. I went back to school in October and only three weeks later, Papa was arrested anew.

Tenente Trotti of PS came with two officers. They gave Papa half an hour to pack.

22: Lambrate

"I CAN DRIVE you home, Commissario."

The smell of roasting coffee and car fumes hovered over the city.

"Take me to the station."

For a while, neither man spoke. Magagna drove past the Alitalia terminal. The evening air was soft.

"I want you to keep an eye on her, Magagna."

Magagna lit a cigarette. "Arresting her would have been the sensible thing to do."

"It's better to leave her free." Trotti smiled. "You don't trust her, Magagna?"

"A policeman shouldn't trust anybody."

"She had no reason to lie."

Magagna shrugged. "We don't know her real motives."

"You think she's involved in Maltese's death?"

With the warm weather, the prostitutes had come out in force along the boulevards. A few cars were crawling by the curbside. The drivers hid behind sunglasses. Flat, emotionless faces assessed the young women, the cheap wigs and the short skirts.

"They were living together and so she probably knew what Maltese was up to. And she knows who killed him."

Trotti sucked at his chipped tooth. "Shaving soap and some underclothes and a few pages of typescript don't constitute proof of their living together."

"But it explains why nobody knew where Maltese was living. Maltese was scared and he holed up with her. It makes sense. It wasn't on a permanent basis—perhaps they weren't lovers. But it was somewhere where he felt safe. Why else would he have hidden the manuscript with her?"

"The neighbors would have noticed him."

Magagna inhaled thoughtfully and the red tip of the cigarette glowed. "There's always a back exit—and perhaps she was in disguise. Maltese was living with her there at least some of the time. He went into hiding after the Night of the Tazebao. He knew his life was in danger and apparently nobody knew he and the girl were friends."

Trotti turned and looked at Magagna. "Incidentally, how did you manage to find Guerra?"

Magagna shrugged and beneath the sunglasses the lips broke into a grin.

Almost against his will, Trotti smiled too. "Congratulations."

"I've been with Narcotici for eighteen months. I've started to build up a nice circle of contacts."

"Cocaine?"

Magagna frowned. "What?" He braked for the traffic lights at Piazzale Cinque Giornate and his face was tinted by the red light. Behind the police car a driver hooted impatiently.

"The powder you found—it was cocaine?"

"Heroin." Magagna shook his head. "And poor quality. The sort of stuff that a buyer wouldn't pay more than two thousand dollars for the kilo. In Afghanistan or Turkey."

"And how much in Milan?"

Magagna shrugged. "Heroin is morphine that has been processed. Heroin is the stuff she's killing herself with, the white powder, the stuff she's got to buy. But Ragusa and his friends import morphine base and they transform it—that's where the money is. A kilo of morphine can be converted into a kilo of heroin. What some tribal clansman in Pathanistan got paid two thousand dollars for can be sold—once it's been transformed into heroin—on the street for anything between a hundred and twenty and a hundred and fifty thousand dollars." He smiled.

"Narcodollars. And with the Soviet invasion of Afghanistan the prices have gone up—a seller's market."

"An expensive habit for the daughter of our late city architect."

"Nobody made her stick the needle in her arm."

"But once she did, she was hooked. An addict."

"We're all addicts of something or other." Again the smile as Magagna let out the clutch and the car moved forward. "I know people who get irritable, who show withdrawal symptoms, who almost lose control of themselves if they're not getting their dose of drugs . . . of glucose. In the form of rhubarb sweets."

Trotti laughed. "Or women."

"Commissario, I'm a married man. I hope you're not attributing to me improper or immoral thoughts." He threw the cigarette out of the window. "Nice legs, though. Pity Guerra's an addict—although I quite like that cadaveric, underfed look. Better than when she was a fat lesbian."

Trotti's smile vanished. "I must get home."

Trotti did not speak again until they reached Lambrate. Magagna parked. Trotti did not wait for him but walked directly onto the platform. It was lit up by the high sodium lamps. On the far side of the tracks stood a long, silent and immobile train. Incomprehensible words and characters were stenciled on the canvas tarpaulins. Beograd, Zagreb.

Magagna approached Trotti.

"I need to find Novara."

"Go home and rest, Commissario. Maltese's death isn't going to go away. There's no hurry and you should still be in bed. You don't look well, your face is still bruised . . ."

"Maltese worked with Novara—and he knew he was risking his life when he gave information about the Banco Milanese and South America. Find Novara—and perhaps we find the explanation behind Maltese's death."

"You don't need to wait for the train, Commissario. Please let me drive you home. I can get you back to your doorstep in under three quarters of an hour—and you won't have to hang around waiting for the Diretto."

"I want to go through Maltese's manuscript again. I can do that on the train." He paused. "Short, though."

"Short?"

"For somebody who was a journalist—four pages. Short for somebody who knew that his life was in danger."

"I'll drive you home, Commissario."

Trotti placed his hand on Magagna's shoulder. "It's kind of you—and I appreciate it. Forgive me, Magagna, forgive me. I realize what you're doing for me and I'm grateful." His face was haggard. "I know it's not easy for you to take time off the Ragusa thing—I know that."

A crowd of railway men stood chatting by the open door of the station bar. One wore a raincoat, the others wore their uniforms and their peaked caps of blue. They laughed. The station master held a red stick beneath his arm.

"Guerra knew me and so did Maltese. Yet when he sat down beside me in Gardesana, he didn't say a word. I didn't get the impression that there was any recognition. Why was he there? What was he doing?"

Magagna shrugged. "A coincidence."

"I don't trust coincidences when people are getting killed."

"He wanted to speak to you but in private." Magagna raised his shoulders.

"How did he know I was at Gardesana? The only person who could have possibly known that was Pioppi—or me."

Magagna lit another cigarillo. A few minutes later, a pair of lights—red and angry, like the eyes of a dog in the gathering dusk crept into the station. The Diretto. Carefully, ponderously, it drew alongside the platform, pulling with it old, dirty carriages.

Magagna assisted Trotti onto the train and accompanied him to a wooden bench. "Sure you don't want me to take you home?"

The yellow lights of the compartment were turned on.

On the platform, the station master threw away his cigarette. He put a whistle to his mouth.

"Novara," Trotti said. "I've got to find Novara."

The station master lifted the red stick.

23: Minerva

HE HOBBLED OUT of the station.

It was not yet ten o'clock but the city was strangely empty.

There was a taxi. Trotti approached it. The man behind the wheel was reading a newspaper. He caught sight of Trotti and climbed out.

"It's you, Commissario." He gave Trotti a large, friendly grin that appeared anemic beneath the lights of the railway station. "You've hurt your leg."

"I got into an argument."

"You must let me take you home." The man held open the door of the car and helped Trotti onto the back seat. "You don't look very well."

"It's nothing."

"The rowdy life you lead, Commissario." He climbed into the driver's seat and turned on the engine. "How's your wife?"

"In America."

"Lucky woman. And Pioppi?"

"At the university and working like a madwoman—determined to get thirty out of thirty for every exam she sits. Thirty summa cum laude." Trotti added, "And she gets her thirty every time."

"A clever girl."

"She gets her intelligence from her mother."

"And her determination from her father."

The taxi was new and in good condition.

The driver took the car slowly down the empty road and turned left at the granite statue of Minerva—a stern figure standing above the rising swirls of mist. Angela, the transvestite, stood in a lonely pool of light at the curbside. He was dressed in furs and held his handbag close to his body.

"First time I've seen you in a long time, Commissario."

Trotti shrugged. "Work," he said.

They stopped at traffic lights.

"And the little girl?" Trotti asked.

The driver laughed. "No longer a little girl, our Anna. Quite a lady. Top of the class all the time—best marks in composition and English. She says she wants to become an interpreter and work at the FAO—whatever that may be." He laughed, turned in his seat. The large, round face smiled at Trotti. The passing lights flickered across the pale skin. "And she's like a mother to her baby brother." He added, "I've got a lot to thank you for, Commissario."

"You forget that I'm the little girl's godfather."

"You should come and see us more often. Why don't you come for a meal—come on Sunday and Netta will cook something special."

Trotti laughed.

"What do you say, Commissario? We'd love to see you." Then with one hand on the steering wheel, he turned on the roof light and fumbled with a leather wallet. He extracted from it a photograph that he handed to Trotti. "Torre a Mare," he said.

The white, flat buildings of the countryside around Bari—Trotti could almost smell the tang of the Adriatic and see the sun glinting on the rocky beaches. There was Anna—she had grown taller, had filled out and was already an adolescent. The fringe had disappeared—her dark hair was pulled back in a ponytail. She stood in front of her father and stepmother. Simonetta was holding a baby in her arms.

The driver said with pride, "You know that we called the little boy Piero?"

They turned into via Milan and Trotti closed his eyes. "Piero," he repeated.

The car stopped.

It was late and there were no lights on in the house.

"You must come in for a drink."

"Another time, Commissario. Pistone comes on in another half-hour and I've got to be back. Netta doesn't like it when I'm not back on time. But perhaps during the week—or better still, you come and visit us. Bring Pioppi and the signora."

He helped Trotti out of the car.

"And anyway, I don't drink now—not outside meals. Haven't touched anything other than the glass of wine for over three years."

"Come in for a quick cup of coffee—strong and sweet as you like it."

"Another time, Commissario."

Trotti put his hand into his pocket. "How much do I owe you?"

The other man shook his head. "How much do I owe the man who helped me when I needed help?"

24: Phone

THE BOOKS OF urban architecture had been left open on the kitchen table. An empty glass stood in the sink. Trotti picked it up and smelled it. Mineral water.

Through the bedroom door came the regular fall of Pioppi's breathing. The myopic teddy bear stared down from where he was perched on the top of the wardrobe. The glass eyes were dusty.

Trotti entered his own bedroom and undressed. Then he showered, cleaned his teeth and looked at the jagged edge of the broken tooth the mirror. He gently touched at his bruises; they were still ugly and dark but the pain had considerably lessened.

Commissario Trotti went to bed.

No sound of traffic from the road. No sooner had he closed his eyes than he could feel himself falling asleep. Even the gentle throbbing in his ribs could not keep him awake.

The phone rang.

He awoke with a grunt, and the stiffness returned to his body. It required a considerable physical effort to reach out for the phone. A quarter past three—the hands of the clock took on a thick, luminous glow.

Early evening in New York.

He pulled the telephone towards his ear. "Agnese?"

"Commissario Trotti?"

"Who's speaking?"

"Commissario Trotti?" It was a voice he had heard some-where before. "You are an intelligent man."

"What d'you want?"

"And a happy man. You have got all you want. Please don't spoil everything."

The sleep drained from his eyes and from his body. "What do you want?"

"It's not what I want." An educated voice, lisping slightly. A voice from the past. "It's what you want that's important."

"What d'you want?" Trotti repeated and he could hear his own stupidity.

"Forget Ramoverde, Trotti—he's not important. But your job is important. Your job and your family. Forget you ever met Ramoverde. He's insignificant. And he's dead." A friendly voice, giving friendly advice. "Do I make myself understood?"

Trotti was silent.

"Ramoverde is dead." For an instant the voice laughed. "But for the time being you are still alive." A friendly, bantering laugh. Then the man hung up.

25: Farmyard

PISANELLI DROVE, HIS shoulders hunched over the wheel and his eyes squinting against the sunlight.

They went over the bridge, then skirted the center of Piacenza, taking the road up into the hills. After a while, the buildings and factories fell behind them. It was a good road. The apple and cherry trees were in blossom.

"An aerial over there, Commissario."

They had turned off the main road at Castello Piacentino and after a few kilometers of winding turns, they found the unsurfaced track.

"Park here," Trotti said.

His ribs hurt less but he was grateful for Pisanelli's help. Together they walked along the track until they came to a farmhouse. It was pretty, a stone building with brightly painted woodwork and flowerpots set along the ground. Geese fluttered across the open courtyard. Cow dung lay on the ground.

"A place like this that you'll retire to, Commissario?" Pisanelli had lost his look of harried concentration. Perhaps it was the effect of the clean air of the hills. Amusement formed wrinkles at the edge of his eyes.

"A few years to go before I retire."

There was a jeep—a Fiat Campagnola—standing near the farmhouse door. Men materialized from the building and the adjacent stables. A horse neighed somewhere. A man—he was wearing camouflage fatigue and a beret pulled down on one side of his face—came running towards Trotti. He carried a machine gun. His right hand kept the muzzle pointing towards the ground. With the other hand, he saluted.

"Commissario Trotti?" He smiled briefly at Trotti then glanced at Pisanelli.

"Pisanelli," Trotti said. "He's here to help me."

For some reason, Pisanelli blushed. He lowered his face, then fell into step behind Trotti and the man who led them to the door of the farmhouse. He did not knock. He lifted the heavy latch.

"So at last you've got here, Trotti."

Spadano was sitting behind a wooden table. Beside him were two other men in uniform. They looked up, but neither smiled. The air smelled of cigar smoke.

"We've located your Sardinians."

They shook hands hurriedly. The tip of the cigar glowed in the poor light of the farmhouse. Spadano did not introduce the other men. He gestured for Trotti and Pisanelli to sit down. A bottle of red wine stood on the table.

"My Sardinians?"

"Or perhaps you're not interested in who murdered Maltese. And who beat you up."

"What's Maltese got to do with you?" Trotti frowned. "I thought you were in the city, Spadano."

"And I thought you were going to take a well-deserved rest—but instead you choose to get shot at." He grinned. He looked alert and his uniform was freshly pressed.

Trotti wondered how long he had been up here in the hills.

"Care for some wine, Trotti?"

Trotti shook his head.

Spadano was still smiling. "You forget that this is a Carabinieri enquiry."

"This?"

"Maltese was sitting next to you when he was murdered—but Gardesana is under Carabinieri jurisdiction."

"So nice to see the Carabinieri willing to collaborate with the Pubblica Sicurezza."

"I'm not collaborating with the Pubblica Sicurezza." The smile had vanished. "You know what I think of the PS."

"Then why invite me out on a country excursion?" Trotti added, "To a place where neither you nor I belong. This is Piacenza."

"Trotti, you and I can work together. I trust you."

"Work together at what, Capitano?"

"It's possible that we're both dealing with the same thing."

"What?"

"Dealing with organized crime, Trotti. Both you and me—and it would make things a lot easier if we could pool our information."

Trotti shook his head, not understanding.

"Trotti, you know what I think of a lot of your colleagues. But I'm not always very keen on mine either. And I don't like the way that some of our own people refuse to share information—particularly when sharing information can mean saving time." He took the cigar from his mouth. "Their names are Uras and Suergiu. Sardinians. Small-time criminals from Orgosolo in Nuoro province. Shepherds who've been driven out of Sardinia by lack of work. They have records for kidnapping in Sardinia. Then robbery with violence on the mainland. Stupid, but tough and reliable. But what's interesting—"

"And you think you found them?"

"What's interesting is why they're involved in the first place. Not planners or organizers. And not marksmen. They're the sort of people who work with sawn-off rifles—not with guns."

"So?"

"Sure you don't care for some wine, Trotti?"

Trotti shook his head.

"And your friend?"

Pisanelli had his eyes on the bottle but Trotti shook his head. "We try not to drink on duty in the PS."

"Highly commendable." Spadano poured a thumb's worth of red wine into his glass and an equal amount into the glasses of the two officers.

He removed the cigar from his mouth while he drank.

"What makes you think that these Sardinians . . ."

"Suergiu and Uras."

"What makes you so sure that they were involved in Maltese's death?"

There came the soft crackle of static from a radio that had been set down near the window. From the aerial socket, a thick cable ran across the floor towards the open window.

Spadano replaced the cigar in his mouth.

"And how did you locate them?"

"You underestimate the Carabinieri, Trotti. Of course, we are unimaginative Southerners—but at least we have the merit of doggedness. We plod away at things. And these days we've got computers to help our slow, southern brains. So you won't be too surprised to learn that it didn't take Nucleo Investigativo very long to identify the murder weapon."

"Murder weapon?"

"Which killed Maltese."

"And?"

"A P38."

"Which is precisely what I told Capitano Mareschini."

Spadano held up his palms. "Nobody is criticizing you, Trotti."

"But is it to state the obvious that you have asked me to drive the sixty kilometers to this place? Or was it to taste the local wine?"

"I want to collaborate—but there are people—Mareschini among others—who feel that your attitude towards us is cavalier."

"Spadano, a man died in my arms—and I'm still not certain that it was him the killers were aiming at. Forgive me if I get impatient when a captain of the Carabinieri wants to play the amateur detective before he goes into retirement."

Spadano smiled slightly behind the cigar.

"Where are these Sardinians?"

"Perhaps you ought to have been informed, Trotti—but there again, Nucleo Investigativo knows that you're no longer involved." The smile disappeared. "The same gun that was used to kill Maltese was used in the robbery at the Banca San Matteo."

For an instant, Trotti was silent. "That doesn't make sense."

The door opened.

Spadano turned to face a young man in fatigues. His face was covered with black grease and in one hand he held a walkie-talkie.

"Movement in the house, Capitano."

"What sort of movement?" Spadano glanced at his watch.

"The door's been opened."

"Anyone come out?"

The man shook his head.

Spadano gave Trotti a brief grin, looked again at his watch. "Then I think it's time we moved in."

26: Scythe

THE BUILDING STOOD at the bottom of the valley.

To either side there were empty fields of pasture which as they rose up the side of the valley became dry bracken and bush.

A Carabiniere in camouflage was lying in the grass. He had a machine gun lined up on the door of the house. Spadano crouched down easily beside him. Pisanelli helped Trotti lower himself onto the grass.

"Keep your head low."

No movement in the valley.

The house looked deserted, the sort of place where a shepherd could live during the summer months of pasture. Along the roof—tiles that had already begun to cave in, revealing wooden rafters—birds moved backwards and forwards. From time to time, one would fly away, flutter, hover and then return to the point of departure.

Spadano took the man's walkie-talkie and spoke into it.

A figure ran out from the trees where he had been concealed. He ran fast, doubled over. In his right hand, he carried a light-weight rifle. He headed for the house, reached it midway along the wall, and stopped with his shoulders against the bricks.

He wore a mask that covered his face.

It was late afternoon and the sun was beginning to move behind the hill.

The man was joined by three more Carabinieri. They did not speak to each other but communicated with fast hand signals. Then the first man, moving stealthily, approached the open door. The others went to either side of the open window.

More men ran across the grass.

A thud and Trotti felt a fear in the pit of the stomach. A sound that he recognized, that brought back memories.

Two more dull explosions, then from where they were hiding, Trotti and Pisanelli saw smoke that started to curl out of the window.

Spadano said softly, "Let's go."

Trotti tried to run. He followed Spadano and Pisanelli helped him, careful to stay on the left of the machine gunner's line of fire, should the man decide to pull the trigger.

There was nobody to fire at.

Pisanelli grinned, but there was sweat along his forehead.

By the time the three men reached the building, the action was over.

The Carabinieri had pulled off their masks and they stood, with their rifles pointing at the ground, waiting for orders.

They cast long shadows on the grass.

"Where the hell are they?" Spadano was angry.

One of the men shook his head.

Spadano looked inside the building, pushing at the rotten door.

Eddies of tear gas billowed outwards, caught in the draught and he coughed.

"They must have moved out."

Spadano gave the man a withering glance and lit a cigar.

Nobody had noticed the man.

He stood on the edge of the field, a man in black trousers that came down as far as his ankles and his muddy, peasant boots. In one hand he held a scythe; with the other he shaded his eyes against the western sun.

"And what the hell is he doing here?" Spadano was angry, very angry. "He could have been blown apart. Where's Attilio?" Spadano walked towards the peasant who waited in immobile silence, his hand to his forehead.

The two men spoke but they were too far away for Trotti to hear anything they said.

The man pointed towards the copse. It was only then that Trotti, following the line of the outstretched hand, saw the car.

An Opel.

It had been driven across the grass and hidden beneath the trees.

Branches had been placed over the dull metalwork in an attempt to camouflage it.

Spadano turned away from the man and came running back. His face was taut and angry. "Attilio's going to pay for this cock-up." He took the cigar from his mouth to give a few brisk orders. "Anti-terrorist training, for God's sake, and they can't even do up their laces without having me there to hold their hands. Shit, it might be booby-trapped."

Later, when the Carabinieri had been placed along the ditch at the edge of the field—Trotti found himself next to the peasant who muttered under his breath, and who repeatedly crossed himself—two men approached the Opel.

The man smelled of garlic. And goat.

It was his car, Trotti's car. It looked normal, humdrum, reassuring.

One of the men carried a geiger counter.

Overhead a helicopter appeared.

Somewhere a grasshopper was chirping, but it forgot its song as the helicopter approached.

A man had crawled beneath the Opel. He stayed there, with only his legs visible. When he reemerged, he was grinning, his teeth white against the black grease. He called to the other man. One pointed at the trunk. The man with the counter spoke into his walkie-talkie.

He then came running back towards the ditch.

The officer approached the trunk of the car. He was no longer grinning. His hand touched the chrome lock.

Trotti heard the click distinctly.

27: Baccoli

SIGNORA BACCOLI INSISTED upon accompanying Trotti down the gravel path to Villa Ondina. It was dark, stars had come out and on the far side of the lake, the fairy lights zigzagged up the side of the mountain.

"We see you so rarely, Signor Piero." The woman smelled of the hot kitchen that she had just come from; under her arm, she held a casserole. "If I'd known you were intending to come, I would have prepared something special."

"It's not necessary, signora. I am with a friend—and we have just eaten at Guerino's."

"At Guerino's." She laughed mockingly. She wore an apron over her black dress. Thick woolen stockings came halfway up her legs and her open wooden shoes scraped on the gravel. "There's always plenty of pasta for two hungry men, Signor Piero." She lowered her voice as she shifted the weight of the casserole on her hip. "I heard about the young man."

"Let me carry the saucepan for you, signora."

"There has been talk in the village. I don't like to gossip, as you know—and anyway we live outside the village, Ruggiero and I, and we prefer things that way. The grocer is a thief—and if we were a bit younger and if we had a car, we'd go into Salò or up to Riva to do the shopping. I've lived here all my life, Signor Piero, but the shopkeepers of Gardesana don't believe in friendship, or loyalty—or anything. All my life—my father used to grow lemons—and his father brought the soil over from the other side, ferried the earth across from the Veneto side in order to make the terraces—but that doesn't concern the shopkeepers. All they believe in is money. They treat us in just the same way that they treat the visitors from Milan or the tourists. The tourists—the Germans—they've got money. But we haven't. A war pension, Signor Piero—what's a war pension for an old couple like us to live on?" She stopped walking. "Do you know how much Fratebene charges for his tomatoes—not local tomatoes, mind you, but tasteless imported ones?" She added contemptuously. "Common market."

"What young man, Signora Baccoli?"

"Three thousand lire, Signor Piero. Common market tomatoes."

"What young man, signora?"

She turned her head, the pale features just visible in the dark. "They say you were with him when he was shot." She moved forward, the gravel scraping against the shoes. "There's never been anything like that before. Not here."

Trotti said nothing.

"Not even when the Duce was here. There was fighting—he went away to Milan—but there was never . . ." She lowered her voice. "There was never murder. Not in Gardesana."

"You were here at the time of Mussolini?"

She gave a dry laugh—a sound like that of her shoes on the gravel. "I'm no longer a girl. I lived here throughout the war while Ruggiero was in Russia. That's where he lost his fingers." She raised her shoulders. "Frostbite."

They had reached the front door of the Villa Ondina. From above the porch, the electric Madonna threw feeble rays against the surface of the wall, the climbing bougainvillea and clematis.

"And you saw Mussolini?"

"As near to me as you are now." She nodded at the recollection. "He was a very big man—and very strong. But he was good. He cared about the village. Of course we didn't see him very often—he was in the Villa and scarcely left it—but he cared about us. We knew that he was ill and he should never have left his wife. A terrible thing, to leave her for that other woman, who was no better than a . . ." She looked up at the Madonna and Signora Baccoli repeated, "The Duce was a good man."

"He lost the war."

"He gave his life." She shifted the weight of the casserole and Trotti opened the front door of the Villa Ondina. The woman entered the hall and made her way towards the kitchen. "Twenty minutes," she called over her shoulder, "and the pasta will be ready."

Pisanelli had already settled in.

He gave Trotti a grin. He sat in the empty dining room, his feet on a chair. He was still wearing his suede jacket and he had a glass in his hand.

"Make yourself feel at home, Pisanelli."

The television screen was alive with the fuzzy image of an old Alberto Sordi film. The picture was grey and unsteady, coming from one of the private stations on the other side of the lake.

Beneath the grin, the face was taut and the eyes unhappy. He put his head back to acknowledge Trotti's remark and drank some more wine.

Trotti went to the phone. In New York, she should now be back from lunch. He picked up the receiver and dialed—he knew the long number from memory but had to dial three times before getting a line.

A voice in English.

"Signora Trotti, per favore." Trotti added in English, "Please."

The distant secretary said something but Trotti did not understand.

Again he asked for Agnese. There was a moment of awkward hesitation and then somebody spoke in Italian—a woman's voice with a strong American accent. "Signora Trotti is not yet back in the office."

"When will she be back?"

"I don't know."

"This is her husband."

"I know."

"Please." He ran his hand across his forehead. "When she

gets in, would you kindly ask her to ring me back?" He gave the phone number. "Tell her that it's important and I'm waiting for her call."

The voice repeated the number and then hung up.

Trotti went upstairs and showered. The water was not hot yet and it ran slightly brown with rust. He let the water run over his body—the bruises had almost disappeared on his chest, but on his thigh a small patch of blue was turning yellow. Trotti rubbed himself dry on a towel and went into the bedroom. Enclosed space and floor polish. He opened the blinds and a smell of clover, grass and the cold water of the lake rose to his nostrils. He breathed deeply, taking in the air. Prompted perhaps by the smell, he remembered the weekend—it must have been in '55 or earlier—when Agnese and he had come to the lake without telling anybody. They had walked around the villa on tiptoe. And holding hands. Trotti smiled to himself at the thought.

"Nearly thirty years ago," he muttered.

A milky whiteness lit up the sky beyond the silhouette of Monte Baldo's shoulder. Soon the moon would be rising over the lake and casting its silver reflection onto the gentle ripples across the surface.

A knock on the door. "Signor Piero, the food is ready."

Trotti turned to look at the woman.

She stood there, hesitant, a hand lifted to her face, as if she had toothache. "It's about that man."

"Pisanelli?" Trotti shrugged apologetically. "I'm afraid that's the way he is."

The woman shook her head.

She had never approved of Trotti. She had always identified with the interests of Agnese's family and had considered him as an intruder. For Signora Baccoli, the young mistress—so beautiful, so well educated—could have made a better match—a husband more like her, someone belonging to the same background, someone better than the dull policeman from the hills beyond the Po.

But Baccoli and her husband were pragmatists and the peasant woman realized where her interests lay. In the evening of her life, she did not want to be thrown out of the little house that stood on the edge of the grounds of the Villa Ondina, overlooking the terraces of vines and tomatoes that ran down to the lakeside. Agnese's parents were dead and Signora Baccoli—a tough, peasant woman who was always referred to as "la contadina"—knew that her two daughters were too busy to spare her much time or thought. She had always been severe with them when they were little, scolding them and threatening them with the harsh punishments of a retributive and cruel Christianity.

Signora Baccoli did not like Trotti—she never had. But she needed him.

An irony, then, that while the old woman—she never wore anything other than black—still admired Agnese and put her interests first, it was Trotti who had always refused Agnese's pet project to sell the Villa and in so doing force the old couple to leave their house.

Trotti followed the woman out of the room.

"The man," she said, "the man they murdered."

"Well?"

She spoke in a whisper. "I'm not a person to gossip, Signor Piero. But you are a policeman and it is only right that you should know."

Trotti felt a sudden sense of excitement. "Know what, signora?"

"It's Pia—you know, my sister who lives in an apartment above the bakery. Perhaps she should have told the Carabinieri, but the man is from the south and his breath smells and you can't trust them because they're not like us."

"Pia?" Trotti said. "What's she done?"

"You know she used to work in the town hall?"

Trotti nodded.

"And you know she has insomnia, ever since she worked with Sindaco Fermi—the last mayor but one—who used to make her drink so much coffee?"

"Yes, yes," Trotti said impatiently.

"The day he was shot . . ."

"Who?"

"The man who was shot at Guerino's—well, Pia saw him. She told me at Mass on Sunday. She saw him when he arrived in Gardesana. It was early, before seven o'clock. She saw him when he arrived, when he got out of his car."

"His car? What car?"

The woman shrugged. "Pia says that there were other men in the car."

"What car, signora? Can you describe it?"

The face smiled. "Pia knows nothing about cars. And neither do I. But she told me that it was a big car—a German one."

"A Mercedes?"

The woman shrugged. "A big car."

28: Vino

SIGNORA BACCOLI HAD set out the plates for supper in the kitchen. Already Pisanelli was placing his napkin on his knees.

"I thought you'd lost your appetite, Pisanelli."

The contadina filled two plates and poured wine into the glasses.

"Drink, signore," she said to Pisanelli and for a moment she placed her work-worn hand on the shoulder of his jacket. "It's my husband's wine. He made it himself—with the grapes from the vineyard."

Pisanelli drank and nodded his appreciation.

Trotti sat down in front of the food and the old woman left the kitchen. "I'll prepare the guest room for your friend."

They ate in silence. Pisanelli had not lost his appetite and the cannelloni was good—made with cream and parmesan cheese and spiced with pepper.

From time to time, Trotti looked at his watch.

Behind Pisanelli's head there was a thermometer attached to the wall. Also on the wall, a colored photograph of Pope John XXIII.

Trotti said, "Maltese came here in the Mercedes."

Pisanelli was sitting forward, slumped over his plate and traces of cream at the edge of his lips and on his mustache. The cuffs of his jacket were propped against the kitchen tablecloth. He raised his eyes—brown, intelligent eyes.

"How d'you know?"

"He was seen in the village—at seven o'clock."

Pisanelli smiled. "At seven o'clock—then he couldn't have followed you."

"Precisely—I didn't reach Gardesana until nearly eight."

"Somebody must have told him." Pisanelli grinned. "D'you talk in your sleep?"

Trotti glanced at him and the sheepish grin vanished. Pisanelli looked at his glass of wine. The top of his head and his forehead were completely bald.

"He came in a Mercedes—which means he came with his killers. He thought he was going to set me up—and instead the bullets were for him."

"The killers were perhaps aiming for you, Commissario."

Trotti shook his head. "They were professionals."

Pisanelli wiped the smears of cream from his mouth. "Why would Maltese want to set you up?"

"Revenge, perhaps. Revenge for what happened to his father—and he held me responsible." Trotti shrugged. "But I don't think his father held me responsible. Like everybody else, I didn't agree with Dell'Orto. I didn't think there was any real evidence against Ramoverde." Trotti pushed the empty plate away. "And I told Ramoverde that. Towards the end of the trial, I became—well, we grew to understand one another."

"What was he like?"

"Self-assured, distant—but I'd like to think I got through to him. A strange friendship—it was as if he wanted someone to confide in—but didn't dare. I had the impression that he knew a lot more than he let on."

Pisanelli raised his eyes to look at Trotti. "Was he guilty?"

Trotti poured more wine into the glasses.

Pisanelli drank thirstily before asking, "Was he guilty, in your opinion, Commissario?"

Trotti shook his head. "I don't know." He added, "I didn't know then—and I still don't."

"But you had an opinion."

"I liked him—but I didn't believe him."

"Then he was guilty?"

Trotti threw up his hands. "Drink your wine, Pisanelli."

Pisanelli did as he was told; then he emptied the bottle into his glass. "It really is very good."

"Glad you like it."

"You think Maltese came here to see you?"

"I told you, Pisanelli. I don't know."

"One thing is certain." The same foolish grin. "Uras and Suergiu aren't going to tell anybody." He paused. "Perhaps that's why they were killed."

"Well done."

Pisanelli shrugged. "I don't see how else you can explain their deaths."

"The Sardinians?"

"You saw, Commissario. Shot in the back of the neck and left in the trunk of your car. Organized crime, Southern crime—it's the way the Mafia works."

The two bodies had lain like mangled fetuses in the trunk of the Opel. Blood covered the rubber matting, giving it an unpleasant, metallic odor. The Carabiniere, who only a second ago had been risking his life, turned away to vomit. And from out of nowhere the flies appeared, settling on the two maimed corpses.

The right hand of each man had been severed at the wrist.

Pisanelli emptied his glass. "They have been silenced."

"But the photograph was there."

"What?"

"I left a photograph in the glove box—a photo of the Guerra girl and they—"

The phone rang.

Trotti went out into the hall.

"Commissario Trotti?"

"Speaking." Outside the warm kitchen, the hall was cold.

"Mareschini here."

Trotti said, "Ah."

"I heard you were back in Gardesana."

"Word travels fast, Capitano."

"I heard you were back and I wondered if I could ask you to

drop by tomorrow. I would have come and visited you personally this evening—but after the events outside Piacenza . . ."

"Then you know that Uras and Suergiu have been found murdered?"

"Commissario Trotti, there are certain points concerning your statement . . ." He coughed. "Points that aren't exactly clear."

Trotti waited in silence.

"So if you could drop by tomorrow . . ."

"I'll try."

"I must ask you to collaborate, Commissario. The whole affair is very unfortunate and I want to get to the bottom of it as soon as possible."

"In the morning, Capitano." Trotti hung up.

Back in the kitchen, he took Pisanelli's plate and put it in the sink.

"Would you like a cup of camomile before you go to bed—it'll help you sleep?"

"It's a bit early to go to bed."

"We've got a lot of work to do tomorrow." Trotti rummaged through the cupboards and took out a glass jar. "If you want to go to bed, why not take a shower?"

"Excellent wine."

Trotti poured water into a saucepan and then set it on the gas ring.

Before long the water was bubbling. Trotti poured the steaming liquid onto the dried camomile flowers. He looked at Pisanelli. As if seeing the face for the first time, Trotti realized that Pisanelli had aged.

"A bullet in the back of the neck." Pisanelli shook his head. "And neither of them older than me." He sighed. "They deserved better than a car trunk for a grave—even if they were murderers."

Trotti sucked his teeth. "Uras and Suergiu weren't murderers."

"They killed Maltese."

"Sardinian shepherds—what would they have known about professional killing?"

"And they beat you up, Commissario."

Trotti said nothing and Pisanelli, after waiting for a bit, stood up and went unsteadily out of the kitchen. "Goodnight."

"Goodnight."

His shoes creaked on the marble as he walked along the hall and began to make his hesitant way up the stairs.

Trotti drank the camomile in the dining room, in front of the silent television; his own reflection bounced off the curved grey screen. He thought about Maltese.

Trotti put his head back on the soft leather of the armchair—it used to be the favorite of Agnese's father and nobody else was allowed to sit in it—and stared at the ceiling.

Somebody had been setting Maltese up—and Maltese had gone like a lamb to his own slaughter.

Trotti closed his eyes. His grip on the hot cup loosened.

29: Women

"PIERO, THE DOOR was open."

She was standing beside him, looking down.

"How did you get in?"

"I met Signora Baccoli as she was coming up the drive."

"And what's she going to say about your visiting a married man at this late hour?"

"Piero, Signora Baccoli has known me for more than forty years."

The laughter was light, almost girlish.

Trotti stood up and kissed her on the cheek. Donatella smiled, a genuine smile that was wide and friendly. For a few seconds, they stood looking at each other with their hands loosely clasped.

"I hear you're a grandmother. Congratulations."

"And not a day over forty-three."

Trotti said, "I was forty-three once."

"And you've still got your hair." Her hand brushed his forehead.

Trotti turned away, slightly embarrassed. "Would you like something to drink?"

"Papa told me you were here." She pulled up an armchair and sat down, crossing one ankle across her knee. She had the same golden hair—years ago, the boys in the village used to call her "la Tedesca" because she was as blonde as a heroine from

Grimms' Fairy Tales. Her face was still smooth and young—soft features, light eyes and skin that was Mediterranean in comparison with her hair.

"The contadina has made some cannelloni. Would you like to heat it up?"

"Dear Piero, always worrying, always anxious." She shook her head in amusement and the large smile revealed the gap in her teeth. "Tell me how you are. Two years is a long time, Piero."

"I saw you last year, Donatella."

She wagged her finger. "You can't be bothered to come and see me in Sesto San Giovanni—and you never come to the lake anymore."

"I was in Sesto a couple of weeks ago." Now he smiled. "But I thought you had got married?"

She threw her head back to laugh; then she caught sight of the framed photograph. "And your wife?"

"Agnese's in America."

"She's still very beautiful?"

"Yes."

"That's just like you, isn't it? Very detached, distant—but I can remember when you were first married—and you were so in love with your wife. You've always been in love with her." Again she glanced round the room. "You know, Piero, I've only been here once before." She looked at the photograph of Agnese's father. She stood up and went to the mantelpiece. "Where was this taken?"

"At the Istituto Zootecnico that he had in Brescia."

She turned, holding her hands behind her back. She was smiling.

"There's a moon over the lake. Let's go outside for a moment."

"You need a sweater—it's cold out. I'll go and fetch one."

When he came back, the dining room door was open. Donatella's light perfume still lay on the air. He went out onto the verandah—outside the air was chill—down the iron steps and through the small gate. He walked across the beach; the pebbles scraped beneath his shoes.

"I'm over here."

She looked like a little girl in the dark. She was sitting at the end of the wooden jetty, her hands clasped round her knees. The moonlight glanced off her hair; otherwise she was in the shadow. "Piero, come and sit down beside me."

"You'll catch your death of cold."

"Always worrying, Piero." She tapped the wooden plank. "Sit down and you can keep me warm."

Beneath them the softly splashing water lapped around the wooden posts of the pontoon.

"Papa told me what happened."

"The shooting?"

She nodded.

"The man—it was Ramoverde's son."

"Ramoverde—I can remember that." She was leaning her cheek against her knees. "I can remember, you were here on the lake—and you had to leave your wife. She wasn't very pleased."

"Understandably. She was pregnant with Pioppi."

"How is Pioppi?"

Trotti did not reply.

"Well?"

"Donatella, what d'you want me to say?"

"Tell me how your daughter is."

"She's a brilliant student . . . and she gets top marks in everything at the university. She wants to become a town planner and she says she wants to work in Bologna."

"Then you ought to be very proud of her. She's acquired your intelligence. And if she's anything like her mother, she must be very beautiful—very beautiful indeed."

"She looks like a skeleton."

"A skeleton? Why?"

"She doesn't want to eat."

"Why not?"

"If I knew, I'd try and do something to help her."

"What do the doctors say?"

"Pioppi refuses to go to the doctor. She says there's nothing wrong with her—simply that she's not hungry." Trotti shook his head. "She can't keep her food down. Sometimes she vomits."

"But, Piero, you must send her to the doctor."

"My daughter is no longer a child—and she does as she pleases."

For a moment, neither spoke. Then Donatella said, "Only yesterday. Time flies—I can remember Pioppi when she was in her pram—and now . . ." She sighed. "It seems scarcely more than a couple of years ago. Pioppi's a grown woman—like my own daughter Valeria." She shook her head and the moonlight danced on the blonde hair. "Time passes so fast and we don't have time to enjoy our children." She hugged her knees and stared out at the water. "Valeria's married now and has a child of her own."

"She's happy?"

Donatella took his hand but without looking at him. Her perfume was sweet; not one of Agnese's French perfumes, but light, with a hint of lemon. "I was always jealous of your wife." She turned and an oblique ray of light was caught in the iris of her eye. "It was 1960, wasn't it? That's when Papa bought the bar—we'd been living in Rome. 1960 and that's when I first saw you with your wife. She was pregnant and you were so proud of her. I saw you once walking along the road to San Giorgio—now they've built a luxury residence for all the Germans—but in those days, there were just the olive groves and the meadows that ran down to the edge of the lake. I saw you picnicking there." Again the light laugh. "I can even remember the checkered cloth that you were sitting on."

She fell silent.

"That was a long time ago, Donatella."

"I was jealous of her—and that's why I wanted to be pregnant. It wasn't very difficult, I can assure you—behind the old parish church with Gianni Potta. My God, that was a mistake. He never wanted to marry me—and I shouldn't have forced him. In his way, he's not a bad man. Violent—and I soon realized that I could never live with him. But at the time, I wanted Valeria to have a father. So we got married and in those days, there was no divorce." She turned and in the light, he saw the brightness of her smile. "Poor Gianni—he now works in Sweden. Married and done well for himself."

"You've done well for yourself, too, Donatella. You have a beautiful daughter—and now a grandson."

"Time hurries past and you don't notice a thing—it's other people who seem to be getting older. And then one day you look in the mirror and you see all the wrinkles and you know that you're old. And you know that those days—days that you thought would last forever—are never coming back."

"You're young and pretty."

"I'm an old woman!"

Trotti said, "We can go back inside."

Donatella placed her head on his shoulder. "Hold me, Piero. Keep me warm."

30: Pia

"Piero!" The woman gave him a large smile and held out her hand above the high counter.

"Signora Pia, how are you?"

The smile vanished. "But how are you, Piero? I saw you nearly get killed on Friday—if you hadn't jumped backwards, that car would have killed you."

"I'm all right—a few bruises."

"And that stupid Massimo—he's a good boy but he doesn't always understand." She shrugged. "It's not always easy to find people who want to stay on in the village. They go away to Brescia or Milan—where they can escape from their families. Massimo is a good boy but . . ."

The air was warm with the smell of fresh bread and Signora Pia, standing behind the counter, wearing a white overall, was smiling at Trotti. Unlike her sister, Pia's face was gentle, despite the marks that time and worry had left upon it.

Pisanelli stood by the window, eating a doughnut. Already the granules of sugar had nestled into his mustache.

"I would like to ask you a few questions, Signora Pia." Trotti glanced at the other customers. "In private if you don't mind. Just for a few minutes."

The woman came out from behind the counter—she had a short, sturdy frame, and although she was nearly seventy, she moved briskly. Her legs were strong. Her white hair was held in tight permanent waves. She went to the door and pulled down the blind. Then hurriedly she served the remaining customers.

"And you, signore?"

Pisanelli shook his head.

"The gentleman is with me," Trotti said tersely.

Signora Pia led Trotti into the back of the shop. High ovens and a smell of flour. It was very hot. Trotti recognized Massimo, who was standing near an automatic mixing machine. The boy looked up and nudged at his thick glasses. There was no recognition in the eyes.

She looked carefully at the bruises on his face. "You must look after yourself, Piero," the woman said, placing her hand on his arm.

"I'm all right—but I need your help." He lowered his voice. "Your sister tells me that you saw the car."

"I nearly saw you run over. And if Massimo hadn't braked in time, he might well have been killed—and what would his mother have done without the wages that he brings home?"

"They murdered the man—and he died in my arms." He looked at her. "But you didn't tell the Carabinieri."

She placed her hands on her hips. "You know what I think of southerners—they're all the same. When I worked in the town hall, there was the horrible Lepetit who thought he could put his hands on me when he pleased—and me a married woman."

Trotti smiled. "And how's your daughter?"

The woman shrugged. "She's happy—or so she says. But in my opinion, she should never have married a southerner. My opinion and the opinion of her poor father, too. And do you know, because of that man, she couldn't afford the money to come to her father's funeral? Her father, who had carried her on his shoulders."

"But you see her?"

Pia said dryly, "She comes at Christmas." Then a smile. "And I get to see the little children who are lovely—despite the Neapolitan accent."

Trotti took a packet of sweets from his pocket. "Signora Pia,

I won't keep you—but you must tell me if you saw those people before."

"What people?"

"You saw the big car—the Mercedes." Trotti gestured with his thumb towards the via XX Settembre. "And you saw how they tried to kill me." His voice dropped to a whisper. "Your sister says that you saw the Mercedes earlier in the morning—at seven o'clock."

There was a short silence. The woman frowned and her forehead was creased in thought. "I told my sister in secrecy."

"The man who died," Trotti said, "he was a friend."

She sighed before speaking. "I saw a big car."

"And you saw Maltese—the murdered man—you saw him get out?"

"A young man? Fairly thin and with dark glasses? A man who needed a shave?" There was a ring on the shop doorbell.

"Yes." Trotti spoke fast. "And what time did you see him?"

"There's only one road into Gardesana—and only one road out. I thought the car was leaving the village—you know, one of those rich Germans up at the residence who was spending the day in Milan and wanted to get there early."

"What color?"

"I can't remember." She shrugged apologetically. "Perhaps it was black."

"At what time did you see the car, Pia?"

"It must have been before seven. And the car parked just outside."

"You recognized the car? It was a German car?"

She shrugged. "A big car."

"Did you see the number plates?"

She shook her head.

"But it was the same car that tried to knock me over?"

She put her hands together and rubbed them. "It was a big car, Piero. I can remember that it was a big car."

"And you saw the two other men?"

Now she frowned. "The two other men?"

"The same men who tried to run me over."

"There were only two men, Piero. There was an older man."
She nodded with conviction. "He got out of the car and he shook
hands with the young man—poor thing." Again she nodded. "Of
that I am quite sure—an old man. He smiled and I thought they
were friends." Again she nodded. "I didn't see the old man's face
but I noticed they acted like friends—like a father and his son."

31: Trial

"YOU WERE THERE?"

Trotti nodded. "There were one hundred forty-nine witnesses for the prosecution and they had to be sworn in—it was worse than Borgo Genovese on market day."

"And Ramoverde?"

"He never changed. The trial lasted twelve days—and Douglas Ramoverde remained always the same—cold, imperturbable, aloof. It was as if he were a spectator at his own trial."

"You saw him?" Pisanelli asked.

"I was there throughout the trial—I had to be. And even if it hadn't been forced upon me, I would have gone. I couldn't have been more than five meters from him. It was as if he were indifferent. He didn't care about the outcome—or perhaps he was quite sure." Trotti took the packet of sweets from his pocket.

"He was innocent?"

"The evidence was damning in its quantity." Trotti paused. "The car had been sighted on two occasions near the Villa Laura. And then there was the lack of an alibi—he had never been able to prove how or where he had spent the extra hours on his drive back to Piacenza from San Remo. He maintained he slept in the car—but he couldn't prove it. And why sleep in the car when in a couple of hours—less even—he could have been back home, in a real bed between clean bedsheets?"

"It's not proof."

"There was blood on his car."

Pisanelli frowned. He drove but from time to time he glanced at Trotti.

Trotti asked, "Do you want a sweet?"

"Bad for your teeth."

"At my age everything's bad for you." Trotti unwrapped a sweet and placed it in his mouth.

"What blood, Commissario?"

"The Istituto Medicale was certain—it was human blood. But Ramoverde maintained that it came from a boy he'd taken in his car to the hospital in Piacenza—a boy who'd been knocked off his Vespa and cut his forehead. But Piacenza checked—it was only natural, when virtually the entire nation was following the trial."

"And what did Piacenza say?"

"It was true that he had taken a boy to the hospital. The boy even came forward and publicly thanked Ramoverde. But whereas Ramoverde maintained he'd put the boy on the front seat—that's where the bloodstains were—the witness said he'd been put on the backseat."

"More reasonable." Pisanelli shook his balding head. "But that is all circumstantial. What was the evidence against Ramoverde? There must have been evidence."

"Dell'Orto, the investigating judge, was convinced that the motive alone was sufficient. He'd already been forced to release Ramoverde once—and even then with the eye of the nation on our little city, he didn't really have proof. But Dell'Orto was convinced of his guilt. It was like a religion with him. I know that several people—including Dario, who came up from Rome—tried to persuade him from going ahead with the trial. But Dell'Orto insisted. He said that there was a motive."

"What motive?"

"The Villa."

Pisanelli shook his head, not understanding.

"Ramoverde and his wife were frightened that the old man was going to marry Eva Bardizza—the housekeeper. She was a young woman and they saw that he was infatuated with her. According to Dell'Orto that terrified them."

"Why?"

"They needed the money. Ramoverde's dental practice didn't bring in enough." Trotti clicked the sweet against his teeth. "Above all, they didn't want the money to go to the girl. Not after all their years of waiting."

"Did you believe that?"

Trotti shrugged. "Dell'Orto was desperate for a motive. Perhaps he was right—Dell'Orto was no fool. Ramoverde needed the money—he'd been counting on it for a long time. Dell'Orto thought it was because of the inheritance that he'd married Matilda Belluno in the first place. He certainly liked the good life—eating out, the theater, occasionally betting on a horse in Milan or going to the Casino in San Remo. But there was something else—a point that the prosecution insisted upon throughout the trial. There was hostility between Bardizza and Ramoverde's wife. It had come to a head about seven months before the murder—in the villa at San Remo."

"What happened?"

"Douglas Ramoverde slapped Bardizza."

"What on earth for?" Pisanelli grinned.

"The girl insisted upon sitting at the table with Belluno and the Ramoverde family. Matilda Ramoverde told her to wait until they'd finished eating—and the girl had replied tartly that she wasn't a maid. According to Ramoverde, the reply was deliberately insolent, intended to insult his wife. He always admitted to slapping her—once on either cheek—for her insolence. He maintained that at the time he wasn't aware of any negative reaction from his father-in-law. But two days later, the lawyer was called in and Belluno insisted upon rewriting his will. And he bequeathed virtually everything to Eva. Furthermore, he got his lawyers to inform his daughter and son-in-law that he was putting the San Remo villa up for sale."

"Belluno broke with his daughter?"

"That was never made very clear." Trotti shrugged. "Both Ramoverde and his wife denied that there had been a break with the old man. But there were several witnesses who claimed that Belluno didn't want to have anything more to do with them. And that's probably why they spent the month of July in San Remo."

"July 1960?"

Trotti nodded. "Belluno's daughter was trying to patch things up. Probably she felt she could heal things with the help of her son. The old man Belluno was very fond of his grandson."

"Who we know as Maltese?"

"He changed his name later."

"And there was a reconciliation between Belluno and his daughter?" For some reason, Pisanelli was still smiling.

"According to Ramoverde, things got better. He was working throughout July and he could only take the weekends off to visit his wife and son at San Remo."

"Wait a minute." The grin disappeared and Pisanelli frowned; his eyes remained on the road ahead. His forehead was wrinkled in concentration. "Belluno was murdered at the Villa Laura, not at San Remo?"

"Belluno and the girl were on holiday in San Remo but they returned to Villa Laura because he had work to do."

"Work?"

"Belluno was still involved with his publishing firm. Apparently there were proofs that he had to read—and he preferred to work away from the sea. But it was his intention to get back to San Remo early in August."

"And during that time, Signora Ramoverde was alone at San Remo with her son?"

"Yes."

"Strange that the father threatened to sell the villa and then allowed his estranged daughter to stay there in his absence."

"Things were supposed to be getting better." Trotti placed his arm through the open window. They were traveling fast on the autostrada to Milan; beyond the green haze of the fields and the electric pylons, he could distinguish Segrate and the high blocks. "Then on the second day of the trial, the prosecution produced a bit of evidence that took Ramoverde by surprise."

Pisanelli laughed. "What?"

Trotti spoke in a neutral voice. "He always maintained that he had turned off the autostrada—and anyway in those days, there weren't as many autostradas as today—it was still the beginning of the Italian Miracle. Or perhaps you don't remember."

"I may not be as old as you, Commissario," Pisanelli said, turning, "but I'm already beginning to lose my hair."

"Increase your sugar intake—eat a few sweets."

"What was the surprise evidence?"

"Ramoverde said he'd turned off the autostrada at Voghera and that he had slept in his Fiat 1100 for a couple of hours. But then the prosecution came up with his logbook. Ramoverde was a strange man—in a way. Very precise—like a machine." Trotti's face broke into a smile. "Perhaps it was his scientific background. Anyway, he kept a logbook. And he kept it religiously. On the night—July twenty-first, I think—when a car had been sighted by midnight runners near Villa Laura—Ramoverde had noted the mileage in the logbook. I can't remember exactly what the mileage was. And I can't remember what it was the following day, when he noted it down again. But the difference—and this was hammered home by the prosecution—was two hundred eighty-five kilometers. According to the logbook, between San Remo and Piacenza, the car had covered a distance of two hundred eighty-five kilometers. But the real distance was only two hundred fifty kilometers."

"So what?"

"So what?" Trotti glanced at Pisanelli. "The prosecution maintained that Ramoverde never slept that night—as he claimed he did—by turning off the main road. Instead they accused Ramoverde of having driven the extra thirty kilometers or so to Borgo Genovese—to the Villa Laura where he hid his car."

"Mere conjecture."

"Of course, Pisanelli."

Pisanelli drove in silence.

"Conjecture," Trotti repeated. "And that's what Ramoverde should have said. Or he could have said that he had taken his car for a run on the following morning . . . that he went to Zio Orazio. If he had wanted to, he could have invented an explanation."

"What did he say?"

For a moment, Trotti was silent, lost in thought. He stared out of the car window and the wind pulled at his thinning hair. Pensively, he pushed the sweet against his cheek.

"What did Ramoverde say, Commissario?"

"He said that the odometer was defective." Trotti gave a brief smile. "He said that it wasn't working properly. That was how he explained the extra thirty kilometers. And of course, the judge immediately demanded that a test should be carried out on Ramoverde's car."

"Well?"

"The odometer was in perfect running order."

32: Cats

" WELL? "

Pisanelli did not reply. He sat behind the steering wheel of the car, nibbling at his mustache.

"Well, Pisanelli?"

He looked peeved. "There are times, Commissario, when you refuse to make allowances."

Trotti looked at the Villa Laura. It had scarcely changed; it was the trees and flowers around it, the flowerbeds and the lawn that had altered with time.

Trotti could not remember so many cypress trees. Tall, they moved almost imperceptibly with the wind from the river.

"Not everybody has your experience, Commissario. You should realize that. However, I try to do my duty and I hope that I do it to the best of my ability." He added, after biting his lip, "I've spent the best part of the last twenty-four hours with you—I believe that I'm entitled to a rest. I should like to go home."

"Pisanelli, if you wanted short hours and English weekends, you should never have joined the PS."

"It's only the Squadra Mobile that works day and night, Commissario Trotti." The young man's face had hardened and for a moment Trotti did not speak.

"One day you will be a good policeman, Pisanelli." He

placed his hand on Pisanelli's arm. Then without waiting
for a reply, he climbed out of the car and started walking
towards the Villa Laura. The sun was almost overhead and
the air was full of promise. Soon it would be summer. Somewhere, a solitary grasshopper was singing its private song.
Through the trees, Trotti caught sight of the grey, glinting
Po. Apart from a couple of sluggish chestnuts, all the trees
were already in leaf.

Trotti went up the short flight of marble stairs and rang
the bell. A distant tinkling echoed feebly within the building.
Pisanelli joined him, pushed back the hair that had fallen forwards. Trotti said, "The two officers climbed in through the
back window. Belluno's room's there—look, that window up
there." He pointed.

The sound of steady, purposeful footfalls and then the bolts
were drawn back. The door came open.

"Pubblica Sicurezza."

The girl wore neat shoes and a blue skirt that looked new, a
white blouse open at the neck and a gold crucifix. She blinked
in the sunlight. "How can I be of use?"

"Commissario Trotti of the Squadra Mobile." As an afterthought, he added, "And Brigadiere Pisanelli. I wonder whether
we may come in."

"Signora Buonaventura is resting."

"Signora Buonaventura?"

"Who were you looking for, Signor Commissario?"

"The proprietor of the Villa Laura."

"I have told you, Signora Buonaventura—the proprietress—is
resting."

"And who are you?"

The girl looked surprised. "I live here. The signora needs
someone to look after her." She sounded offended.

Pisanelli coughed. "Kindly let us in, signora."

She looked at Pisanelli and said coldly, "Signorina. Signorina
Moroni." She glanced again at Trotti and then stepped back.

They entered Villa Laura.

The hall was large and gloomy, with at least six cats sitting on a single settee. It was an old piece of furniture, upholstered in a deep green brocade that had lost its color with the years. The cats were pulling at the fabric with their claws.

The air smelled of cat urine; there was also the hint of excrement.

Pisanelli gave Trotti a lopsided grin. He held a long finger to his nose.

"Signora Buonaventura normally sleeps at this time of day. Until four o'clock. Perhaps the gentlemen would like to return later."

"No."

The same look of offended pride appeared on her young face. "Then perhaps I can offer you some coffee?"

"You are very kind," Trotti said and sat down on the grubby settee.

The cats jumped away in fright and disappeared, almost in single file, up the stairway.

"That's where they found the corpse," Trotti whispered after the young woman had turned away and was walking briskly towards a far door.

Absent-mindedly, Pisanelli stared after her disappearing legs and the well-formed calves. "Pretty."

"That's where they found old Belluno," Trotti repeated. "Belluno lying on the first flight of stairs—there—head downwards. Naked except for a singlet and a pair of underpants that had been stuffed into his mouth."

"And the girl?"

"In the bathroom. She had been battered and then drowned in the bath water."

Pisanelli mumbled something behind his hand.

"What?"

"Were they living together?"

"Who?"

"The old man and his housekeeper . . ." Pisanelli paused, blushing. "Were there relations between them?"

"Were they screwing, you mean?"

Pisanelli nodded hurriedly.

"It was never proved or disproved. What was certain was that there'd been no intercourse in the period preceding death. But the girl wasn't a virgin, either. The doctor insisted upon the fact that Bardizza had been menstruating at the time of death."

"But were they living together?"

"It was all a long time ago—over twenty years—and there weren't the research techniques that we've got now. It was never proved that they had been lovers. No stains on the sheets or mattresses. But of course, Ramoverde and his wife insisted that they were having an affair. Ramoverde wanted to prove that the old man was infatuated and imply that he was losing control of his mind."

Pisanelli shook his head. "If the girl wanted to marry him—marry him for his money—she'd've been better advised not to give in. Not before the wedding day."

Trotti laughed and a single cat darted from under the Venetian chest-of-drawers. "For somebody who can't tell one end of a woman from another, you know a lot of things."

The young policeman frowned. "A year at the Faculty of Medicine, Commissario—and I have three older sisters."

Trotti leaned back on the settee and laughed. He noticed that the fabric was covered with minute hairs.

The interior of the hall was as he remembered it: dingy walls, cornices of plaster and a mural on the ceiling with cherubim and rosy-cheeked goddesses of plenty. There was the painting of the army officer. It was in the same place, next to a tall mirror. It must have been painted just after the Great War. The name Diaz was on a piece of paper at the officer's feet.

Pisanelli asked, "How can people go on living in a place where there's been a murder?" He shivered.

Trotti did not answer.

The telephone was new, and with its red cord, it looked inelegant and out of place. It stood on a small table, on top of a pile of directories. Trotti was about to stand up when the young woman returned, carrying a tray. With her she brought the reassuring aroma of strong coffee.

"Ten years, signorina?"

"I beg your pardon?"

"You've been working here for ten years?"

"No." She put down the silver coffee pot and looked at Trotti. Her waxy, pale features were devoid of expression. "I've been here for three years—answering an advertisement in the paper." She added, not without pride, "I am from the Valdosta. I came because Signora Buonaventura fell and broke her hip. She needed someone to look after her."

"I understand."

The girl poured the coffee efficiently and in silence. Pisanelli watched her movements with interest; then the two men drank.

"Very good," Trotti said. "You wouldn't have any grappa?"

"There's no alcohol in this house." She stood with her arms folded.

She reminded Trotti of a well-behaved adolescent who had to accept—but only with reluctance—the rules imposed by strict parents. She was pretty, but very pale.

The sound of feet on the stairs.

"I thought I could smell coffee. Patrizia, be an angel and fetch me a cup."

For somebody who had just risen from a siesta, Signora Buonaventura was immaculately dressed. She wore a silk blouse with long collar tips that came down over the soft, expensive material of her cashmere cardigan. She was a plump woman and she wore an ample skirt that matched the beige of the cardigan. The bangles of silver at her wrist jangled and around her neck hung two rows of large beads. There was another necklace—this one of silver—that supported a crucifix. "And who are these gentlemen?"

Trotti stood up.

She moved down the stairs slowly, almost theatrically, leaning on the thick banister of polished stone and moving both her feet onto one step before venturing down onto the next. "I hope they like cats."

"Pubblica Sicurezza," Trotti said and nodded towards Pisanelli who moved forward to help the woman.

She shook his proffered hand away. "And what do you want?"

"I'm making a few enquiries, signora."

When she reached the bottom of the stairs, Trotti was surprised to see that she was almost as tall as he was, one meter seventy-five or so, with white hair in rinsed waves and a strong face. The eyes seemed to have retreated behind the layers of pouched and wrinkled skin.

"Where's my stick?"

Signorina Moroni reappeared carrying a stick that she gave to the old woman. She received no word of thanks.

"Well, gentlemen?"

Beneath the double row of beads and the crucifix, a pair of glasses also hung from her neck. The woman raised them without placing the arms alongside her temples, but holding them as if they were pince-nez. "Ah," she said.

"Commissario Trotti of the Pubblica Sicurezza." He added, "And Brigadiere Pisanelli."

Pisanelli smiled inanely.

"Well?"

"There are a few questions that I should like to ask you, signora."

"Why?"

"Because I need the answers."

She lowered the glasses. "And what's your reason for coming here?"

"I believe you are the sister of the late Signora Ramoverde."

Under the thick layers of white face powder and the deep red lipstick, which gave an almost ghostlike quality to her face, the similarity to Maltese was striking. It was a similarity that Trotti found reassuring. At the same time he was aware of the fact that Pisanelli was intimidated by the woman. Tall, well over sixty-five years old, with expensive, slightly outdated clothes, she reminded Trotti of a severe schoolmistress.

"So what?"

Trotti was still standing and he held his empty cup of coffee. He moved to the table where the girl had placed the tray and set down the cup. "I can assure you that I have no intention of wasting your time."

A deep voice, like a man's. "Have the decency, young man,

to tell me what you're here for." She came forward, leaning on the stick with both hands and lowered herself onto the settee. There was no longer any room for the two men.

"Where are my darlings?"

Two cats jumped up beside her.

"So beautiful, aren't they?"

Trotti nodded politely.

"Sit down, for heaven's sake."

In a dark corner of the room, there were two old chairs. Pisanelli fetched them and gave one to Trotti.

"You see," Trotti said in an apologetic voice, "I must ask you when you first came to the Villa Laura."

"Does that have anything to do with you?"

"Please answer the question."

"What question?"

"Did you come here after the trial of your brother-in-law?"

"Whatever makes you want to bring that up? That was a long time ago and I'd rather not be reminded."

"I understand that the will was contested at the time of the trial."

"Not at all." She put her head to one side. "You are indeed a dull fellow. My father had left everything to that peasant girl—but the poor, greedy thing made the mistake of getting herself killed along with her benefactor."

"So who did the property go to?"

"Property! There wasn't much, you know. Three villas—but they can be expensive to maintain." She stroked the cat beside her; the animal's eyes closed with pleasure. "It reverted to my sister and me."

"Matilde?"

The woman nodded reluctantly.

"And where is she now?"

"You are an uncouth man. My sister—if you insist upon knowing—is no longer with us. She passed away, God rest her soul. In 1975. Perhaps not one of the Creator's most marvelous inventions—she was not an intelligent woman in my opinion—but He, in His infinite wisdom, loves us all. And intelligence is not the same thing as goodness."

"I wouldn't know," Trotti said.

Pisanelli coughed.

"Signora," Trotti asked, "when did you come to the Villa Laura?"

"Do I have to answer these fatuous questions? I'm an old woman and at my age, I have very little time for what goes on beyond these four walls."

"Please answer my question."

A sigh. "I was in Africa. Helping."

"Helping whom?"

"My husband."

"You're married?"

"I was. I no longer am. Orazio is dead." Her hand returned to stroking the cat. "A good man in his own way."

"And what were you doing in Africa?"

She shrugged, and the necklaces moved in unison. "My husband died—and there was nowhere for me to live in Mogadishu. What was I supposed to do? Stay on in that benighted country? When at any street corner I could run into some dark-skinned urchin that might well have been one of my husband's countless brood." She leaned forward. "Are you married?"

"Yes, signora."

"I trust that you are a faithful husband." She raised a shoulder. "Anyway, all policemen are unimaginative. I imagine you don't have the time or inclination for . . ." She folded her arms.

Trotti glanced at Pisanelli and for a moment, wondered whether he had fallen asleep. "About Africa, signora."

"Nothing about Africa. I came back to Italy. At the time, it seemed a reasonable thing to do. It may not be civilization—it most certainly isn't civilization—but after the land of those grinning monkeys, anything is better. At least in this country, the monkeys are white and they grin less." She allowed herself a little shudder. "Africa is a land of communists and Muslims. I can't say I approve." Then, recalling that she was thirsty, she turned on the settee. "Child, I'm still waiting for my coffee."

The girl entered, carrying another tray.

"With sugar. Hurry up. You should know by now how I like my coffee."

Trotti noticed that the cup handed to the old woman was considerably larger than his or Pisanelli's. He also noticed that she had big, strong hands.

"And Ramoverde?"

The woman took no notice. Receiving the cup from the younger woman, she raised cup and saucer to her puckered lips.

"And what happened to Ramoverde?"

The woman drank. "And darling, isn't it time you fed the children?" Seeing the look of puzzlement on Trotti's face, she added, "The cats."

"Where is Douglas Ramoverde, signora?"

"A fool—as much a fool as my poor, beloved sister. God knows, I shouldn't speak ill of the dead. At least Douglas had a pretty face."

"Where can I find him?"

She looked at Trotti over the edge of her large cup. "I am not a medium."

"He's dead?"

"Are all policemen as swift of thought?"

"How did he die? And where?"

"How d'you expect me to know?"

"You lived with your sister for several years. She must have told you."

Signora Buonaventura smiled. "I see that you know more about me than you admit."

"Well?" Irritation had crept into Trotti's voice.

"What exactly is it that you want to know, young man?"

"The truth."

She held out her cup and the girl moved forward to pour more coffee. "I'm afraid that I'm not the purveyor of truth that you take me for." She paused, sipped her coffee. "I'm merely an old woman—and I wish to be left alone."

The cat jumped from her side and approached Trotti. It stopped, arched its back. The dark hair rose upright. It bared its small, white teeth.

"What happened to your brother-in-law? Douglas Ramoverde?"

"He went to Argentina."

"With his family?"

"Of course."

"They stayed there for a long time?"

"A couple of years. You understand, there was the scandal—it ruined Ramoverde, although, if you care to know my opinion, he deserved it. Never was reliable—and his nose began to twitch when he saw a woman." She shrugged. "All men are the same— even policemen." She glanced obliquely at Pisanelli.

"When did your sister come back to Italy?"

"For all I know Ramoverde was responsible for Papa's death."

"When did your sister return to Italy?"

"Is this *Lascia o Raddoppia*? Or some other stupid television quiz?"

"Please answer my question. When did Matilde return?"

"I've just told you. Her husband died—what remained for her in Argentina? The boy had grown up—he had a life of his own. He went to Milan University. Not a very persevering child—he gave it all up to become a journalist. A second-rate journalist."

"When did your sister return? What year?"

The woman put her cup on the floor where one of the cats moved towards it stealthily. "I don't know what your name is—oh, yes, I do, it's Trotti and I've heard about you, Commissario Trotti—I've heard a lot about you. I should be most grateful if you and your comatose friend would leave me alone. You're behaving like thugs. You ask me awkward, useless questions. I don't remember these things—and anyway, they're best forgotten. Ramoverde—Douglas Ramoverde was a mistake of my sister's making. It was nothing to do with me. And anyway, it was all a very long time ago." Her head turned and for a moment Trotti had the impression that the old eyes were staring at the flight of stairs where the body of her father had once lain.

"D'you ever see your nephew?

"Why does that matter?"

"Last week, a young man was gunned down in cold blood. In Gardesana, on Lake Garda. He called himself Maltese. But I have good reason to believe he was your nephew."

"How strange."

33: Arrondissement

"HAVE YOU SEEN the newspaper?"

Trotti looked at his watch. "What time is it?"

"I think you ought to have a look."

Trotti sat up in his bed. It was still dark, although first light was creeping round the edge of the shutters. "Why do you have to wake me up?"

A brief laugh. "On page two of the *Popolo d'Italia* there's a photograph of your friend. Of your dead friend."

"Who?"

"Novara—the journalist."

"What are you talking about, Magagna?"

"Shot dead in the street of the . . ." He paused, as if he were reading. "Of the sixteenth arrondissement."

"Who?"

"In Paris. You asked me to find him, Commissario. Open the paper and he's there. Novara—the man behind the smear campaigns." Again the laugh followed by raucous, heavy breathing.

"You smoke too much, Magagna."

"Shot in the back of the head as he was returning from a local restaurant." Magagna paused. "More effective than cigarettes, you'll agree."

"Where are you phoning from?"

"Monza. I'm still on my case."

"Drugs?"

"This is a public phone," Magagna said sharply. Then he added, "Why else do you think I'd want to come to Monza?" A brief, humorless cough. "If Novara knew anything about Maltese's death, he's not going to tell you. Not now."

It was a moment before Trotti replied, "Novara and Maltese were journalists—and they knew what they were up against. Unless they were complete fools, they knew the rule."

"The rule, Commissario?"

"Information is dangerous if you're the only person to possess it. Information is power, but if you are alone in having access to that power, you—and the information—can be eliminated. With a bullet."

The sound of a cigarette being lit.

Suddenly Trotti felt very clear-headed. "Maltese knew that he could be killed. That's why he was hiding—but he wouldn't have been stupid enough not to share his knowledge. A life insurance."

"A life insurance that didn't pay off." Magagna added, "Now Novara is dead."

"There's still the girl." Trotti said. "The Guerra girl. Unless I'm mistaken, she knows more than she admits to."

"Good luck, Commissario." Magagna laughed and hung up.

34: Anorexia

WHEN HE WOKE again, Trotti could feel the heat of the sun on the wooden blinds, and when he opened the windows, he realized that summer had come to the Po Valley. Beyond the new block of flats, with their rows of matching green sun blinds, the fields stretched out flat and windless, broken only by the occasional line of gaunt plane trees. There was a morning mist and from somewhere came the peal of church bells.

Morning traffic hurried along via Milano. Petrol fumes mingled with other, more pleasant smells of summer.

It was time he took the Ganna out of the garage and oiled it. He had grown flabby over the winter and cycling to work each day would help him get rid of the extra kilos. And perhaps, Trotti shrugged, he would give up eating sweets.

Trotti yawned, stretched and then found that he was humming. In the mirror, he smiled at his own reflection. *Turandot.* He wondered whether summer had arrived in New York.

Pioppi had left for the university.

He put on the coffee, then showered and shaved. With just a towel around his waist—the bruises had all but disappeared—he sat down for breakfast while listening to the radio. The same advertisements for antacids and more news from Argentina. The radio on the refrigerator spoke of the British fleet moving south. Belligerent words from London and Argentina.

Argentina.

On his father's side, there was a whole section of the family that had gone south. Originally it was to farm, but later a couple of uncles had entered the building trade. They had left the countryside and with a slow, steady accumulation of wealth, they had settled in the residential suburbs of Buenos Aires. Sometimes at Christmas there was a card from Placido Trotti, a distant cousin and now a wealthy lawyer.

Children with Spanish names.

The English did not need the islands.

Again Trotti found himself smiling as he felt the irrational antagonism rising. The heritage, perhaps, of a fascist childhood and the posters and slogans painted on walls that reviled the English. Five meals a day and a place in the sun. Half the world painted red and up in arms because Italy dared to invade Abyssinia.

In the last months of the war, Trotti had met several Englishmen. Later, much later, he discovered that one of them—a pilot with a broken jaw and tanned skin—had gone on to become the Prime Minister of his country somewhere in Africa. They had all treated the Italians like animals.

Trotti had preferred the Americans, who were generous and handed out cigarettes and chewing gum and kissed the girls. The Americans—even the black men with their round, shiny faces and brilliant teeth beneath the lopsided helmets—had seemed more human.

He drank the coffee and glanced at his watch. It was not yet eight o'clock.

It was early for Pioppi to have left. He looked round the kitchen, wondering whether she had eaten any breakfast. The place was spotless. He opened the refrigerator. Nothing had been taken.

"Papa!"

For a moment he thought he was dreaming. It was Pioppi's voice. He stood up and went to the window. On the radio, the man was making an announcement about washing powder. Trotti opened the kitchen blinds.

"Papa!"

The same plaintive call for help. It ran through him like a cold shiver, like the time she had fallen and hurt her back. Trotti spun round and went into her bedroom.

It was dark, the blinds were drawn and there was an unpleasant smell. The smell of sickness.

"I thought you'd gone to the university."

A bed lamp had been left on by the desk; held in its ring of brightness, several books lay open. Pioppi was on her bed. Thin like an insect, like a locust. The gaunt, drawn face that once had been so pretty. The eyes moved slowly, with difficulty, with pain. She was crying.

"What's the matter?"

She looked like an old woman. His daughter had not even taken off her jeans. "Papa," she said and tried to form other words but the lips merely trembled. The eyes looked at him with imploring intensity.

Her breath was fetid. Trotti moved to her bedside and he was aware of pain in his chest—of a pain that he had never known before. Something tangible that he could feel swelling up, almost preventing him from breathing. An anger. A burning resentment for his own loneliness.

He realized in that moment that he hated Agnese. She had forsaken him and she had forsaken her own daughter.

"Papa, help me." Pioppi's voice was hoarse. "Papa, please help me."

35: Bottone

"SHE'S ALL RIGHT."

The nurse was a girl with the accent of Emilia and short hair beneath the white cap. She took Trotti by the arm. She was gentle but firm.

"My daughter must not die."

She laughed kindly. "Your daughter will be out of here in twelve hours."

"She doesn't want to eat, you see."

"You must go home, Commissario. Go home and relax."

"I'll wait."

"That won't help." She smiled. "I will fill in the forms for you and you can go home. We'll feed her."

"But she won't eat, you understand? She refuses to eat. Sometimes she'll pretend to eat and then later she'll go into the lavatory and force herself to vomit."

What he said did not affect the nurse's smile. "We'll feed her."

Trotti shook his head vehemently.

The girl accompanied the smile with a small shrug. "Please don't worry. Not through the mouth but directly into the body."

"She won't eat, I tell you."

"Commissario!"

Another voice.

"For six months now—ever since she started her course on town planning at the university—she's been refusing to eat. It's my fault. And this morning, when I didn't see her, I thought she'd gone to university. That's all she ever does. The university and on Sunday she goes to church. If only she could . . ."

"Commissario Trotti!"

A hand was placed on his arm and almost reluctantly, Trotti allowed himself to be pulled round. "I thought I recognized you."

The round rims of the glasses glinted. The emaciated face broke into a hollow smile. The tall man held out his hand. In the same moment, he gave the nurse a sideways glance. She nodded and hurried away, going through the swinging doors that closed in rubberized silence behind her.

Trotti watched her go.

Dottor Bottone linked his arm through Trotti's. "Come, Commissario." He led him out of the cool hall into the morning sunshine.

"I've always tried to give the best to Pioppi."

The old florist and his daughter were doing brisk business on the other side of the road. A cart covered with flowers and several vases with their tight-budded roses and their neat carnations.

"I always think, Commissario, a hospital's the last place for talking about these problems."

36: Nonna

THE NONNA WAS waiting for him and for an hour he sat with his mother, holding her cold hand and wanting to cry. His mother said nothing, but rocked herself back and forwards.

At six he drove back to the hospital but he was not allowed to see his daughter. A nurse informed him that Pioppi was sleeping.

He made a meal for his mother and then went back to his house on the other side of the garden. It was as he went up the stairs that he heard the telephone.

"Pronto?"

"Piero?"

A woman's voice and for a second he thought it was Agnese.

"Yes?"

"I wanted to thank you for the other night."

"Thank me, Donatella? What for?"

"You were very gentle." There was a long pause. "I would like to see you again, Piero. Not in another four years but soon."

"Pioppi's in the hospital." He added, "She's very weak and they're having to feed her."

"Oh." Along the line, her voice sounded distant, muffled. "Can I be of help?"

"For the time being, she's in the doctors' hands."

"Would you like me to drive down, Piero? I'm here in Sesto and in an hour . . ."

Trotti smiled into the mouthpiece. The muscles of his face

were weary and his eyes felt gritty. For an instant he imagined Donatella, the brown eyes, the look of concern, and the blonde hair. "Not now, Donatella. I need to think. But thank you. Perhaps later."

"Who's going to look after your mother?"

"I'll ask one of the neighbors."

"I can help you, Piero, if you want me . . . That's what women are for."

"Thank you."

"Kiss Pioppi for me. And ring me, won't you, if there's any news."

37: Ink

The same porter.

The black shoes creaked officiously. "Wait a minute, dottore." The small man crossed the green linoleum floor. He had taken off his peaked cap and held it beneath his arm. The other arm swung like a soldier's. The blue serge suit was well-pressed but shiny. A non-commissioned officer in retirement.

The university porter tapped at the window of ground glass. He held his body slightly bent, in preparation for future obsequiousness.

The man entered the office and for a moment, Trotti waited. Unesco magazines on the table, an old typewriter and this morning's *Provincia Padana*. A student was reading at the table, a mousy-haired girl with an unhealthy complexion who sat poring over a series of books. She wore glasses, a roll-neck sweater and her ample chest was supported by the edge of the table.

The girl's fingers were ink-stained.

"Professor Baldassare will see you in a few minutes." The porter reemerged from the door and whispered like an acolyte at High Mass.

Trotti brushed past the man and entered the office.

It was untidy.

Baldassare was sitting behind a desk with his feet propped against the edge. He was smoking and he raised his eyes in faint surprise.

Trotti stepped forward.

"I'll be with you in a few minutes."

"Now," Trotti said.

Another man sat near the desk. Large patches of damp had formed at his armpits. The smile on his face was frozen.

"Now, Professor Baldassare," Trotti said. "And in private."

The other man hesitated.

Trotti jerked his thumb towards the door. Then he laid his hand on the man's arm. Trotti's grip was firm and the man did not resist. He allowed himself to be pulled to his feet and accompanied to the door.

"Arriverderci." Trotti gave him a push and then closed the door behind him,

"Very impressive, Commissario."

Baldassare still had his feet on the top of the desk.

He wore tinted sunglasses with large frames and lenses that became progressively bluer and darker towards the top of the rims. Receding grey hair that was long and deliberately unkempt gave him the appearance of a well-groomed bohemian. A pale blue shirt and a tie, a loose linen jacket. The shoes were new and expensive. As Trotti sat down on the chair vacated by the other man, he noted that the soles to the shoes still retained their initial varnish. They had scarcely been scuffed by wear. Dark green corduroy trousers.

Baldassare was older than Trotti had imagined. In good condition, but at least fifty-five years old.

"I don't believe we've been introduced."

"Squadra Mobile."

"Ah." Amusement danced at the corner of the lips and behind the tinted lens, the skin formed wrinkles. Thin lips, a long nose and a pointed jaw.

"Commissario Trotti of Squadra Mobile."

"Not a name on everybody's lips."

Trotti pointed. "You know my daughter."

"I don't believe I've had the pleasure." Even the frown suggested amusement. "I have many students and my classes would appear to be popular among the student body. But," he placed a hand to his forehead, "I don't think I know of a Signorina Trotti."

"She is at the Policlinico at this moment—where she is being fed intravenously."

"The poor child."

"She weighs just over forty-five kilos. And since last year, she hasn't been eating. She refuses to eat." Trotti rubbed the back of his hand across his mouth, aware that the saliva was forming at the corner of his lips. "Over six months, Professor Baldassare—about the same time that she has been going to your classes. Classes on urban planning."

Slowly, almost casually, Baldassare took his feet from where they were propped. They fell noiselessly to the floor and then Baldassare leaned forward, placing the weight of his arms on a pile of documents. "I don't think I understand." The smile remained, but the lines hardened.

"I think you do."

"Please explain, Commissario."

"I've nothing to explain." Trotti knew that he was losing control of himself. The word *intravenously* echoed angrily around his head.

"Am I right in thinking, Signor Commissario, that you are attributing your daughter's problems to me?" A snort, part indignation, part amusement, worked its way through the long, narrow nose. "I don't know Signorina Trotti. If she is anything like her father, she must have difficulty in being a charming person."

Trotti moved forward and grabbed him by the tie. The movement was rapid and Baldassare's face sagged. "Careful," Trotti said. His jaws were clamped together.

Baldassare slumped back. He adjusted his tie. "I know nothing about your daughter."

"You're a liar."

"Our marvelous, democratic police force." Baldassare attempted a smile.

"I'm also a father." The anger was draining from him—Trotti could feel it seeping away, like water through the earth. "You have been playing with the emotions of a young woman. You have made use of your position as . . ."

"Trotti, I don't know your daughter." He raised a finger. "I don't know her and I don't want to know her."

The vision of his daughter in bed, the liquid dripping into her emaciated arm. His daughter—the child of his flesh—of his and Agnese's.

The anger was now cold, but it was still anger. Anger with the evil man in front of him. With a brushing movement, Trotti cleared the desk of everything. Of the books and papers and the desk lamp. They fell to the floor; the lamp clattered noisily against the side of the desk, still supported by its flex.

The eyes remained fixed upon Trotti. "You're mad."

"How can you explain this?" Trotti stood up. He fumbled in his pocket. He took out the wallet that Agnese had given him many years previously and from the pouch he took the visiting card. "I found this among her possessions last night. Among the secret things that she wanted to keep hidden—like the purgatives that would stop her from putting on weight. My daughter, Baldassare, my only daughter and I found this in her drawer." With a hand that trembled of its own accord, Trotti held the card under the other man's nose.

"A policeman—even with your own daughter. No privacy, no right to a life of her own, but you've got to be snooping. A sleuth, a clever little spy." Baldassare laughed. "And you riffle through her possessions like a thief in the night."

"My child is dying—do you understand?" Trotti knew he was shouting now. It was as if he were a spectator—an outsider watching his behavior with detachment.

"Trotti, I don't give a shit about your daughter."

"She's dying and I care for her. She is my child, and I know that you are responsible for what she is now having to go through. Urbanistica, urbanistica—that is all she can talk about. A poor child who's fallen in love with a married man. And you, you exploit her. You exploit her innocence."

Baldassare sat back and folded his arms. "I've no idea what you're talking about."

"You deny that this is your card?"

He shrugged. "If I was having an affair with one of my students, I certainly wouldn't want to advertise the fact—or advertise my identity." A patronizing laugh. "Come, Commissario, even a policeman can understand that."

"And this isn't your handwriting, *With many, many thanks*? And this isn't your signature? And this isn't your phone number?"

A long silence.

"So help me, if you don't answer, Baldassare's, I'll kill you."

Baldassare shrugged. "I didn't know she was your daughter."

"What the hell does that mean?"

There was no amusement in Baldassare's smile, even though he showed bright teeth. "Poor thing—like a miserable, unhappy animal."

"What?"

"I felt sorry for her."

"You'll soon be feeling even sorrier for yourself."

"Your daughter followed me." He shrugged. "What could I do?"

"You've been exploiting her—making use of your position, of your authority. Baldassare, I'm going to have you annihilated."

The two men looked at each other. Trotti had regained control of himself but the anger was still there, burning like a flame that could burst into life at any moment. He put his hands on the desk to stop their trembling.

Baldassare shrugged. He turned away from Trotti and regarded the scattered paper and books on the floor. Trotti looked, too, and he noticed for the first time that a bottle of blue ink had smashed, spilling a few dark tears onto the paper and the linoleum floor.

Baldassare leaned over and picked up a framed photograph. He set it on the table.

Trotti asked, "Who's that?"

"Frank Lloyd Wright."

"Who's he?"

"A friend of mine from Pizzighettone. He repairs carburetors."

As Trotti struck him, the sunglasses flew from his face.

"I'll have you thrown in jail—don't get clever with me. D'you understand, Baldassare? Thrown into jail as an accessory to murder!"

He looked older, more vulnerable without his glasses. Baldassare ran his fingers through his hair.

"Don't use long words and don't make intellectual jokes. I'm a dumb policeman. But that won't stop me from causing you trouble."

"You shouldn't threaten me, Commissario." Although flat, the voice was full of menace.

"I'm talking about murder."

"You're dangerous, Trotti."

He took the chair and sat down. "Now perhaps, we can talk seriously."

The naked face gave a thin smile. "You're not going to get away with this."

"Perhaps you don't understand, but I'm talking about murder. Murder, Baldassare. And that can mean life imprisonment on some Sardinian island. Don't become all tough little intellectual with me."

"You're mad—and you're dangerous. What do I know about your daughter? A poor thing who looks like an underfed rabbit and follows me around like a faithful puppy." He shrugged. "I thought that she was ill—some disease, some incurable disease. She pestered me, always asking questions, always trying to attract my attention. I felt sorry for her—and now I understand. Her disease is her father." His elbow was on the table and he wagged his finger at Trotti. It was a strange gesture. Baldassare was afraid, physically afraid; yet there was no fear in his defiance. "Listen, Trotti, I am not a doctor, but I read the magazines. It didn't occur to me that your daughter was starving herself—I didn't realize that. But I read the papers and I've heard about anorexia. And I know what causes it."

The skin on Trotti's face felt numb.

"Nothing to do with me, Trotti. That's your little pipe dream and if you want to think that your daughter's starving herself out of love . . ." He shrugged, and the mocking smile had returned behind the upheld finger. "But from what I've read about anorexia, I thought it was a way of asserting yourself. Not a broken heart, Commissario, but a way of showing yourself and showing the rest of the world that you're in charge—that you're an autonomous adult. Control your body—and you control your life."

"Be careful what you say, Baldassare."

"A way to assert your freedom—freedom from demanding parents, freedom from people who don't consider you a real human being but merely a pawn. A pawn in their own private game of conflict and domination."

The numbness had spread. It had reached the back of his neck. Trotti felt cold, very cold. A lump of ice within his chest.

"A poor kid who's crying out for attention and love. But attention and love are things a man like you doesn't need to think about. It's easier, isn't it, to come round here"—Baldassare gestured to the pile of scattered books on the floor and to the stream of dark ink that had almost reached his shoes—"and to accuse me of murder? Accuse me of having killed your daughter. But then, you're a policeman—you can throw your weight around with other people, just as you throw your weight around with your daughter." He shook his head. "Poor Commissario Trotti."

"Save the pity for yourself."

"Trotti, you're finished. As a human being, you must have died a long time ago. As a policeman, you're not worth the paper your identity card is printed on." Baldassare rubbed his face, then leaned over and picked up the sunglasses. "By God, I'm going to see you pulled through the mud."

Trotti stood up.

The ice was there in his heart, but his head was clear now and his body was washed of any need for revenge. He went over to the window.

It looked onto the Cloisters of Magnolia. A couple of students were sitting beside the well, enjoying the sunshine. The sun was warm and a man was sweeping the cobbled courtyard. The birch broom moved in regular, short strokes. The man was sweeping away the accumulated dirt and detritus of winter.

For the first time, Trotti noticed the smell of the magnolia.

"No, Baldassare, no." Trotti turned and now he was smiling. "You can't escape the facts. There's only one person who knew where I was going last Friday morning—and that was my daughter. Nobody else—nobody. And yet a journalist found me there. A journalist, Professor Baldassare, who had been living with Signorina Guerra. Which is, I am sure, a name that is not totally unknown to you." Trotti paused. "Your wife's maiden name."

The long face was looking at him. Baldassare ran a hand through his hair.

"My daughter told you—and through you, the message reached Maltese. Only now, Maltese is dead—murdered in cold blood by two men who knew that he would be at Gardesana on Lake Garda at eight o'clock in the morning. Two men who were waiting for him."

One of the tinted lenses had been smashed in the fall.

"Tell me, Baldassare, why did you want Maltese killed?"

Baldassare smiled as he tapped the lens; small shards of glass fell onto the desk.

38: Carmine

THE BEAUTY OF the city—Roman brick, Renaissance architecture, Hapsburg ochre walls and the trees in blossom—did not
touch Trotti. Nor did the gentle smell of flowers coming from
the private gardens. His footsteps echoed against the high walls
of the narrow streets.

Piazza Carmine was full of rows of parked traffic. The church
was of red brick and in the walls, blue and white dishes had been
embedded. It was said that they were gifts brought back by local
dignitaries from the Crusades. Trotti brushed past a group of
old women and pushed open the heavy door, worn and dirty
beneath the touch of so many hands. He entered the cool chill of
the church. The smell of candles reminded him of his childhood
and Zia Anastasia, stiff in her black clothes and her hand firmly
on his wrist, pulling him towards the altar and—she hoped—a
more Christian existence.

Pioppi was a regular churchgoer and sometimes Agnese
accompanied her—perhaps because she enjoyed dressing for the
occasion, perhaps because she met old friends, people like her.
They would never think of coming to visit her in via Milano but
were happy enough to chat with her on the neutral ground of the
church steps and to speak of other, anodyne things—of clothes
and prices and children—but never of the policeman whom she
had married.

Trotti stood by the door, looking at the burning candles. He felt that he was an intruder upon a world that he had renounced many years earlier. A clumsy genuflection. Crossing himself while his eyes adjusted to the gloom. He went to a pew and sat down.

The creak of shoes as a man—the sacristan, perhaps—busied himself before the high altar. There were rays of light coming from a window. Specks of dust fluttered and danced in silence.

Trotti placed his head on the back of the chair in front and closed his eyes. He did not move. He did not pray—did not know how to. He sat motionless for over an hour. He remembered Pioppi—when she was little, pointing at the fish that darted beneath the surface of Lake Garda. The silence of the church brought him comfort. The grittiness behind his eyes seemed to lessen and when he raised his head, he felt refreshed.

39: Siemens

"RAMOVERDE WAS LIVING in Buenos Aires until about 1968, when he had a heart attack."

"Leave me alone, Magagna."

"He died in 1970. The Argentinians have been slow in sending us any information—very slow. I don't think that they're pleased with Italy or the Italians. Perhaps they feel that we've let them down in their moment of need."

Trotti stared at the empty wall in front of him; the cream paint had been smeared by the passage of time and by the movement of people along the hospital corridor. He turned to look at the younger man, but Magagna did not look up from his notes. Magagna said, "His wife died a couple of years later, but the body was repatriated."

"Leave me, Magagna. Go back to Milan."

It was then that Magagna took notice of Trotti and of what he was saying. He smiled brightly. "You can't stay here for the rest of your life."

"Pioppi needs me."

"You've seen her—she's asleep."

"I must stay with her."

"You're not doing her any good—nor yourself." He removed his sunglasses and there was compassion on his face. There was also stubble along his upper lip where he was growing a new mustache. "You're only hurting yourself, Commissario."

"What the hell do you want me to do?"

It was still early morning, and beyond the door, in the parking spaces by the trees, doctors were arriving for work. They looked naked without their white laboratory coats.

"Take this." Magagna handed Trotti a packet of sweets. "It might help you to get a bed in the diabetes ward."

Trotti shook his head. "What am I supposed to do?"

"I've driven down from Milan to see you, Commissario."

"I phoned America. I left a message saying it was urgent, and still my wife hasn't phoned."

"I think," Magagna said, putting his glasses back on, "that we ought to go and see the girl."

Trotti's shoulders were slumped. He sat with his hands hanging between his knees and he stared at his shoes. Further down the corridor, a woman was singing—a cleaning woman, whose voice rose above the clanging of her pails and broom: "Amor, dammi quel fazzolettino."

"I should be in Monza—but there's not much point. Ragusa knows that we've got all his phones tapped for the simple reason that he's got friends in Siemens . . . the telephone company."

"Siemens?"

"Perhaps we ought to go back to the shop and ask Guerra a few more questions—questions that we should have asked her the first time."

Trotti looked up.

"You told me that there must be some form of insurance that Maltese took out to protect himself. If he knew anything, he probably told the girl—or entrusted her with evidence."

Trotti said nothing.

"Unless, of course, she knew he was going to get killed," Magagna said.

40: Canary

TROTTI DID NOT talk. He sat beside Magagna, his chin on his chest and his shoulders slumped forward. Magagna could not see whether his eyes were closed or whether Trotti was staring out of the window, looking at the fields or the sluggish canal where fishermen held their rods over the polluted water.

Past the Certosa, past Binasco—where Magagna was held up by the blue coach turning into the station. Afterwards, determined to make up for lost time, he sped along the road and before long they were on the outskirts of the city. Suddenly the flat fields became a jungle of new tower blocks, and the morning sky was acrid with fumes. Cars hooted at each other, driven by a magic, manic force.

Milan.

"For God's sake, stop that whistling."

Magagna turned, surprised. "I was whistling?"

Trotti did not reply.

At Ventiquattro Maggio, Magagna turned left, almost hit a truck—Reggio Calabria registration and the driver sweating, despite his cotton singlet—and moved through the traffic at speed.

Trotti was gripping the armrest. "Where are we going?"

"To the shop." He bumped the car across a tramline, took another turn. A woman with a poodle, about to cross the road, gesticulated angrily.

"Women!" Without stopping to catch his breath, Magagna added, "Either she sent him to his death without knowing it—or it was deliberate."

"Guerra?"

"If—as you say—her brother-in-law knew that you were going to be at Gardesana, it would seem reasonable to assume she told Maltese." Magagna pulled the car onto the pavement. "The question is, did she know he was going to his death?"

Trotti said nothing. He got out of the car and Magagna soon joined him. Magagna pushed the sunglasses on the bridge of his nose. Guiding Trotti by the arm, he crossed the road.

It was not yet eleven o'clock. Already a hot day. The neon light seemed insignificant.

The bell rang overhead.

"Gentlemen?"

The woman was wearing the same vivid lipstick, but she had changed her jeans. Now she had on a bright pair of canary yellow slacks.

"Pubblica Sicurezza."

The woman threw her eyes to the ceiling. "We've met."

"Where's the girl?"

Her eyes watched the two men with ill-concealed hostility.

"Well?" Magagna looked at the shelves, glanced at the display of new and second-hand clothes, the single black and white poster of Totò, the Neapolitan actor, drinking a cup of coffee, his eyes sad, and a burning cigarette between two fingers. Then he looked again at the woman. His face had grown older, more feral. "A few questions that we want to ask her."

The woman shrugged.

From between the racks of jackets a client emerged. A man in a raincoat. He mumbled "Buongiorno" and left hurriedly, accompanied by the dying tinkle of the overhead bell.

"Strange customers," Magagna said.

"I didn't invite you."

"Where is she?"

"Who?"

"The girl—where is she?"

She looked at Trotti in surprise and raised an eyebrow of plucked hair and paint, "I haven't seen her." She gave a sudden, ingratiating smile. Lipstick on her false teeth.

Magagna asked, "Why not?"

"I don't know—perhaps because she hasn't been in since you went off with her—perhaps because she's a lazy bitch. Or perhaps she's staying out of trouble." She added, "I am not a relative of hers."

"Lucky girl."

Then the woman lost her temper. "Who d'you think you are? I'm a respectable woman and I run a respectable shop. Please leave—your presence here is not good for business."

"Your presence in Questura will be even more harmful to business, signora."

Trotti brushed past the woman—she took a step back on her high-heeled sandals—and went to the door at the back of the shop. He turned the handle: it was locked.

"Please open it."

"Why?" The tone was querulous, with a hint of fear. "I've told you, she hasn't been in. Not since the last time you were here. And anyway, I didn't want her—I don't like having flatfeet coming here when I've a legitimate business to run. There are criminals, you know, real criminals—why don't you go and bother them? Leave honest folk to get on with their business. Go and catch criminals and terrorists."

"Please open the door, signora."

The woman hesitated, bit her lower lip and as she did so, her jaw swelled with the displaced dentures. She turned and glanced at the front door.

"All you have to do is unlock this door."

"I haven't got the key."

"On Monday, you had it."

Again the head turned and with her bloodshot eyes, she looked despairingly at the front door. "It's not me who has the key."

"Then we'll have to knock the door down."

Her face lit up, inspired. "Do you have a warrant?"

Magagna shrugged and turned to Trotti. Trotti said nothing. She repeated, "Do you have a warrant?"

With his thumb, Trotti gestured towards the closed door. Magagna nodded, but before he could approach it, the woman fell on him.

"No!" she screamed.

He pushed her away. Theatrically she threw her head back; the knees crumpled and she started to fall towards the floor. She released a slight, hissing gasp as her head hit the coarse weave of the jute carpet.

Magagna put his shoulder against the door. Without moving his feet, he swung his body and pushed hard. The lock gave way immediately.

The last time, the room had been almost empty, dry and dusty. Now it was full of parcels—parcels wrapped in brown paper and attached with string.

Magagna produced a penknife and cut at some string; then he ripped at the brown paper.

Magazines—glossy magazines.

41: Theory

"YOU CAN'T TRUST women."

Magagna said, "Why did you marry one?"

"You can't trust men, either. Magagna, take me home," Trotti said tensely, "or take me to the station and I'll catch a train."

"I think you ought to see the girl."

"I want to get back to my daughter."

"Let's talk to Guerra first."

Trotti did not reply; he stared at the dingy buildings that followed the via Isonzo. With the sudden arrival of the summer, this part of the city appeared shabby, unprepared for the brightness of the sun. Soot hung in the air.

"I need to get back to Pioppi."

Magagna said, "Five hundred thousand lire."

"What?"

"That's how much the Carabinieri found on Ramoverde."

"Well?"

"Perhaps he wanted to give it to you, Commissario. Perhaps that's why Ramoverde went to Gardesana." Magagna paused for an instant. "Or perhaps the girl gave it to him."

Trotti looked out of the car window.

"She knew he was going to be killed—and she wanted you to associate him with the robbery at the Banca San Matteo."

"There's no connection between the money and the robbery."

"Other than that's what the Sardinians were looking for."

"I don't understand, Magagna, what makes you think that the Guerra girl wanted Maltese killed. Why, for heaven's sake? They were living together, weren't they? It was you that pointed out he pissed down her sink—a sign of intimacy, you'll agree."

"Money, Commissario."

"Explain what you mean."

Magagna lit a cigarette. "An expensive habit to maintain, heroin. Where could she get the money? She must have known that after the Night of the Tazebao, there was money on Ramoverde's head." Magagna gave a thin smile and nudged his glasses. "The Danish magazines? I knew that they've been circulating—I didn't know they were coming out of Senigallia—but I've been out of things at Monza. I've got you to thank for bringing me back into the city." He opened the car door—they had parked on the end of viale Lodi, near the traffic lights. "Heaven knows why anybody should want to buy that rubbish."

"Loneliness."

"With children, Commissario? That's sick—for maniacs, not for human beings. For depraved sex maniacs."

"We're all maniacs at some time or another. Or d'you think that the perverts who masturbate over those pictures—d'you think they'd be wasting good money—giving away good money to the Mafia—if instead they were able to go home every evening to Ornella Muti?"

"They ought to be castrated."

Trotti did not reply.

Magagna inhaled on his cigarette and looked disapprovingly at Trotti.

On the other side of the street, a tramp, still wearing the heavy clothes of winter, was rummaging in a garbage can.

"Lonely or not—people like that ought to be castrated."

They got out of the car and crossed the road.

"Why d'you think she's at home?"

"Where else can she go, Commissario?"

They went up the stairs, up the flights of flint steps and then walked along the outside balcony that gave on to the grimy courtyard below. The air now smelled of soot and boiled cabbage.

The door was closed and Magagna knocked. He rapped against the wood—a dull hollow sound.

"Doesn't seem as if she's there."

"She's here, Commissario."

"How d'you know?"

"I know addicts—eighteen months in Milan has taught me that they don't move around—just enough to meet their pusher or go to the chemist's." He rubbed his chin. "I know she's there."

"She could be with friends."

"Addicts don't have friends."

Trotti frowned. "She's well enough to work—she didn't look like an addict to me. It hadn't got to the stage where it was interfering with her life."

Magagna clicked his tongue. "Looks like my day for knocking doors down."

"Magagna, take me home."

The other man held up his hand and gave a brief, placating smile. He threw away the cigarette and Trotti watched it as it swirled down into the courtyard, landing between the lines of washing.

"I don't want to be party to what you're intending to do. Not here with people watching us. I've no jurisdiction in Milan, Magagna, and knocking down a door without a warrant can get me into trouble."

"You didn't mind in the shop."

Trotti shrugged.

Magagna smiled.

Trotti gestured towards the door. "Are we going to stand around here all day?" He pointed at the three locks that formed a glinting punctuation on the dirty, varnished wood.

Magagna turned and thumped again.

"There's no one there. Let's go." Trotti moved towards the top of the stairs. On the balcony of the building opposite, a woman appeared. Her hands were wet and she was staring at the two men as she took a towel from where it hung on the metal balustrade.

From the other apartments came the sound of life—people eating, radios blaring the midday news. Somewhere, somebody was shouting in a Sicilian dialect.

In the narrow space, Magagna took three steps, turned and charging, his shoulders hunched and his face taut, he hit the edge of the door. The wood scarcely moved.

"I'll have to kick it down." His face was red.

"You don't have a warrant, Magagna—and I'm not staying here—too many people have seen me as it is."

"Guerra may be dead!"

"And you want to lose your job?" Trotti waved his hand in a gesture of salutation. "I'll wait for you in the car."

He went downstairs.

42: Empty

LOST IN THOUGHT, Trotti was sucking disconsolately on a boiled sweet when Magagna came across the road. He walked fast, opened the driver's door and slid in behind the wheel.

"She's dead."

"Guerra?"

Magagna nodded, unhooked the microphone from the dashboard and made a brief call. The answering voice was tinny, a woman's voice distorted in the ether.

Magagna got out of the car, leaving the door open. Trotti followed him.

On the far side of viale Lodi, a train was shunting noisily and the screech of its brakes accompanied the two men as they went upstairs. Magagna broke into a run, taking the stairs two at a time. There was white dust on his jacket where the shoulder had rubbed against the wall.

From behind a closed door came the sound of a radio; the midday news was now over, replaced by the familiar advertisements, the same timeless jingles—everyday life in Italy. It was reassuring.

Trotti climbed the stairs with mounting apprehension. "My fault," he said under his breath.

A crowd had gathered on the fourth floor. They stood on the landing. There was an old woman talking in a hoarse whisper.

She wore black and spoke in a dialect that Trotti could not understand. Wisps of white hair hung about her face. The other bystanders stared at the door. It hung on its hinges. The wood around the locks had been torn apart and there were splinters and flakes of dust on the stone floor.

"I needed a bit of help," Magagna said when Trotti reached him.

Trotti recognized the smell of blood. "Where's the body?" The room was bare. Blood was everywhere, and the strange metallic smell was overpowering. A dry puddle and streaks across the floor and wall that had turned black.

Trotti repeated the question. "Where's the girl?"

Magagna shrugged.

The mattress was as it had been; the can of shaving cream was where Magagna had left it on the first visit. But the poster on the wall advertising the Sila in Calabria had been pulled down, torn and smeared with blood.

"Where is she?"

"I don't know."

"You said she was dead." Trotti went to the window. He felt sickened and for a moment he rested with his hand on the window ledge, the feel of wood beneath his skin comforting. He stared unthinkingly at the shunting yards on the far side of the street. He saw the locomotive. Trotti also noticed a man leaning out of the control cabin while another man hurried alongside the railway track, trying to keep up with the moving train.

Trotti turned.

The floor of the room was bare except for a smashed syringe and an ashtray that had been knocked over, spilling its contents of ash and cigarette tips onto the cold stone. And the dead, trampled-on carnation.

"Not very convincing." Trotti said.

Magagna was crouching down and with his fingernail he was chipping at the edge of a smear of blood. He looked up.

"Breaking down doors—making a noise and attracting the neighbors." Trotti shook his head. "That's precisely what Guerra wanted."

Magagna took no notice.

Outside, the strident wail of a police siren was approaching viale Lodi.

Trotti said, "I'll make my own way to the station." He walked out of the room and pushed through the crowd of onlookers.

43: Orchidea

"You're still at university?"

"I sit the occasional exam."

Magagna came back and smiled at Trotti. "Our friend here is a student in sociology. But before long, he'll be working full time for the Faculty of Medicine—unpaid."

He could not have been much older than twenty-five, but there were premature wrinkles about his eyes and in the unflattering light of the bar he looked pale and unhealthy. He had not shaved, and the ends of his drooping mustache lost themselves in the dark stubble. His eyes were bloodshot, the iris dilated. "Faculty of Medicine, Signor Magagna?"

"It's not often they have young corpses to work on—it makes a pleasant change after the tramps and the old people from the hospice."

The man said nothing.

"You want something to eat?"

"I'm not hungry."

"Business good?"

The man shrugged.

"Have something to eat," Trotti said, turning to call the Moroccan waiter to prepare a couple of sandwiches.

From behind the bar, the waiter nodded. He put down the dishcloth.

"I"m not hungry," the man repeated. He placed his hands on the table—long fingers and dirty nails. He bit his lip.

Magagna said, "I think Marco is scared."

"Scared? I've got nothing to be scared of."

"Perhaps you've been hiding something from me, Marco."

The sounds of Milan—the trams, the traffic, the ceaseless bustle of people—did not reach them. They were sitting in the back of the Bar Orchidea in the Brera. A basement bar, furnished with dark wood and photographs of Juventus of twenty years earlier. One or two signed and framed photographs on the wall—football players, boxers and cyclists. In a room off the main bar, there was a rod-football machine. Young people—probably students—were playing noisily, banging the rods and laughing. From time to time, the hollow bang as the ball went into the goal.

"I've got nothing to keep from you, Signor Magagna. That was the agreement, wasn't it?"

"You don't look at all well, Marco." A mocking tone.

"I'm okay."

"Somebody been lacing your powder with strychnine?"

"I'm okay."

"Then perhaps you'd like to tell my friend"—Magagna gestured towards Trotti—"perhaps you'd like to tell him what you told me about the money?"

Marco gave an ingratiating smile that succeeded in making him appear uglier. He reminded Trotti of a drowned rodent. Marco had narrow shoulders and was wearing a shabby cardigan that had lost its form and color. The zip down the front was broken; underneath he was wearing an orange roll-neck sweater of nylon. It was smeared with dirt. "Your friend is from Narcotici, too?"

"Buoncostume."

Marco visibly paled.

"But he's very broad-minded." Magagna tapped Marco's wrist. "And he knows all about your particular tastes."

Three dirty fingers went to the forehead and worried at the wrinkles. "Signor Magagna, we had an agreement."

"You had an agreement, Marco."

"But you promised that if . . ."

"And what happens if you go off and do one of your little tricks again, Marco? What are my friends in Questura going to say? Have you thought about that?"

"I haven't done anything, I swear."

"Your young friends in via Moscova—I hope you haven't been hanging around there lately, Marco. You haven't been pestering anyone, I hope."

"My God . . . I'm too . . ." He stopped, ran his hand over his mouth. "I assure you I'm not up to any of that—not now. I don't feel well enough."

The barman arrived. He placed a plate of sandwiches on the scarred wood of the table-top. "And to drink?" he asked, without looking at the three men, but staring at old posters on the wall. He had acquired a Milanese accent.

"A beer for me," Magagna said. "What would you like, Marco?"

"A mineral water."

"Nothing stronger?"

"It's for my kidneys."

"Surprised you've got any left." Magagna laughed.

Trotti ordered a cup of coffee. To Magagna he said, "I don't want to miss my train."

"You could've left this afternoon."

"Pioppi was still sleeping when I phoned Bottone at the Policlinico."

Magagna turned back to Marco and pushed the plate towards him. For an instant, Marco looked at the sandwich. Then he shook his head.

"You must eat."

"I'm not hungry."

Magagna spoke in a low, threatening voice, "Eat."

Reluctantly, Marco took one of the sandwiches—two thick slices of southern bread, the crust dusty with flour. Sliced tomatoes, spices and olive oil. A thick slab of mozzarella. Marco made a face as he took a small bite. He forced himself to swallow.

"You see, it's good for you."

Marco nodded and mouthed a silent, "Yes."

"Now, Marco, I want you to tell my friend about the girl."

"The girl?"

The side of his hand struck Marco across the cheek. The sandwich fell from his hand and onto the table, scattering its contents. "Don't flirt with me, Marco."

Marco looked down at the pieces of food and started to pick them up. Trotti wondered whether the man was going to cry.

"All you have to do is tell my friend about the girl."

"Guerra?"

"You see," Magagna gave a big, approving smile, "you're beginning to be reasonable. We're going to get on well tonight, aren't we, Marco?"

"What d'you want me to say?" The hand that now held the sandwich was shaking; the dilated pupil looked at Magagna while the eyes seemed to be immobile.

"Just tell my friend what you told me."

"About the money?"

"Very good!" Patronizing, like a schoolteacher.

"She came to see me—that's all. She wanted some stuff."

Trotti asked, "Stuff?"

"Snow—she was fairly desperate. And she wanted the best—from Lebanon." He looked to Magagna for reassurance. "D'you want me to explain to your friend where it comes from?"

"My friend wants to know about Guerra."

"She paid in cash—brand-new bills of fifty thousand lire. That's why I was suspicious."

"Suspicious?"

"In the past it was small bills—just change." Again the three fingers pulling at the forehead. "Money that she had managed to scrape together. One time she was quite wealthy—that was when she was whoring in San Babila. But fifty-thousand lire bills?" He shook his head. "And she wanted ten grams."

"You sold it to her?"

"I didn't have it to sell."

"Why not?"

"It's the Sicilians—they do it on purpose. They think that the price is getting too low, so they hold the merchandise back, waiting for demand to put the prices up again. And in that way, they can find out who's cutting in on their market. There was . . ." Marco stopped suddenly as his mouth came closed.

"Go on," Trotti said.

His adam's apple bobbed in the scraggy neck.

"Go on, Marco. My friend wants to hear what you've got to say."

He hesitated briefly. "A Bulgar—a character with black glasses—he called himself the 'Positive Hero'—and he was selling it cheap—good stuff that hadn't been cut and that you could make a decent profit on. When stuff comes from behind the Iron Curtain, it's normally good. But it's dangerous, unless you know who you're dealing with." The eyes moved from Trotti to Magagna.

"Well?"

"The Sicilians found him."

"So what?"

"They run this city."

"And?"

"They left his head on the front seat of a car in Porta Ticinese."

"And the rest of the body?"

Marco shrugged. "Never found."

"My heart bleeds," Magagna said coldly, pushing at the frames of his glasses. In the light of the bar, his features appeared harsh. The big city was already leaving its mark on the young policeman from Pescara.

Trotti said, "Do you know where Guerra is now?"

"She lives in viale Lodi."

"Not anymore." He drank some coffee. "When did you last see her?"

"When she came for the deal." Unexpectedly, Marco smiled behind his hand. There were large drops of sweat along his forehead. "That's what I told Signor Magagna. I'd never seen her with money like that—she was spending like a sailor. She said she could afford the best."

"Eat your sandwich, Marco." Magagna pushed the plate against Marco's narrow ribs.

"What made you tell Magagna about the money?"

"I was scared."

"There was nothing to be scared about."

Reluctantly, Marco started eating. He mumbled something.

"What?"

"I thought it was organized crime money."

Magagna snorted. "You shouldn't have accepted it in the first place." To Trotti, he said in a low whisper, "He told me about the money when he knew I was looking for Lia Guerra."

"I needed the money." Marco shrugged, lowered the sandwich and looked at the small tooth bites. "It occurred to me that it was a pay-off to the girl." He added, "I wouldn't have trusted her."

"You knew she was living with a man?"

"A pimp?"

"It was in this bar that they met."

Marco shrugged. "She's a lesbian—she's not interested in men."

"When did you last see her?"

"A couple of weeks ago." The hand across his mouth. "Perhaps less—I don't know. I find it hard to remember things." He began to nod.

"I might have to jog your memory, Marco," Magagna said. "Me or Buoncostume."

The look of a tracked beast returned to the bloodshot eyes. "It was last week," he said hesitantly.

"And she didn't tell you where the money came from?"

"A wonderful man—that's what she said. A wonderful man who was going to make her happy."

"Who?"

"I don't know. I didn't pay any attention. I told you—she's a lesbian."

"She didn't mention any names?" Trotti asked.

Marco shook his head. "She had the money under her shirt. She showed me one hundred fifty grand—three notes. I was just glad to find somebody willing to do business. I got the stuff for her that afternoon from the Sicilians—and she gave me the money."

"Where?"

"In the metro." He paused, looking at Trotti and there was something frightening about the glazed eyes. "Loreto—there's a place by the escalators when you're changing lines." He paused. "A good place, no cops."

"And you contacted Magagna?" Trotti asked.

Magagna snorted. "I found him, the miserable runt. When you asked me to find Guerra, I went through all my contacts—my addict friends. And Marco recognized the photo."

Trotti stood up, the cup of coffee in his hand. "I don't want to miss the train." He finished the coffee in a gulp. "I've got to get back to the hospital."

Marco was looking at the sandwich. Suddenly he turned his head and leaned over the end of the wooden bench. He started to vomit a white, viscous liquid.

44: Flowers

THERE WERE A couple of books on the night table.

"What are these?" Trotti picked one of the books up.

The young nurse shrugged. "I think your daughter's bored."

One of the titles was in French. Trotti recognized the word *"planification."*

"I thought she was supposed to be resting."

The nurse nodded.

"Then she shouldn't be studying, for heaven's sake."

"You'll wake her, Commissario, if you shout." In the half-light, the nurse's face was worried, as if she now regretted letting Trotti into the small room. "Sit down if you wish. But you must let the poor thing sleep." She pushed a chair against the back of his legs and Trotti sat down slowly. "And her mother?"

"Still in America."

The woman nodded and smiled. "Would you like me to bring you something to drink?" Lightly her hand touched his shoulder. Trotti looked up at the regular features and the short hair that caught the reflection of the bedside lamp.

"You're very kind."

Soon it would be midnight and Trotti was tired. Twice his eyes closed and he came awake with a violent jerk. He wanted to sleep, but at the same time he wanted to be with his daughter. He tried to think about her—how she had been when she was a little girl—the dolls, the strange, sweet lisp that he had almost forgotten about. He thought about these things—but from time to time, he found his determination lagging and his head began to loll forward.

The nurse brought him a cup of coffee. "Café Hag," she said.

"Thank you."

She stood beside him, her hands clasped loosely together. "Your daughter is very beautiful, Commissario."

"She takes after her mother."

"She must have many admirers."

Pioppi had remained a child for a long time—longer than her friends at school. But when the change came, it came suddenly and from that moment on—without even admitting it to himself, and while very happy to have a pretty, adolescent daughter—Trotti knew that he was going to lose her. Something that was special between them—a day would come when it would have to come to an end. There was going to be another man in her life, younger than him, better educated, richer, and the time would come when Pioppi would have to leave him. Trotti knew that his love for his daughter was tinged with jealousy.

But at the same time, thoughts of being a grandfather, of going up into the hills, of living in Santa Maria, were always there at the back of his mind.

"A man came in the afternoon to see her."

Trotti looked up in surprise.

"Oh, he wasn't very young," the nurse from Emilia said and she laughed. Her gentle laughter was like water on pebbles.

"Who was it?"

"He didn't say—it was just as I came on duty." She raised her hand. "It was he who left the flowers. Would you care for some more coffee, Commissario?"

"He didn't say who he was?"

"He just left the flowers—and he said that he hoped to see you tomorrow. A nice gentleman—I thought perhaps it was your father or your father-in-law."

Trotti frowned.

"He was very polite."

45: Ribcage

"WHERE'S PIOPPI?"

"Where are you calling from?

"Where's Pioppi, Piero?"

"She's in the hospital."

"Why?"

"Why do you think, Agnese—because she's ill."

"What's happened? I keep trying to phone you but you're always out."

"So you wake me up in the middle of the night?"

"What's wrong with her? God help me, Piero, but if anything happens to my child, I will hold you responsible."

"If you really loved your daughter, you'd be here with her."

"What's happened? How is she?"

"She collapsed."

"Why?"

"Because she doesn't eat enough. Because she's underweight, as you know full well. She wasn't eating properly when you left—but that never affected your decision to go to America. And how are things in Pearl River?"

"Piero, you know I had no choice. And don't try to make me feel guilty."

"She's your daughter."

"Is she eating now?"

"My God, Agnese, if you really cared about your daughter,

you wouldn't be asking these questions. You wouldn't phone me up in the middle of the night and treat me like some messenger boy. She's your daughter and you should be by her side. Pioppi needs you and I can't spend all my time at the Policlinico. I've got a job to do."

"You've always had a job to do, haven't you, Piero? Your wonderful job and all your wonderful friends in the Questura—you've always put them before me and your daughter."

Trotti slammed the phone down.

He looked at his watch—just gone four and it was still dark. No noise from via Milano. The house was empty.

He pulled the blanket up over his ears but could not get back to sleep. His heart thundered silently against his ribcage.

He hoped that his wife would ring back.

46: Old times

GINO SAT AT the desk with Principessa beneath it, at his feet. Neither stirred as Trotti got out of the lift. Gino held the newspaper as though he were reading it, but behind the thick glasses, the pale eyes were immobile.

"Buongiorno."

"Ah, Commissario." The old face broke into a smile. Gino had changed into his summer wear. The collar of his shirt was open, revealing grey hairs on his chest. It was rumored that he had once worked in the merchant navy and that it was in China that he'd been blinded when the ship's boilers exploded. It was even said that he had a wife and child in Shanghai. "There was a man to see you."

"A man?"

"Late last night—but I told him that you'd gone to the Policlinico."

"I was in Milan with Magagna."

"Magagna?" Gino smiled. "Enjoying marriage, I hope."

"He certainly enjoys his work with Narcotici."

Gino said, "Magagna's an innocent."

"The big city seems to have changed him."

"Don't you believe it, Commissario. Magagna's an innocent. You know, when you can't see, you develop other senses—and about Magagna, I know I'm right."

"Did this man leave any message?"

As Gino shook his head, the sleeping dog stirred, yawning

to reveal a long, pink tongue. "He said you'd be pleased to see him." He lowered his voice, and placed his hand on Trotti's elbow. "An elderly party—seventy, seventy-five years old. Wearing American glasses."

"I don't know who it could be."

"He'd be waiting for you, he said. In the bar in Piazza Vittoria—at half-past nine." Gino frowned briefly, trying to recall something. "A friend of the family, he said—and since he was in town for a few days, he said he wanted to see you. Remember old times."

Trotti was puzzled. "Remember old times?"

47: Allegra

THE SAME AGE as him.

As the woman came towards him smiling, her legs like the legs of a young girl, Trotti found himself wondering whether they had made a mistake in Registrations. Signora Allegra did not look a day over forty-five.

She was carrying a silver tray with two cups. "Commissario, how nice to see you!"

The sun formed deep-etched shadows along the medieval porticoes of Piazza Vittoria and for a moment, her face was caught in the penumbra. Then Trotti saw her smile, large and friendly.

The Bar Duomo.

"Not too late for a cappuccino?"

"Commissario." She laughed and entered the Bar Duomo.

Trotti moved towards the man.

At first he did not recognize him. He sat alone at one of the tables set out in the piazza, enjoying the morning sunshine. Despite the pair of tinted glasses, he held the open newspaper at arm's length. One eyebrow was raised.

On the white tablecloth in front of him was a tea pot.

Trotti approached.

"Ah!" The man turned and smiled.

Trotti, too, smiled, pleased to see the old investigating judge. The man stood up and they embraced.

"What on earth are you doing here?" Trotti frowned through his smile.

He was wearing a black waistcoat. He tapped the left-hand side. "The old clockwork, Piero—it needs a bit of reservicing."

"I thought you were in Arezzo. That's where I've been sending your Christmas cards these last ten years."

"And I still am in Arezzo. But I've been staying in Milan—nearly three weeks now. The doctor has given me permission to go home but I wanted to see you before I return to Arezzo and to my dear wife."

He lowered himself into the chair, his hand still on Trotti's arm. "And how are you, Piero? It must be years since we last met." He smiled. "And is it my imagination or are you losing your hair—the hair that you were always so proud of?"

"I am no longer a young man, Signor Giudice. In a few years' time, I'll be sixty."

"Sixty!" He clapped his hands. "A marvelous age—the best. The women love a sixty-year-old—you're old enough to be their father and women are all incestuous." A frown fluttered across his forehead. "And don't call me 'Signor Giudice,' Piero—I've been retired these last fifteen years."

Slightly smaller perhaps, and the shoulders more sloping, but otherwise the old giudice istruttore had hardly changed. Of course, Trotti realized, Dell'Orto had always looked old—even twenty years before, when for nearly two years he was one of the most talked about lawyers in Italy. The change was in his clothes. The pince-nez had disappeared and he now wore a pair of tinted sunglasses—rather like Magagna's. His thin, white hair had been well cut and waved; his suit and waistcoat were clearly of the best quality. And instead of the old wing collar that he had always worn, he now had on a fashionable tie of lovat green.

"You're looking very well."

"That's not what the doctor says."

"What does he say?"

"Senile and confused." He tapped his chest. "And my heart isn't as young as it used to be. I'm an old man, Piero. An old man of eighty-two. Nearly as senile as our illustrious president,

Pertini." Dell'Orto shrugged. "And you, Piero? Your face looks bruised."

"One of the risks of the job."

"You must be careful. Don't take risks, for heaven's sake. Not long before you should be retiring—and your family needs you." The judge leaned forward. "I was sorry to learn that your daughter is in the hospital."

"You were very kind to take her some flowers." Trotti repressed a sigh. "She doesn't appear to want to eat."

"Poor thing—I remember her when she was a little girl. She had your chin, Piero—and your determination. But you must get her to eat. If you want, I know a doctor . . ." Dell'Orto smiled, putting his head back. "If only I had married a girl like that—today I'd be a millionaire. But instead I've a wife who can't turn the page in her women's magazines without caressing the advertisements for spaghetti—grano duro, mind, and her favorite is Number Seven. Something she can get her teeth into."

"How is Signora Dell'Orto?"

"Getting fatter every day. And yet nimbler on her feet than the day we met. In L'Aquila, on June twenty-ninth, 1929."

"Your marriage has been blessed."

"Piero, if anybody has a gorgeous wife, it is you."

"Perhaps."

"Perhaps." He laughed. "Just like you to say that, Piero Trotti. But you adore Agnese, you adore the ground she walks on. And she loves you—as much as when you were first married. It was she who contacted me, don't forget, when there was that problem."

"Problem?"

"In seventy-eight and they kidnapped Moro—although, quite frankly I never had any time for the man and his mock humility. He could've been a priest—and enough of his close collaborators were feathering their nests instead of running this country. You were having a slight problem with the Questore, I seem to remember. It was Agnese who contacted me. She was so worried, poor thing. Not worried about herself—but worried about you, Piero."

"She never mentioned a word."

"She knew you had other things on your mind."

"Why did she contact you?"

"What was his name, the Questore? A stupid man."

"You mean Leonardelli?"

"I believe he's in America now."

Trotti realized that he had allowed his mouth to gape. "You mean to say that you were instrumental . . . ?"

Dell'Orto held up his hand.

"But, Signor Giudice, I nearly lost my job—I thought I had lost it—and then nothing."

Dell'Orto smiled. "Nearly sixty years old, Piero, and you manage to remain naive about this country."

"And you . . . ?"

"I still have friends—and in this country, friendship is important. Real friends, Piero—not southerners or, God forbid, Sicilians—but people whom I can count on." He shrugged. "Your poor wife was distraught. There are times when I think you take her for granted."

Signora Allegra arrived at the table, bringing Trotti's cappuccino and two small cakes on a saucer. "A little treat for our Commissario," and she gave a laugh that Trotti found provocative. He looked at the woman as she bent beside him and their glances met. She smiled. She was wearing a lot of makeup, a lot of foundation, but beneath all the powder, she was still very attractive. "It is not often that an old lady has the opportunity of spoiling her favorite client." She turned. "Another pot of herbal tea for the signore?"

Dell'Orto responded to her smile. Gallantly he nodded his appreciation. "You are very kind, signora. But the doctor . . ." He lifted his open palms. "More than one cup of anything pleasant is strictly forbidden."

"Then perhaps something else. Something that will do your health good. An amaro—or a vermouth."

Dell'Orto tapped his chest. "You tempt me sorely, signora—but I must look after the clockwork. Unfortunately—or so the medical profession assures me—alcohol causes rusting."

She smiled, took the empty pot and returned to the bar.

"Old Franceschini's daughter—a charming woman."

The cappuccino was hot.

"I was in Milan, Piero." He tapped Trotti's arm. "I wanted to see you, anyway . . . see how you were doing. And now things have been forced upon me."

"What things?"

He had put the paper down on the edge of the white table-cloth and his hand smoothed the wrinkled pages in a reassuring gesture. "At my age, I'd like to feel that I was entitled to a little rest and a little privacy, without having to put up with people who think they can pick up the telephone at any hour night or day. Just because—or so people like to think—there was a time when I was a powerful man."

Trotti sipped at the coffee.

"Good?"

"What?"

"The cappuccino—ah, you can't imagine how much I miss coffee. The other things in life—at my age, who needs them? A good bed, three meals a day—I don't ask for much more . . . Although I must admit that I'm not yet completely insensitive to a pretty face and there seem to be a lot about, don't there, Piero?" He shook his head. "But it's not women that I miss. And I have my dear Genoveffa, bless her soul." Behind the glasses, the old eyes wrinkled. "Is it good, Piero, is it good?"

"Signor Giudice, the Bar Duomo is the best bar in the city. You know that. One of the few places where they don't skimp on the coffee."

"Arabica." He tasted the word as if he could taste the coffee, letting it move along his tongue. "The doctors won't even let me have coffee-flavored sweets." He laughed abruptly. "Do you still eat those sweets? And you've still got your teeth?"

"Like my hair—dropping out."

Their eyes met. There was no mirth in Dell'Orto's smile.

"What was it you wanted to see me about?"

"I see that the *Provincia* has an article on the death of the Ramoverde boy." Dell'Orto shrugged. "I heard about his death in Milan. I was very upset. Very upset—I see he had changed his name to Maltese. You might not believe me, Piero, but a day doesn't go by without my wondering about the whole thing."

Trotti finished his drink and began spooning out the last drops of foamy milk.

"After all these years—I still wonder whether I did the right thing."

"The Ramoverde affair was a long time ago."

"Not for me."

"I don't think you need worry yourself."

"I hear, Piero, that you were with the boy when he died."

Trotti nodded. "But I didn't know he was Ramoverde's son. That was something the Carabinieri found out later."

"Did he suffer?"

"No," Trotti lied.

"Strange that it was with you that the boy should die."

"A coincidence." Trotti put down his spoon.

"My niece's husband teaches at the university." A pause as the old fingers moved across the newspaper. "In the Department of Urbanistica."

"Baldassare?"

"I'm sorry, Piero—this is as embarrassing for me as it must be for you." He lowered his voice to little more than a whisper. Trotti leaned forward; the old man's breath carried the odor of herbal tea. "Never really liked him and I have no idea why Guerra's daughter ever married him. He's almost twice her age. But the other child did no better—as you know. She ended up a terrorist."

"Do you ever see her?"

"Her?"

"The second daughter—Lia Guerra?"

Dell'Orto shook his head.

"Do you know where she lives?"

"Piero, after her problem with the Questura, she broke off all diplomatic relations with me." Without pausing for breath, he continued, "Baldassare's a man who is full of himself. Arrogant and not really very intelligent, in my opinion. But he thinks he has power—power because his father-in-law was city architect. He wants you thrown out of the police."

"Is that all?"

"A horrid man. I feel sorry for my poor niece."

"And Baldassare contacted you?"

"At eight o'clock in the Hotel Ambassador last night. Just as I was about to go to bed."

"And that's why you wanted to see me, Signor Giudice?"

"Piero, you're a good man. You know that I've always had considerable esteem for you. But you must be careful."

"It is possible that he's involved in Ramoverde's death."

Dell'Orto raised a white eyebrow behind the glasses.

"I think he knew that I was going to Gardesana."

"You've just told me that your being there was a coincidence."

Trotti looked away.

"What did I tell you? All those years ago, what did I tell you, Piero?"

Trotti did not reply.

"Motive."

"Signor Giudice, you believed that you'd found a motive for Ramoverde to kill his father-in-law. A trial with judge and jury came to a different conclusion." Immediately, Trotti regretted the sharpness that he had allowed to enter his words.

"The jury did not agree with me—but that didn't necessarily make me wrong."

Trotti shrugged. "It was all a long time ago."

"Not for me, Piero. You knew the dossiers—there were times when you were my right-hand man. Tell me, Piero, was I wrong?"

"I think that there may be a connection between Maltese's death and the fact that Baldassare knew I was going to Gardesana."

"How did he know?"

Trotti did not reply.

Dell'Orto said softly, "You thought he was guilty, didn't you?"

"Who?"

"Douglas Ramoverde?"

It was then that Trotti noticed a plaintive note in the old man's voice. He looked at Dell'Orto and for a fleeting moment, he felt sorry for him in a way he had never felt sorry for him before. In the twenty years since the trial, the two men had met rarely—and then in 1968, Dell'Orto had gone into retirement, had returned to his villa outside Arezzo. But Trotti could see that the doubts had never left the old man. In his voice, he heard the years of self-questioning.

"You thought he was guilty, didn't you?"

He was tempted to shrug, but Trotti knew that it would not have been an answer. It was not to repeat Baldassare's threat that the old man had come to the city. It was for the sake of a long forgotten murder trial that was as important as the faded yellow pages of *Vita e sorrisi*. A sense of responsibility—perhaps of guilt worried him. And it continued to worry him, like a disease that would not go away, like a cancer slowly eating away at the host tissues.

"Because even if the jury set him free—and I was glad when he was absolved—Douglas Ramoverde's life was already over. It ended the day I had him arrested. It was you, Piero, who went to the Villa Laura—you saw his face that day. He was resigned for the worst, wasn't he? He knew he would never be a free man again. The insinuations stayed with him for the rest of his life. And was all that of my making? Was it all my fault, because I looked to the motives?"

"Douglas Ramoverde returned to Piacenza."

A dry laugh. "And then he left Italy for good. He took his family and he no doubt hoped to start a new life in Argentina. And there he died. He died in exile. Like some Roman emperor, it was I who sent him into exile." He allowed a weary smile to crease his face. "I still have my doubts, Piero."

"Now his son is dead, too."

Dell'Orto looked at Trotti in silence.

Trotti said, "I don't believe in coincidences."

"And you really believe, Piero, that Baldassare is involved in Maltese's death?"

"A lot of people wanted Maltese dead—he had helped write

an article which virtually destroyed the director of the Banco Milanese—the director and all the people behind him. Maltese knew that—and he had gone into hiding. He knew that he could get killed—and he was. But somebody wanted him to die in my presence."

"What on earth for?"

"I've no idea, Signor Giudice."

"And the Banca San Matteo affair, Piero?"

Trotti looked at Dell'Orto. "What about it?"

"I read about it in the paper." He shrugged. "And I saw your name."

"It's been taken out of my hands. Under the control of the Finanza."

"You know Pergola?"

"Yes." Trotti asked, "Why do you ask?"

"What do you think of him?"

"He's lucky to be alive. Two bullets in the leg."

"But what's your opinion of him?"

Trotti said, "I try not to have opinions."

"Do you think there could be a connection between the robbery at the Banca San Matteo and what's happening at the Banco Milanese?"

"Why do you ask?"

Dell'Orto smiled. "My wife has invested quite a lot of money in the Milanese."

"Why do you ask about Pergola?"

Dell'Orto did not reply. There was silence while he looked at Trotti; it was as if he were trying to decide something in his own mind. "*Cherchez la femme*," he said softly and then he put his hand to his waistcoat. "I wonder if you remember those letters that spoke about a woman in Piacenza. At the time of the trial."

Trotti frowned.

"*Cherchez la femme*, Piero."

"What do you mean?"

"You know, perhaps there was a woman. Perhaps Ramoverde really wasn't at the Villa Laura on the night of Belluno's death. A woman—a mistress. Adultery—something he would never have dared admit to his wife. Or to anybody else, for the sake of his good name and his dental practice."

"What letters?"

"Perhaps I should have paid more attention to them." Dell'Orto's smile was weary. "But perhaps I was afraid to admit to my own determination to see Ramoverde found guilty by a court of law."

"Why are you telling me this?"

"There are times, Piero, when I wonder how honest I am."

Trotti shook his head.

"I didn't come to see you about Baldassare, Piero."

"You've had a long time to come to terms with your doubts over the Ramoverde affair."

Again the smoothing motion of Dell'Orto's hand across the *Provincia Padana*. "You're right, of course."

Signora Allegra stood waiting in the shadow of the portico. One hand rested on her hip. Trotti wondered whether she was looking at him—her eyes were in the shade—and gave her a brief smile, which she did not return.

"I received a letter, Piero." The retired judge slipped a piece of paper from the inside pocket of his well-cut suit.

He handed the letter to Trotti.

The paper was thin and had acquired a looseness from having been folded many times. The print was irregular, clumsy—carried out by somebody who was not used to working with a typewriter.

> *You destroyed the only man I ever loved.*
> *And now you have killed his son.*

No date. No signature.

48: Maserati

"DELL'ORTO NEVER KNEW Maltese."

Trotti shrugged. "He saw him at the murder trial."

"That was years ago." Maserati gave a self-conscious smile. "Why should he feel guilty about the murder of someone he scarcely knew?"

"The letter—it shocked him."

"Judges receive threatening letters all the time."

"But not twenty years after the event."

Maserati was one of the new generation of policemen—one of the young men who had been recruited during the years of political tension. They were not interested in policing the streets or coming into contact with the public. Many of them had been to university or technical institutes and Maserati was a technician who was only really happy when given a laboratory coat and a precise task to perform.

"I don't see how I can help you, Commissario," Maserati said, adjusting his tortoiseshell glasses.

"Maserati, the records must be here."

"What year?"

Trotti found himself irritated by Maserati. He was intelligent and hard working—there could be no doubt that since his arrival in 1980, Sezione Archivi had been revolutionized. It was Maserati—without any particular training in archive work—who had insisted upon the computer which now stood in the corner of the chill room, a green dot blinking on the screen. Now when the need arose for a cross reference, Trotti no longer found himself being forced to hang on to the internal telephone waiting for a piece of information that the woman could never give. Or if she could, it would nearly always be incomplete. Maserati had imposed his scientific approach upon the section. He was competent, extremely well-organized and had a thoroughness that was almost Teutonic. But he was also humorless. To the fastidiousness of an old maid and the cold precision of a Swiss watch, he added a kind of boorishness as if he felt ill at ease with anything other than his machines and their printouts.

"1960—or 1961."

The laugh was unexpected. "I'm afraid you're out of luck."

"Out of luck?"

"Do you realize all the work that this job involves, Commissario? Having to get everything scheduled? Not easy, you know. And Signora Paternoster is away on maternity leave." Behind the lenses, the eyes were offended and moved erratically. "I'm still working on 1968 and you want 1960."

"I would like to see the old files."

"I haven't gotten around to them yet."

"But they're available?"

Another laugh, this time self-justificatory. "You'll have to go downstairs to the basement. And look under the dust."

"I'm looking for a series of letters. They're in the file."

A sigh.

"Dell'Orto mentioned a series of letters. I need to see them because it's possible that there's a connection between the Villa Laura and Maltese's death." Trotti added, "It's possible that Maltese was working on the trial—perhaps he was writing an article. And it's quite possible that he came up with information that could have caused difficulties."

"Maltese was murdered because he knew about the Banco Milanese."

"Why was he killed in Gardesana, then?"

"It might've been the only place where the assassins could get to him."

Trotti said, "It's important that I see the dossiers."

"I see." He wore a white coat and the sleeves were rolled up to his forearms. A repressed sigh and Maserati stood up. "Then there's nothing for it but to go and look."

Trotti followed him out of the laboratory and together they went down the two flights of stairs to the basement of the Questura.

Maserati turned on a light.

The walls had been partially painted—the Questura dated from the late fascist era—and in places the grey cement was showing through. Linoleum had been put down. It deadened the sound of their feet. The air was musty and carried the odor of damp paper.

"1960," Maserati said to himself.

"The Villa Laura killings were at the beginning of August."

Maserati had reverted to the role of the absorbed scientist. He did not seem to be aware of Trotti's presence. "1960," he repeated.

Trotti waited.

The young head turned. "You think it'll be a child's game to find the Ramoverde dossier, Commissario?"

"I'm sure you'll do your best."

"Just look." He gestured to the rows of bookcases.

Faded manilla files tied together with string, a piece of yellowing paper to identify them slipped beneath each knot, masked two walls.

"You people upstairs—you're all the same. You get angry—you want everything immediately and you think I'm not doing a proper job because I'm still bogged down in 1968." He nodded towards the files and then rubbed his hands. "Two more years' work here—and looking for your files will be like looking for a grain of sand on the beach at Milano Marittima."

49: Squadra

TROTTI RECOGNIZED THE tuneless whistle.

"Where are you going?"

The thin silhouette was caught against the light coming from the entrance. With the suede jacket thrown casually over his shoulder, Pisanelli was about to leave the Questura.

For a fraction of a second, he froze. Then Pisanelli swung round.

"Where the hell d'you think you're going, Pisanelli?"

"To lunch."

Trotti reached the top of the stairs and he walked towards Pisanelli. "Not now." Trotti shook his head. "There's work to be done."

"I haven't eaten, Commissario."

"Maserati needs your help."

"Maserati never needs help."

"He's downstairs in the old archives. Go and help him."

"But Commissario Trotti, I haven't eaten."

"You work for the Squadra Mobile—not in a restaurant."

Pisanelli glanced at his watch. He said, "I'm meeting a friend."

"She'll have to miss you."

"But we intend to get married!"

"Then she'll have to get married by herself."

Pisanelli slid the jacket from his shoulder and looked at Trotti. The attempt to appear angry was only partially successful. "Etta and I are getting married next month—and she's expecting me at the Bella Napoli pizzeria at one thirty." He added forcefully, "In three minutes."

"I'll phone the Bella Napoli and leave a message."

"You can't do that."

"You want a pizza, Pisanelli? A margherita? A quattro stagioni?" Trotti brushed past him, heading towards the entrance and the granite steps that were bright in the sunlight. "I'll have them send you a pizza."

"But . . ."

"There's three days' work sifting through the files. Go and help Maserati—then perhaps you'll be able to see your Etta before the end of the week."

"What work?"

"Maserati will explain."

Trotti stepped out into Strada Nuova, now deserted of traffic. An old woman stood on the far side of the road, near the War Memorial. Two black shopping bags were at her feet and she was looking at the limp flag.

"And where are you going, Commissario?" Pisanelli called out after him. He stood at the top of the steps, one shoulder slightly forward, as if to give himself courage. "You don't feel that you ought to help your subordinates?"

"I'll be back in half an hour. I'm going to the Policlinico."

"And in half an hour, I'd be back from the Bella Napoli."

"Stop moaning, Pisanelli."

Pisanelli turned away in silence, reentering the darkness of the Questura while Trotti headed towards Piazza Castello to find a taxi. The air was warm, but not yet hot and windless. He regretted that he had not taken the Ganna out of the garage.

Apart from one or two students, the street was deserted.

Trotti walked past the Teatro Civico, where white and red posters announced forthcoming attractions—posters almost identical to those used by La Scala. Cool air and muffled music came from the porticoes. Bruckner, perhaps, deadened by the thick doors. The Hungarian National Orchestra on tour in Italy, and not enough money to pay for a midday pizza. Instead, they were practising.

Trotti went past the new tavola calda, with its odor of hot oil and tomatoes.

"Commissario!"

He turned round and squinted his eyes against the light.

"Can I talk to you?"

At first Trotti did not recognize the tall man with the sad face.

"But not here, not in the street." He gestured with his arm, and walking with a forward stoop, he hurriedly crossed the road and headed towards the university.

"Let's go to my office in the Questura."

The man took no notice and Trotti followed him. It was as they entered the coolness of the main quadrangle that he realized who his companion was.

"Over here."

He stopped beneath the main flight of steps that led to the university library. There was a service door and because the man stood in the shadows, only the observant passerby would have noticed him.

"You work in the Servizio Estero, don't you?"

The man nodded. He did not hold out his hand but looked at Trotti with his hangdog eyes. "Grandi—head of the exchange counter."

"I think we could talk more easily in the Questura."

Grandi shook his head. "I won't take up your time, Commissario Trotti." He was carrying a leather bag slung from one shoulder. He undid the strap and took out a newspaper. "I saw the photograph in this morning's *Provincia*."

"What photograph?"

"Commissario, I'm a law-abiding man. But I've my family to think about. And I don't like taking risks." He coughed, but the sad eyes remained on Trotti. "The photograph of the man who got shot on Lake Garda." He opened the paper and tapped at the passport-like photograph of Maltese.

"Well?"

"I've seen this man."

Trotti felt his heart miss a beat.

"A few months ago—he came in to see the director."

"Director?"

"At the Banca San Matteo—Signor Pergola."

50: Matron

"I WANT TO see her."

"I'm afraid she's sleeping."

"She's my daughter. I'm allowed to sit with her."

"The doctor gave express orders that the patient shouldn't be disturbed."

"My daughter's been here for three days. Nobody's ever stopped me from seeing her."

"I must obey the doctor's orders." The woman was matronly in appearance—ample chest beneath a white smock and greying hair that was pinned up above the nape of her neck. She wore a white cap. She stood with her arms akimbo. "The patient needs rest."

"The patient is my daughter." Trotti was aware that he had raised his voice.

"You must come at another time. I have my orders."

Trotti placed his hand on the door handle. "I wish to be with my daughter."

The nurse looked at him, squinting her colorless eyes. "You leave me no choice but to call the doctor on duty." She folded her arms beneath her chest and walked down the corridor, past the plaster statue of San Matteo in his whitewashed niche.

Trotti entered the room.

Pioppi was asleep. Now the tubes that ran into her arms had been removed. Her black hair billowed out on the pillow and the light from the table lit up her pale face. There were flowers at the window and also beside the small transistor that was tuned to a local station. Soft, rhythmic music.

Trotti noticed that the books had disappeared.

The body rose and fell with slow, regular breathing,

Pioppi stirred and in her sleep she was smiling. He bent over her. He pushed the dark strands of hair away from where they had fallen into her eyes. Then he heard the door open behind him.

"You must leave, I'm afraid."

"Go away."

"Your daughter needs to rest."

"She is resting. I won't disturb her."

The doctor placed a hand on Trotti's shoulder; the other hand took him by the arm. Then the young doctor, the stethoscope swinging against his chest, tried to pull Trotti to his feet.

Trotti stood up and turned. He caught the man by the throat of his jacket. As Trotti pushed him towards the door, the eyes were suddenly stretched with surprise and fear. The doctor was thin, lighter than Trotti expected. The young man would have crumpled to the floor had he not managed to catch hold of the door handle and support himself in time.

"Now get out!"

The doctor straightened his tie. He turned and left.

Trotti returned to the bedside.

Pioppi's eyes were open. "Papa."

"How are you feeling, Pioppi?"

"Is Mama with you?"

"She phoned from America last night. She's phoned several times."

"And the Nonna?"

"We're all missing you, Pioppi. But you'll be home soon." He took her hand and squeezed it. "Tell me how you're feeling."

Her smile was feeble, hesitant. "I don't feel very strong."

"But once you start eating, you'll feel better . . ."

She frowned.

"Eat and rest. You've been driving yourself too hard, Pioppi."

He leaned forward to touch her forehead. He noticed the eyes flinch.

"You've got to look after yourself, because we love you. We need you. Where would your mother and I be without you?"

Pioppi smiled sleepily. "Kiss me, Papa."

His lips touched her forehead. He could smell her hair. "We're all worried about you, Pioppi. Get well fast."

Her eyes closed.

"I must leave you." Trotti took her hand between his two palms. "But before I go, I want you to answer a question for me."

Her eyes opened again and focused slowly.

"I told you and the Nonna that I intended to go to the Villa Ondina—but I didn't tell anybody else."

Her eyelids were closing again. She was falling asleep. "Did you tell anybody, Pioppi?"

"Tell anybody?" she mumbled.

"Did you tell anybody where I was going?"

Pioppi closed her eyes.

Her father squeezed her hand. "Did you tell someone?"

"Papa . . ."

There were steps in the corridor. Fast steps and angry voices.

"Tell me. I won't be angry with you, but I must know."

The door opened.

"Pioppi, it's important."

Pisanelli.

51: Campigli

THE COUNTRYSIDE WAS flat and Pisanelli sulked.

He drove with his eyes on the road. He did not speak to Trotti except for an occasional monosyllable. Then, when they reached Piacenza, crossed the Po and skirted the city, he appeared a bit less aggrieved. "Good food in Piacenza."

"When we get back, I'll buy you a pizza." Trotti smiled. "You and Maserati did well."

"It was the first dossier I laid my hand on."

Trotti sat with his arm through the window. "Even so, you worked fast."

"There were at least three letters." He added, "I took a photocopy of only one because they were all the same. They all accused Maria Campigli of being Ramoverde's mistress."

"Maria Elisabetta Campigli of Fluviale, Province of Piacenza." Trotti fell silent and Pisanelli drove for another twenty minutes, then took the unsurfaced road. The car bumped on its springs. They moved down towards the river. Through the trees, they could see decaying buildings and a brick wall.

They came to a halt in the courtyard.

It must once have been a small village, stranded in a loop of the river. Three or four houses with tiles of a deep red that had turned black. In places, some of the roofs had fallen in. The air carried the smell of cattle, but there were no animals in sight. The stables were empty. Thin pillars of brick supporting roofs built over long wooden rods. On the floor, no straw or manure.

They got out of the car and waited a few moments. There was a light wind rustling through the trees. The two men listened to the noises of the countryside—crickets, birds and the distant sound of the river. Then they heard the slow movement of feet.

An old man was walking with a stick. His boots struck against the dry earth and cobbles of the farmyard. Slung across his shoulder, he was carrying a gun. He moved slowly, his body arched forward and his legs bowed.

"Signor Campigli?" Pisanelli moved towards the man.

The man took no notice of him.

"Signor Campigli?"

"Well?" He stopped and put his weight on the stick.

"We're from the police."

"I'm too old to go to prison." He spoke in dialect. Though it was nothing like Trotti's own dialect—it was amazing how along the Po, the dialects could vary from one village to the next—Trotti had no difficulty in understanding.

Pisanelli turned to Trotti.

Trotti approached the old man. "It's about your daughter."

"You want to marry her, then?" The face broke into a smile that revealed a mouth without teeth. His skin was like the surface of a walnut. A gnarled hand shaded his eyes from the brightness of the sky.

"Why not, Signor Campigli? I'm sure she's very charming."

The man was even more amused. He leaned forward on the stick and laughed—a laugh that resembled a hoarse cough. He wiped at the specks of saliva forming at the corner of his colorless lips.

"She used to work in the city." Trotti made a vague gesture in the direction of Piacenza.

"She used to work in the city," the old man repeated, changing a few vowels to his own dialect. He laughed again.

Trotti glanced at Pisanelli.

"We'd like to talk to her."

"You're trying to find her?"

Trotti nodded. "I am from the Pubblica Sicurezza."

"Maria Campigli?"

"Can you please tell us where she is?"

This time the old man—he was wearing a faded, collarless shirt and a thick leather belt—leaned forward to place a hand on Trotti's arm. An old hand, scarred and worn by a lifetime of work in the fields. "If you find her, you can send her back." He looked up and his wizened face appeared radiant. "A young, beautiful daughter . . ." With his hands he made a gesture that suggested a female body. "That's what I need. That's what an old man needs. To do the cooking, to help me in the fields, to feed the animals!" He laughed, the toothless gums pushed against his lips. "A young woman to look after me."

"Where is your daughter?"

"They've gone." He turned, moving his body slowly, pivoting on the stick, his eyes carefully watching his own hesitant feet. Then he raised the stick to gesticulate towards the dilapidated stone houses. "They've all gone—gone to the city. Gone away."

"Where does your daughter live in Piacenza?" Pisanelli asked.

"My daughter lives in Piacenza?" He looked at Pisanelli's young face and it was at that moment that Trotti realized there were tears in the old man's eyes. "My daughter lives in Piacenza?"

"Try to help us."

"She is with her mother. Maria Campigli is with her mother."

"Where?"

Old eyes—they looked at Pisanelli and then back at Trotti. "She has been with her mother these last fourteen years. Incurable." He repeated the word, "Incurable and now Maria is with her mother. And with her grandmother." With the same hand that held the stick, the old man crossed himself. "God rest her soul."

52: Confession

THE FIRST THING that Trotti noticed was the eau-de-cologne. It lingered in the air of the corridor, competing with the smell of the coffee from the machine and with the more acrid smell of human sweat.

At least the spilled sugar and the empty paper packets had been swept away.

Trotti entered his office.

Pergola turned and stood up. A hesitant, uncertain smile came to the neatly shaven face. The eyes seemed darker than usual.

"An immense pleasure," Trotti said and nodded briefly. He sat down behind his desk, automatically opened the drawer to see if there were any sweets. "Please sit down, Signor Direttore." He gestured to the greasy canvas armchair. "Kindly make yourself feel at home. And perhaps I can offer you something to drink. Some coffee—or perhaps . . ." He went hurriedly through his pockets. "Or perhaps something to suck on." He held out a packet of rhubarb-flavoured Charms. "Not Smith Kendon, I'm afraid."

A tight smile. Pergola shook his head.

"Well?"

"I've come to see you, Commissario, because . . ." He paused and the prominent adam's apple bobbed unhappily.

"Because you want to confess?"

"Confess?" Pergola put his head to one side, genuinely surprised.

Trotti held up a hand. "Forgive my frivolity." He glanced at his watch. "Half past eight in the morning—and a beautiful May day. I'm just not used to finding a bank manager of all people in my office." He gestured around the small office—at the dingy dossiers that he had recently tidied and that were now piled haphazardly at the feet of the radiator, at the photograph of Pertini that looked as if it had been there since Koblet had won the Giro d'Italia. "I'm afraid that for elegance, my office cannot compare with yours at the Banca San Matteo."

A magnanimous shrug while the eyes watched Trotti carefully.

The pigeons were cooing. The summer heat came through the window and Trotti felt surprisingly relaxed—perhaps the news from the Policlinico, or perhaps the effect of having cycled into work. A few drops of oil and the Ganna was running smoothly, as if it had not spent the last eight months in the garage. "How can I help you, Signor Pergola?"

Hs coughed. "I was not . . ." A gesture of the hand. "I was not totally frank with you, Commissario."

"Frank about what?"

"And it is now something that I regret."

Trotti smiled blandly while his fingers played with the ragged end of the sweet packet.

"When we last met . . . there were things that I should have mentioned."

"It's not too late."

"I saw yesterday's paper and I saw the photograph of Maltese." He nodded. "I wasn't completely truthful with you, Commissario. I knew Maltese—he came to my office."

"Ah!"

"He came to see me."

"When was this?"

"About four months ago."

"Before the robbery?"

Pergola nodded. "It must have been in January. But you see, I didn't realize it was him." Very slightly he raised the padded shoulders of his narrow suit. "I"m a provincial banker—and I know little about what happens up the road in Milan. To be honest with you, I'm not very interested."

Trotti frowned.

"When he came to see me, he gave me his name. Not Maltese. He called himself Ramoverde." Hurriedly, Pergola went on, "How was I to know that he was Maltese? Of course, I had heard of the Ramoverde affair—who hadn't?—but that was a long time ago. And of course, I didn't associate the Ramoverde sitting in front of me with the ex-journalist of the *Popolo d'Italia.*"

"Was this before or after the Night of the Tazebao?"

"I checked in my agenda—when you came to see me." An apologetic smile. "It must've been about a week before."

Trotti nodded. "Afterwards, Maltese disappeared."

"He said he was writing a book—and that he needed to do some research."

"What sort of book?"

"About his father, Douglas Ramoverde. He said that the time had come for the truth to be told. People who could have been hurt were now dead, he said, and he felt that there was nothing to be afraid of. The truth needed to be told, if only for his father's sake."

"Then he knew who killed Belluno?"

For a moment, Pergola paused to think. He looked small and ill at ease; he was sitting forward on the edge of the chair, his buttocks resting on the wooden frame. "That's the impression he tried to give me."

"Did he tell you who it was?"

Pergola replied, "I wouldn't have wanted to know."

"If you weren't interested in the Belluno affair, why did Maltese come and see you?" Trotti raised a shoulder.

The man said nothing, but looked at Trotti with his dark eyes. He bit at his lip.

"What did Maltese want from you, Signor Pergola?"

A deep intake of breath. "I think he wanted information."

"Be more explicit."

Pergola looked anxiously about the office. Then he lowered his voice. "He wanted information about a lodge."

Trotti frowned.

"A masonic lodge, Signor Commissario."

Trotti sat back in his chair and for a moment, he sucked the sweet. "Ah," he said.

"Maltese—if that was his real name—"

"His real name was Ramoverde."

"Ramoverde seemed to believe that I could help him."

"And could you?"

"He wanted to know about the freemason lodge." A flitter of a smile; the skin of his face was drawn tight across the high cheekbones. "Ramoverde seemed to believe that his father had been murdered by freemasons."

"Why?"

"He believed that there had been rivalries."

"What sort of rivalries?"

Pergola shook his head. "I don't know. He got very excited and mentioned a lot of names that I'd heard of—and even more that I had never heard of at all. People that he accused of being involved in Belluno's death. And in his father's court trial."

"What sort of people?"

"I can't remember, Commissario." Their eyes met. "I wasn't particularly interested."

"Then I imagine you threw him out of your office. You told him to be on his way."

"Not quite." He rubbed one hand against the sharp crease of his trousers. "I wanted to hear what he had to say."

"What exactly did Maltese want from you?"

"An introduction." He no longer looked at Trotti but at his two narrow hands, which he had placed on his knees. "Maltese wanted an introduction to the Lodge because . . ."

"Because you're a member?"

Pergola acquiesced with a small nod. "He said it was a case of the son trying to put the record straight over his father's trial." Pergola raised his eyes—dark, intelligent eyes.

"How did he know you were a freemason?"

"In the same way, perhaps, that he knew I was no longer interested in the ritual."

"I see."

"Commissario, you don't see because you cannot understand. I was reluctant to tell you the truth when you asked me about Maltese—but I've been through the initiation ceremony. I've made vows." A small smile. "Now I'm here and I'm talking about these things openly."

"Perhaps you are afraid."

The smile grew larger. "I'm not afraid of the law—if that's what you mean—because I've nothing to be afraid of. I'm a law-abiding citizen—no more, no less. Nor am I afraid of them."

"Them?"

"The Lodge doesn't frighten me because I know what it all means—little men pretending to play at the Ku Klux Klan, men who take their wives to church on Sunday and then when they meet among themselves, they talk rubbish about the Great Architect. They're not genuine masons—they believe in all the childish liturgy as much as you or I do. A front, an organization—that's all. A form of Mafia, a network of contacts, of preferences." He smiled sadly.

"How could Maltese have known that you were no longer very keen about being a freemason?"

The bank manager raised his hands, then let them fall back onto the creases of his trousers. "I can't be sure."

"Nor do I see any reason for him to want to see you."

Pergola stood up and for an instant Trotti wondered what the other man intended to do. He watched Pergola as he walked, limping slightly, to the open window and stared out across the terracotta roofs of the city. Then he turned and folded his arms. "I would like something to drink."

"Coffee?"

He nodded.

Trotti went to the door and shouted, "Brigadiere." In an instant, a young man in uniform appeared. "Two coffees from over the road. And a couple of brioches."

The policeman nodded and moved towards the lift. Trotti closed the door.

"You see, Commissario, I liked him."

"Him?"

"He came to my office and I realized that an introduction was not really what he wanted. He already knew quite a lot about the lodge—for one thing, he knew that I was a member and for another, he knew that I was disenchanted. If he'd really wanted to, he could have got an introduction from somebody else. It was as if he were testing me—or as if he were trying to get something from me without my realizing it. But after a while, we both began to relax. It was then he told me about the book he intended to write." He looked at Trotti, then looked away. "I think I can guess who killed Maltese."

"Who?"

"I have your word, Commissario, that this conversation will rest between you and me. I know that I'm dealing with somebody who is honest."

"You flatter me."

"Twenty years in banking have made me cynical—forty-five years of living in Italy have made me very cynical. But I trust you. And I know that you'll respect my trust."

"You're afraid of something?"

"I'm not afraid for myself. But there are others to think about." He paused. "Do you have children?"

Trotti nodded.

"Then you'll understand. For them, Commissario, not for myself." He moved back to the canvas chair. "Do I have your word that you'll respect the secrecy of what I tell you?"

"I must do my duty."

"By all means do your duty. I merely ask you to treat this conversation as, well . . . off the record."

Trotti nodded.

He relaxed then. He sat back and crossed his legs. One hand clasped his ankle—he was wearing white socks. "He was only seventeen when his grandfather was murdered and understandably it came as something of a shock. He was quite fond of the old man—a fondness which his grandfather reciprocated. Then Ramoverde went to prison, there was all the publicity connected with the trial—things which upset him profoundly."

"Was his father guilty of the murder of Belluno?"

"His father was not a murderer—of that he'd always been certain, even though his father had never discussed the whole business with him openly. Then they left for Argentina. For the boy it was an exile—or an admission of guilt. He saw his father age, start drinking and then die. Later, he returned to Milan where he studied. Then he got his South American job with the *Popolo d'Italia* . . . of course, he didn't tell me which paper, afraid perhaps that I would realize that he was the journalist Maltese."

There was a discreet knock on the door and the officer entered, carrying a tray. He placed it on the cluttered desk and handed a screw-top cup to Pergola, who thanked him. He bowed slightly and left.

"I made the association with the Tazebao much later." He tapped the injured leg.

"You know the director of the Banco Milanese?"

"Bastia?" He shook his head. "We don't gravitate in the same orbits. But like anybody else who reads the newspapers, I know that he is facing considerable difficulties. The night of the Tazebao was merely the last stage in blackmail, when the victim refuses to pay his debts and punishment has to be paid out."

"Who was blackmailing Bastia?"

"You read the papers, Commissario."

"Maltese supplied Novara with information for the posters. But who paid Novara? Who was blackmailing Bastia?"

Pergola shrugged. "If you really want the man, you'll find him in a New York penitentiary—a Sicilian who fled this country for fraud. We Italians are an indulgent people—we have so much dirty linen that we have decided to give up washing it. The Americans, however, see things differently."

"You mean Scalfari?"

"He's serving a prison sentence in America. It will probably keep him out of the way for the next twenty years." Pergola nodded. "Not a very pleasant prospect for a man who has known the 'palazzo' all his life, who has manipulated men, controlled them, used them."

"Scalfari was in his American prison at the time of the Tazebao."

"Precisely."

Trotti frowned.

"Scalfari expected favors from Bastia now that he was in jail. He asked Bastia to help him—when in all probability it was Bastia who tipped him off to the American police."

"And the Tazebao was his revenge?"

"I assume so. Like you, I read the papers."

"Did Maltese mention Scalfari or Bastia to you?"

"When Maltese came to see me, we didn't talk about the Banco Milanese. He simply said that he was interested in the Lodge—that's all. Interested in the Lodge because he felt that directly or indirectly, it was involved in his grandfather's murder."

"Then, in your opinion, where did Maltese and Novara get their information on Bastia?"

"Scalfari knew everything—absolutely everything about the dealings of Bastia and the Banco Milanese. And if he knew everything, it was because there had been a time when he had been propping Bastia up with his own money—drug money, money from organized crime, money from illegal building and from prostitution. It was money that he used to put an insignificant Milanese banker in charge of a major bank—a Catholic bank, respected in the financial community and supported by the Vatican. It was precisely what Scalfari needed. A front—and Bastia was precisely the man he needed. Arrogant, cold, provincial—and not very intelligent. Scalfari knew that he would be able to manipulate Bastia just as he chose, get him to do what he wanted him to do. An ambitious little banker—a nonentity of Scalfari's creation." Pergola did not try to hide the bitterness that had crept into his voice. "Unfortunately, Scalfari's creation turned out to be the more cunning of the two—more cunning than Scalfari. For if Bastia is not exactly intelligent, he compensates for that with his overwhelming ambition." He nodded. "And so to get rid of the old Sicilian, Bastia informed the American police."

"How do you know these things?"

"I've lived all my life in this country." Pergola smiled. "I've had ample time and opportunity to learn how blackmail works."

"Then who, Signor Pergola, in your opinion, murdered Maltese?"

"The actual killer—I don't know and I doubt if you ever will. But now Novara is dead, too. I read that he was assassinated in Paris."

"Who was behind the two killings?"

"It could, of course, be Bastia. Maltese and Novara embarrassed him. Worse than that—with all the revelations on the walls of the Banco Milanese." He gestured. "But once Maltese and Novara had served their purpose—and brought Bastia round to seeing reason—to seeing that he still had to collaborate with Scalfari, neither Scalfari nor Bastia needed them anymore."

Trotti drank his coffee in two fast gulps; as he drank, his eyes remained on Pergola.

"Some time ago I mentioned to a very old friend—a freemason—that I was disenchanted. Like many people, I had joined the Lodge for professional reasons. I no longer needed the Lodge—and I found the quarrelling and the reactionary politics all rather distasteful." He paused. "I must assume that my friend was not very discreet."

"You still haven't answered my question, Signor Pergola."

"What question?"

Trotti lowered his cup and placed it on the desk. Then he picked up one of the brioches and ate it; crumbs fell down the front of his jacket.

"You say that you did not know that Ramoverde was a journalist?"

"We didn't talk about Scalfari and Bastia, if that's what you mean. That didn't appear to be what he was interested in."

"You still haven't told me what it was that Maltese wanted from you."

Pergola repressed a sigh of impatience.

"Well?"

"You do know, don't you, that Belluno was a Venerabile

Maestro?" The banker gave a weary smile. "Maltese wanted to know why the fact that his grandfather had been an important figure in the Lodge of Propaganda Beta was never mentioned during the long trial."

53: P-Beta

MASERATI SHRUGGED.

Trotti repeated, "Propaganda Beta."

"Off-hand, there's not much I can tell you."

"What do you know about freemasons?"

Maserati gave a short, irritating laugh and pushed at the sleeves of his white coat. "Wait a minute." He got up from the stool he was sitting on and walked softly over to the small screen. He began typing; the keyboard chattered with a series of soft, plastic sounds and meaningless words appeared in green on the screen.

"You see?"

Trotti shook his head.

"Over four hundred fifty lodges in Italy. Grande Oriente is the largest. In Rome."

"And Propaganda Beta?"

Maserati typed "Propaganda Beta" on to the screen. He pressed another key and waited. Then he shook his head. "Nothing."

Trotti bit his lip. "Not much use, your computer."

"Learn to ask it the right questions, Commissario."

Trotti turned to leave but Maserati held up his hand. "Wait, Commissario."

"What?"

"Ask it the right question and it'll give you an interesting answer."

"What?"

"For example, the computer tells me that Uras, the Sardinian, was arrested in 1966 for attempted kidnapping. And that the investigating judge was Giudice Dell'Orto."

Maserati gave the monitor a tap of proprietorial pride.

54: Phone

"You knew the girl in the pizzeria, Commissario?"

The air in the elevator was fetid and Trotti could smell the coffee on Magagna's breath. He ran a finger along the handle of the engraved sickle. "You're better without a mustache."

Magagna put his hand to his upper lip—and then stopped, his hand in mid-air. "Pisanelli's girl?" He used a rising intonation and Trotti noticed that he had acquired a Milanese lilt to his voice.

Trotti nodded.

Magagna laughed. "Poor old Pisa."

"Her name is Etta and he wants to marry her."

"How old is she, for goodness sake? She can't be much older than seventeen."

"She's at the university—specializing in psychiatry."

Again Magagna laughed, but he closed his mouth as the elevator door opened. They stepped out into the corridor.

Principessa lifted her head.

"Any phone calls, Gino?"

The blind man said, "No." Then he frowned. "Magagna?"

Magagna grinned. "As sharp-eyed as ever."

Gino stood up and he moved out from his desk. The two men embraced. "How are you?"

"I mustn't complain—I'm with Narcotici in Milan. Hard work but interesting."

"You've put on weight."

"You see everything, Gino."

The old man tapped the frames of his thick glasses. "You don't need eyes to see." He nodded. "At least five kilos. Your wife must be a good cook."

"Dear old Gino," Magagna said and laughed. He squeezed the old man's arm before following Trotti down the corridor. Trotti opened the door and Magagna entered the office, looked around and gave a low whistle. "Hasn't changed much in eighteen months."

"You were the last person to tidy it up." Trotti stepped over a pile of beige dossiers and sat down at his desk. "You shouldn't have made me drink that wine—it's given me a headache."

Magagna lowered himself into the canvas armchair. His eyes went over the desk, the map and the photograph of the president on the wall, the filing cabinets, the cellophane wrappers beside the wastepaper bin. "Just as it always was, Signor Commissario."

"Why do you want to grow a mustache again?"

"There are times when I miss this place."

"Nobody made you leave." Trotti picked up the phone, pressed the plastic button. "Gino, I'll be wanting to make a few calls."

"Nobody made me leave—that's true. But have you tried living on the salary of a brigadiere when you've got a wife and child to support? Do you know how much a packet of Muratti costs now?"

"I don't smoke."

"Then a packet of sweets—do you know how much they cost?" He sighed. "Four years, Commissario—and I was happy here." He crossed his legs and ran a finger along the short hairs of his growing mustache. "I did some useful work."

"You wanted to get married."

"It's not against the law."

Trotti looked up. "I never stopped you from getting married, Magagna."

"But you never allowed me any promotion."

"Promotion takes time."

"And four years is a long time."

"And so you went to Milano." Trotti placed his hands on the desk. He felt giddy. Perhaps it was because of the wine—synthetic chianti of which he had drunk three glasses. His fingers seemed abnormally long. "That was your decision."

"We worked well together, didn't we, Commissario? Your brains and . . ." Magagna shrugged. "My youthful charm."

"Perhaps."

Magagna looked at Trotti; Trotti looked out of the window. The sky was cloudless.

"You know that I would have stayed on."

Trotti gave no sign of having heard. "What did Dell'Orto say?"

"I told you on the phone. He sent Pisanelli and me on a wild goose chase to find Ramoverde's mistress—a woman who had worked for him as a secretary. The only trouble is that she's been dead for the last decade."

"With me instead of Pisanelli, you'd be getting results."

"Magagna, you know you're better off in Milan." Trotti spoke into the telephone. "Gino?"

Magagna moved forward and between his lips he held an unlit cigarette. His glasses were in his hand.

"Put me through to the Hotel Ambassador."

"Which hotel?"

"Hotel Ambassador in Milan, Gino."

Trotti put the handset down and stared through the window. Overhead, the pigeons were cooing. The light started to blink.

"Yes?"

"Hotel Ambassador, Reception. Can I help you?" A woman.

"Pubblica Sicurezza, Commissario Trotti." He paused. "I should like to speak to Signor Dell'Orto."

"Kindly wait a moment."

A series of metallic clicks and someone calling the name Dell'Orto. Muffled laughter.

"Hello?"

A man's voice. "Signor Dell'Orto is not here."

"Where is he?"

"Have you tried phoning his home?"

"When did he go out?"

"Go out?"

"Perhaps he'll be back soon?" Trotti asked.

"Signor Dell'Orto, judge in retirement?" The sound of rustling paper.

"Yes." Trotti glanced at Magagna who was staring at the telephone.

"Please wait a minute."

Magagna lit the cigarette.

"Judge Dell'Orto left yesterday morning."

"He hasn't been back?"

"He left to go home, Arezzo."

"Thank you," Trotti said slowly and he put the receiver down. He looked at Magagna in silence.

"Somebody has been taking you for a ride, Commissario."

Trotti said, "Be quiet." Then he opened the lower drawer of his desk and took out the old leather-bound address book. On the cover, everything was printed in gold-embossed English. There was the logo of the pharmaceutical company. Underneath, PEARL RIVER, NY.

Trotti found the number immediately.

"A line, Gino!"

On the other side of the partition, Gino bumped his hand against the wall. Trotti picked up the phone and dialed. The code for Arezzo was long and the lines were busy. Trotti had to compose the number three times before he got through. Then the phone began to ring and Trotti could imagine the sound echoing through the villa.

"Pronto."

"I should like to speak to Judge Dell'Orto."

It took Trotti a few seconds to recognize the accent. It was a woman's voice. From Africa—probably Ethiopia or Somalia. "He's not here."

"Where is he?"

"He left a couple of weeks ago."

"Where is the judge?"

"He is not very well. He is depressed. He has to go to Milan."

"Where in Milan?"

"Pardon?"

"D'you have an address?"

"Yes. It is Villa Felicità, San Polo, Arezzo."

"An address in Milan," Trotti almost shouted. "Can you tell me where I can find the judge in Milan?"

"Milan?"

"Yes, yes." Trotti paused. "Listen, is the signora there?"

"Signora?"

"I would like to speak to Signora Dell'Orto."

"I am afraid that is not possible. She is no longer here."

"Where is she?"

"She is dead. She died at Christmas." The woman paused. "The judge was very upset."

Trotti said nothing.

"Hello?"

"Can you tell me where I can contact Signor Dell'Orto in Milan?"

"I am sorry, I do not understand."

"Did the judge say when he was coming back?"

"Pardon?"

"When will the judge return?"

"Return?" The African voice was anxious. "The house is still dirty. The painters are lazy and they have not yet finished the work."

"When will the judge return?"

"Perhaps he is with his nephew," the woman said hopefully.

"With who?"

Her pronunciation was difficult but she spoke slowly. "Signor Giudice said he was going to see his nephew. He teaches in the university, I believe."

55: Parrot

"THIS TIME YOU come with a friend."

Baldassare gave a slow smile and the lines along his forehead started to crease.

"I suppose he's going to hold me down while you kick me. Or perhaps he's going to put electrodes on my testicles."

"Surprised you've got any."

The smile vanished and Trotti sat down on the chair while Magagna moved to the window. Baldassare let his shoes fall from the desktop; the heels hardly made a noise as they landed on the green linoleum. Then he held out his two hands. "The handcuffs, Commissario."

Trotti waited.

"Or perhaps you would like to ruin a few more of my books." He nodded towards the table where the books and the inkstand had been replaced in the same disorder as before.

"Where is your uncle?"

There was surprise in Baldassare's eyes.

"Your uncle, Signor Professore."

"I don't have any uncles."

"The Giudice Dell'Orto."

A thin smile. "The uncle of my wife."

"The person to whom you go crying once the police start asking a few questions."

He stroked his chin. "I suppose you could call beating me

up, striking me, intimidating my colleague and casting all my books to the floor—I suppose you could call that asking questions. Semantics is not my field. I must refer the problem to my colleagues."

Magagna said, "Refer it to your lawyer."

"The parrot talks, I see."

"Baldassare, let's be reasonable."

"Commissario, up until now, it's you who's refused to be reasonable."

"I continue to believe that you're involved in the death of Maltese. Your cooperation will no doubt help to dispel such beliefs."

"Ah." The smile remained, but there was a hint of fear in the dark eyes. "Please tell me how I can be of use."

"Where is Dell'Orto?"

Baldassare shrugged.

Trotti leaned forward. "Dell'Orto, Professore. Tell me where he is."

The professor stroked his face. "I suppose this is your way of influencing people and making friends."

"I've no need to make friends with men whose idea of fun is playing with the emotions of impressionable adolescent girls."

"How is your wonderful daughter, Commissario?"

"Tell me where Dell'Orto is."

"You must know, Commissario, that there are laws in this country. Laws that even you are bound to respect."

"Did you know that Dell'Orto was a freemason, Baldassare?"

"I think I must take the advice of the parrot." He reached towards the cumbersome green telephone. "Perhaps it would be better for us all—and for Dell'Orto—if my lawyer were here."

"Your lawyer can wait."

Baldassare shrugged, ran a hand through his unkempt hair and picked up the receiver. Magagna moved away from the window and walked to where the telephone cable joined the wall. He removed the jack from its socket.

"I think, Commissario, that you're trying to intimidate me. I don't want to make threats . . ."

"Good."

"But I must warn you that despite your position . . ."

"Where's Dell'Orto?"

Baldassare bit the corner of his lip. The eyes were small and they looked at Trotti without wavering. "I don't know." He pointed to where the telephone cable lay like an inert snake on the floor. "You have no right . . ."

"Tell me where Dell'Orto is."

"I said I don't know."

"Then guess."

"I don't know where the old fool is—and I don't care."

"But you phoned him up."

"I phoned him at the Hotel Ambassador. I told him that I'd been beaten up by a madman. By an ineffectual policeman with delusions of grandeur but who is incapable of looking after his own daughter. By a man who must go around hitting anybody who has the misfortune to have to deal with his daughter—a horrid, ugly, spoiled little witch. I told Dell'Orto that. I told him than I'd been roughed up by a peasant with grease in what hair he's got left. I told him about Commissario Trotti whose aristocratic wife has got the hottest thighs in the city—and having worked her way through every available man, has gone off to America to try out what's there."

He laughed but there was no laughter in his eyes. His hand rubbed at the flesh of his cheek.

"You know, Commissario Trotti, I think Dell'Orto must have a soft spot for you. Perhaps he was a cuckold, too."

Trotti did not move.

"D'you know who she's screwing, Trotti?"

"Where's Dell'Orto?"

"D'you know who your wonderful, beautiful, so sophisticated wife is screwing in America, Signor Commissario?"

Trotti said nothing.

"That's right. She likes them all. But she loves bankers. Even Pergola. The little runt from the Banca San Matteo. Christ, she must be hard up. What woman would want to climb into the same bed as that narrow-shouldered pansy? A limp-wristed faggot?"

"Dell'Orto?"

"A woman whose every orifice has been profaned by the dignitaries and notables of this little town of ours."

"Dell'Orto, Baldassare."

"Poor, neurotic kid. With a mother who's a nymphomaniac and a father who's no more than a peasant, a thug—is it any wonder that with parents like that the poor child should turn into a starving wreck?"

Trotti stood up and turned on his heels. His face was white as he left the office. He did not glance at Magagna.

A pigeon was strutting across the university courtyard.

56: Matriarchy

PISANELLI WAS SWEATING in his suede jacket. Half walking, half running, he crossed the quadrangle. Then he caught sight of Trotti.

"Commissario."

Hs stopped. Surprised, Pisanelli changed direction and came towards the shop. It was a small bookshop within the university precinct that specialized in academic textbooks. It was now closed.

Trotti stood by the shop window, apparently engrossed in the display. *Matriarchy in the Po Valley* and *The Terrorist State* were on display. A yellow paperback, *The Policeman Is Alone*.

As Pisanelli approached, his eyes went from Trotti to the books and back again.

Trotti did not move.

"I thought you were with Baldassare."

Trotti continued to stare at the books.

Somewhere a girl laughed—a student heading up the marble stairs to the university library. She wore yellow shoes.

"Where's Magagna?"

Trotti gestured with his thumb. Then he turned away and Pisanelli noticed the eyes. They appeared smaller, harder. Trotti's face looked strange, taut and yet devoid of emotion. Lines of red along the eyelids.

"What d'you want, Pisanelli?"

"I've been looking for you."

"Why?"

Pisanelli looked again at the books on display. "I thought Magagna was with you."

"He was with Baldassare."

Pisanelli bit his lip. "There's a message for you."

"In the Questura?" He turned.

Pisanelli nodded. "A phone call from New York."

"Agnese?"

"A man who left a message. I took the call."

"What did he want?"

"Your wife—he said that your wife will be flying into Malpensa this evening on the Alitalia Flight. Flight AL 322. Time of arrival twenty-one hours—Italian time."

Trotti turned back to the books.

"I think . . ." Pisanelli shrugged. He ran his hand through the hair at the side of his head. "I think it might be a good idea to go and meet her. If you wish, Commissario, I can drive you."

Trotti said nothing.

"In five and a half hours' time—and you must reckon on at least an hour and a half to get to Malpensa."

"Is your friend still angry with me, Pisanelli?"

"My friend?"

"The psychiatry student. Etta."

57: Ambulance

"THANK GOD YOU'RE here." She pushed through the crowd and caught him by the wrist.

Trotti allowed himself to be pulled along. Pisanelli followed him.

Sitting in the same chair. The *Provincia Padana* lay unopened on the table in from of him. The head lolled forward onto the chest.

"How long's he been here?"

Dell'Orto.

Signora Allegra's face was pale, worried. "I was surprised when he ordered a cup of coffee. But he insisted. He said that I must let an old man have his way. 'A strong cup of coffee, signora,' he said."

The sound of an ambulance came from the Corso.

Trotti glanced at the crowd of onlookers—shopkeepers and serving girls who had come upstairs from the underground market. Nobody spoke but they stared at the well-dressed old man who sat in the sunlight.

Before long, the sun would move down behind the houses and Piazza Vittoria would be in the shade.

"He wanted a strong cup of coffee," the woman said, "and so I put in an extra spoonful." A tear glistened at the corner of her eye. "You know, he was a friend of my father—when Papa owned the Bar Duomo, Signor Dell'Orto was a regular customer." More tears. "He came to my wedding."

"Is he breathing?"

She took a handkerchief from her skirt pocket. "Like Papa, he was a freemason."

Pisanelli was kneeling down—the crowd had drawn back—and he had put his ear to the old man's chest.

"Papa said that he was a very good man. Very kind. And when my poor husband died and I was waiting for the insurance, he helped me. Without a word—but I received money from him. And when I paid him back, he refused to take any interest."

On the far side of the Piazza a cat was playing with something. A dead bird, perhaps.

"Well, Pisanelli?"

The white ambulance pulled into Piazza Vittoria. Two men in overalls jumped out from the front seat.

Softly, Pisanelli said, "Dead."

Trotti placed his hand on Signora Allegra's sleeve. "The other cup." He pointed to a second cup on the small table. Red marks along the rim.

"Oh, she left a long time ago."

"She?"

"A large woman." She dabbed at her eyes. "I thought perhaps Signor Dell'Orto had found a girlfriend. But she left a long time ago—it must be over an hour ago."

"What did she look like?"

"She seemed very pleasant—but there was a smell of . . ."

"What?"

"There was a smell of cats about her. Like an old spinster. And I couldn't help noticing that she had large hands—very large hands."

The dying sound of the ambulance siren echoed against the walls of the houses in Piazza Vittoria.

58: Malpensa

THE WHITE LETTERS on the electronic board fluttered and then the new times were announced.

"Where on earth is Lahore?" Magagna asked but received no answer.

Trotti stood at the bar, drinking his fourth cup of coffee.

On the drive to the airport he had not spoken but had stared out at the flat countryside as night fell. Now he drank and ate in silence. His third brioche.

Magagna turned back to face him. "Her flight is on time."

"Good."

"Let's go and sit down."

"I'm all right here."

Magagna sighed and took a cigarette from his pocket. "You see, Commissario, it would make sense."

Trotti lifted the cup.

"Both Belluno and Dell'Orto were members of the same lodge. That's why Maltese went to see Pergola. He wanted to get into the Lodge, find out what happened in 1960. He suspected that Dell'Orto had deliberately wanted to keep his father out of the way. And that was why Dell'Orto insisted upon taking Ramoverde to court. Rivalries within the Lodge, things that were kept secret. But by coming back to Italy and digging into the past, Maltese suddenly made things difficult for Dell'Orto."

Trotti finished the cup of coffee.

"He was a journalist—but he realized that because of the Night of the Tazebao he would be out of work for a long time. And anyway, he feared for his life." Magagna shrugged. "So he started work on a book—a book about the killings at the Villa Laura. And as he was hiding in viale Lodi, there wasn't much else for him to do with his time." He ran a finger along the new mustache. "That's what scared Dell'Orto."

There was an announcement, made in Italian and English.

Trotti turned round.

The airport was a different world, already part of somewhere else, of London, or Paris or New York. He looked at his watch, then at the flight arrivals board. Flight AL 322 from Kennedy Airport, New York had already touched down. He could feel a tightening in the pit of his belly.

"The woman saw him."

Trotti turned. "What woman?"

"You told me you talked to her in Gardesana. The woman who lives above the bakery. She said she'd seen Maltese arrive in the village. In a big car. With another man, an older man. Don't you see that was Dell'Orto? Of course, as there's only one road out of Gardesana she thought the car belonged to one of the German tourists who live in the apartments. But . . ."

"What, Magagna?"

Magagna lit his cigarette. "They arrived earlier. They were expecting you and they'd had time enough to drive through the village and turn round."

"And the car?"

"Dell'Orto probably hired it." He added, "That shouldn't be very difficult to check up on. Probably hired it at the Hotel Ambassador. Don't you see? It was Dell'Orto who wanted Maltese killed. It was Dell'Orto who lured Maltese into going to Gardesana."

"To be murdered in front of me?"

"Possibly it was the only way of getting him out into the open." He shrugged, took the cigarette from his mouth and blew the smoke away sideways. "Maltese had gone into hiding—and he had to be gotten out. As for the killing, it was professional—carried out by professionals. The same people who were behind Novara's assassination in Paris."

"How did Dell'Orto know I was going to Gardesana?"

Magagna smiled. "Baldassare told him."

Trotti looked at the empty coffee cup, then pushed it away along the zinc bar. Again he looked at his watch.

"We'd better go to the arrival lounge."

Trotti smiled.

"If you want, Commissario, I can drive you home."

He shook his head.

"Why not? It's no bother."

"Agnese will be tired after the flight."

"It would be a pleasure for me, Commissario."

"Not tonight. Agnese and I—we'll go into Milan and spend the night in a hotel. Perhaps at the Ambassador. A good meal, a good night's rest and a good breakfast tomorrow morning. It'll be like a second honeymoon after being apart for so long."

Magagna laughed, caught Trotti's eye and gave an exaggerated wink.

59: Booth

THEY WENT TO reception and Trotti gave the phone number.

"In America?" The receptionist was a man in a dark serge uniform. A brooch in the form of the letter A on his lapel.

Trotti nodded.

"Are you a guest of the hotel?"

Magagna showed his identity card.

"As you wish, gentlemen." A thin smile. "The number, please." He wrote it down in a large book and then pointed to a telephone cabin on the far side of the lounge.

"You write all numbers down?"

"I beg your pardon?" The man looked up, offended.

"Do you write down all outgoing phone calls?"

"Of course, signore. There is no automatic dialing from the rooms—and records must be kept." Primly, he folded his arms.

Trotti went over to the telephone and waited. The booth smelled of perfume. There was a leather armchair and notepaper by the side of the telephone—notepaper with the same large A for the heading.

The phone started to ring.

"Hotel Ambassador, Milan. Hold the line please."

Trotti said, "Pronto."

Several voices in English. Then the lady who could speak Italian.

"This is Piero Trotti—I'm phoning from Italy. I should like to talk to Signora Trotti—Mrs. Trotti."

"I'm afraid your wife is not available."

"Where is she?"

"There is a meeting of representatives."

"I must talk to her. It's very important."

"I don't think that will be possible."

"Signora, it's very important. Our daughter—she's ill. It's urgent."

"Please hold on."

Trotti sat down in the armchair and his finger ran along the brass studs of the curved armrest. He looked at his reflection in the pink tinted mirror. His eyes stared back at him, unsmiling.

"Piero?"

"Agnese, what the hell are you doing in New York? I got a phone call this afternoon, telling me to go to the airport. I go to Malpensa, I wait an hour for the plane—another hour for you to come through customs. For heaven's sake, is this your idea of a joke?"

"Piero?"

"Well?"

"Give me time to explain."

"As much time as you want, Agnese. Where were you?"

"Didn't you get the message?"

"What message?"

"I asked a friend to tell you that I had changed my mind—there's no point in coming back now."

"Of course there's a point. Your daughter needs you. For God's sake, I need you."

Mocking. "You need me, Piero?"

"Don't you understand, Agnese? Don't you understand that without you . . . ?"

"Is this what you phoned me up for?"

"I want to know why you got me to go to the airport."

"I told you, Piero, I changed my mind. But I left a message."

"I received no message, Agnese."

"That's not my fault."

He raised his eyes to look at the reflection. "So you're not coming back?"

"Not immediately."

"And Pioppi?"

"She's getting better, isn't she?"

"She needs you."

"She's an adult, Piero. She's over eighteen. She can't expect me or you to go on holding her hand all the time."

"Can't you understand that she's ill?"

"She was ill—but she's getting better. You know that if I thought she really needed me, I'd be on the first plane."

A long pause. Trotti waited while his breathing returned to normal.

"Agnese, listen."

"She's a lot better, isn't she?"

"Listen, Agnese, I want you to tell me the truth. About Leonardelli."

"Who?"

"Did you tell Judge Dell'Orto about Leonardelli?"

"Piero, what on earth has got into your head? That was a long time ago—several years ago. You phone me up about some stupid policeman from the Questura?"

"Agnese, have you spoken recently to Dell'Orto?"

"Of course."

"Of course?"

Her laugh was gay. "The poor old thing. He's been very good to me—and to you, Piero, although I know you're incapable of gratitude."

"When did you last speak to him?"

"I often speak to him. He's very lonely, you know—ever since his wife died. The poor thing, he doesn't like to mention that. He's beginning to feel his age."

"You knew that his wife was dead?"

"Piero, what on earth's wrong with you? I sometimes wonder how you manage to do your job. You've got absolutely no memory. Of course I knew she was dead. So did you. I told you. Don't you ever listen to what I tell you?"

The eyes in the tinted mirror did not blink.

"The old girl died of cancer. Her weight went down from one hundred kilos to sixty. Genoveffa—she was a sweet thing."

"Dell'Orto's dead."

"Dead?"

"He died this afternoon."

"My God."

For a moment neither spoke and the line carried the sounds of static over the Atlantic.

Trotti said, "I suppose you told him about your diplomas."

"What are you talking about?"

"You told him, didn't you, that you needed your specialization diplomas?"

Agnese did not hide her indignation. "I told him that it was your job to send them off to me—and that you were never at home—neither you nor Pioppi—to answer the telephone."

"And you told him that I was going up to Gardesana on Friday morning?"

Now sarcasm. "Was that wrong, Piero? Was it wrong to repeat to an old and good friend what my husband had told me a couple of days earlier? Was I revealing some great secret?"

"Who else did you tell, Agnese?"

"Nobody."

"Who else did you tell?"

"What's got into you, Piero? I'm your wife—I'm not a criminal that you're beating up on the third floor of the Questura. This isn't an interrogation, you know."

"Answer my question, Agnese."

"Piero, I'm going to hang up. They must be wondering why I'm hanging on the phone like this."

"Did you tell anybody else?"

"I didn't tell anybody anything. I was merely trying to find you—trying to get you to post off the diplomas—diplomas which I need for my career here in America."

"Agnese, did you tell Pergola?"

Silence.

"You must tell me—Agnese, it's very important."

"Piero, I'm going to hang up. My love to Pioppi," and before he could say another word, the line had gone dead.

He stepped out of the telephone booth and walked across the thick carpet to the reception desk.

60: Hold

IF THE MOROCCAN recognized them, he showed no sign. He came out from behind the bar and approached their table. He did not look at either man. Magagna ordered a beer, Trotti a cup of coffee. He nodded, wiped their table and returned to the bar.

"I'm drinking too much coffee," Trotti said. A pause and then he added, "Maybe she tried the woman at Graffiti."

"Guerra's dead."

Trotti smiled. "The blood on the walls? That took you in, Magagna?"

He raised his shoulders.

"Guerra wants to be left alone. That's why she moved out of the flat—and that's why she smeared the walls with blood. Animal blood."

"Okay, okay." Magagna leaned forward with his arms on the table. "But why do you have to find Guerra now? When I was looking for her, you weren't interested."

"I wasn't interested because you seemed to think that she was responsible for setting Maltese up."

"Why not?"

"She's an addict."

Trotti looked round the bar, at the posters and the fading photographs. "You think he'll come in?"

"You don't know addicts, Commissario. They are capable of

anything—capable of selling their mothers for a few milligrams of joy."

"And Guerra was a hardened addict?"

"She took injections." He shrugged. "Not the sort of thing you do just to impress the boys."

"The scars were recent?"

"I didn't study them. That's not what you asked me to do. You'd need Pisanelli for that—he's the doctor." Magagna grinned and with his finger and thumb he smoothed the short bristles of his mustache. "We should have arrested Guerra—taken her in and sent her to detox."

"I don't work in Milan, Magagna."

He laughed and tapped his chest. "I should have arrested her."

"If she's an addict, she'll be needing her stuff and she's not going to move away from her supply source."

Magagna shrugged and stubbed out the cigarette he was smoking.

The barman brought the drinks.

Trotti looked up. "There is a phone here?"

The Moroccan jerked his hand towards the far room.

"Do you have any tokens?"

He looked at a photograph of Cagliari, 1969/70, while from his apron pocket he took out several telephone tokens that he set down on the table. He had dark eyes, yellow skin that was pale in the light of the Bar Orchidea. A scar ran down one cheek. When he turned, Trotti saw that he was wearing narrow black trousers beneath the apron.

Trotti got up and went into the adjacent room. The games of table football had been deserted but a crowd of silent, smoking men stood round a billiard table. A heavy atmosphere. A cloud of spirals that hovered over the brightly lit baize cloth. Four players and a small man sitting in the corner counting notes. He glanced at Trotti and the notes vanished beneath the table.

A large man with a billiard stick moved towards Trotti. He wore a windbreaker that advertised Fernet Branca.

Trotti picked up the telephone and the man turned away.

Two tokens.

"Pronto."

"Pronto."

"This is Piero—I'm in Milan."

"Piero?"

"Trotti."

"Ah—so at last you phone me."

"Are you doing anything? Because if you're not, I could drive up to Sesto and perhaps—if it's not too late—we could go for a meal."

"Piero, d'you know what time it is?"

"Are you free?"

"It's very sweet of you, Piero, but I'm afraid that this evening . . ." Donatella hesitated. "I'm afraid that I've got guests."

"Guests?"

"Let's say a friend."

"I see."

"But perhaps later in the week, Piero? Another evening?"

"That would be very nice."

Neither spoke and Trotti turned sideways to glance at the billiard players. At the corner of his eye he saw movement.

"Piero?"

"I'll be in touch, Donatella," and hurriedly he put down the receiver.

The man with the Fernet Branca jacket and the billiard cue tried to trip him up. He missed Trotti and raised the cue, as if to hit him over the head. The other men turned. Southern, dark faces, bulging bellies. His path to the door was blocked. Another door behind him leading to the lavatory, perhaps.

Trotti had no time to be scared. He saw the cue coming towards him and he ducked.

He wanted to run but then Magagna was standing by the door, smiling broadly. "PS," he shouted and pointed the small pistol. With a minimum of effort he caught the dealer by the arm and swung him round in a tight hold.

"Now where's little Marco going?"

61: Gabbi

"Did you sleep well, Commissario?"

Like Magagna, she was from the Abruzzi, but not from the city. She had the strong features of peasant stock. She was also clearly intelligent. A small woman, well dressed and with precise movements. Not exactly beautiful—her nose was too long and the mouth too wide, but attractive because of her smile. And Trotti had noticed her readiness to listen.

The apartment was small and comfortable. The furniture was sober, modern and of good quality. A couple of paintings on the wall and a photograph of d'Annunzio's pine forest. A television and placed above it, the wedding photograph.

Trotti had been surprised at the number of books on the bookshelves, surprised to see several de Agostini almanacs and an encyclopaedia that looked well used.

"Very well, Signora Magagna." He smiled. "But you shouldn't have let me oversleep." He threw back the coverlet and sat up.

She pulled the curtains open. "I wanted you to make the best use of the facilities," she said and gave a little laugh. "We've been lucky, Commissario. We managed to get an apartment which is near the center and at the same time fairly quiet. And private gardens for the children to play in."

"You're planning to have children, signora?"

She put her hand to her belly and smiled.

Through the window he saw the cloudless sky.

"Look," she said, "while you men were sleeping, I had time to go downstairs and get fresh bread. And fresh brioches. Gabbi told me that you were fond of them." She gestured towards the kitchen table where she had set out the breakfast things—including napkins. "And fresh honey from home."

"You are from Pescara, too, signora?"

Bright, lively eyes. She was a lot younger than he had imagined. "A village—on the border with the province of Chieti." She raised her shoulders. "Just a few houses near the railway-line—but at this time of the year, when the flowers spring up in the meadows and in the distance you can see the Gran Sasso . . ."

"What ever brought you to Milan?"

"Milan, Commissario? If I had the choice, I would leave this town tomorrow. Noise, dirt and violence—and a corrupting influence on Gabbi."

"Gabbi?"

"My husband."

"Why d'you call him that?"

"Because it's his name." She laughed. "What do you call him?"

"I rarely call him anything." Trotti could not help smiling. "And when I do it's simply Magagna." He paused. "Gabbi?"

"Gabriele—after d'Annunzio."

"Yes?"

They turned. Magagna stood in the doorway in pajamas. "How did you find sleeping on the divan?"

Trotti said to Signora Magagna, "I don't think he looks like a Gabbi."

The phone rang and Magagna disappeared, taking the call on the bedroom extension.

Trotti got out of bed.

In the kitchen, Signora Magagna poured the coffee. It was good, strong and she had a machine that put froth on the milk. Trotti said, "I've always loved breakfast."

"Then why have you waited a year and a half to come and see us?"

She smiled but he saw that her eyes were watching him

carefully. He also noticed the slight muscular movement at the corner of her lips.

"I'm not often in Milan."

"Gabbi hoped so much that you would come to the wedding." She hesitated. "I think he was a bit upset."

Standing up, Trotti drank some coffee.

"We were both hoping that you would be there. Gabbi has always said that you have been good to him . . . Commissario, you must try the honey. Acacia from home that my brother brought up to Milan for us. Please try it—and if you like it, I can give you a kilo to take home." She added softly, "Gabbi has told me about your daughter. You must give her honey—real honey—and you'll see that she'll love it. You must take a jar."

Magagna reappeared in the doorway. "For you, Commissario."

"What?"

"The telephone—it's Pisa."

Trotti put the cup down and went into the hall.

"Pisanelli." A vase of flowers on the little table—lily of the valley.

"Commissario, at last. Where've you been?"

"Mind your own business!"

"Have you been to the Policlinico this morning?"

Fear in the belly. "Why?"

"I'm phoning from the hospital. There's a woman here—she says she's been looking for you."

"Pioppi—how is she?"

Pisanelli laughed on the other end of the line. "Your daughter's well, Commissario."

"Then what woman are you talking about?"

"She refuses to give her name."

"What does she look like?"

Pisanelli lowered his voice. It became hoarser and more sibilant. "Blonde hair, made up, fairly short—one meter sixty-five. Pretty—looks a bit German."

"And what does she want?"

"She's got something for you."

"What?"

Pisanelli mumbled something.

"Stop lisping like an old woman, for God's sake. What does this woman want?"

"A key, Commissario."

"I don't have any keys."

"She's got a key to a private safe. At the Banco Milanese. And she says she wants to give it to you in person."

62: Wig

THEY WALKED ALONG the Galleria Vittorio Emmanuele and from time to time, Signora Magagna took Trotti by the arm. She spoke about her home and asked him questions about Santa Maria in Collina. He enjoyed her company and felt flattered by her attention.

At ten o'clock they stood at the entrance to the Metropolitana and waited for Pisanelli.

Milan, Piazza Duomo.

Before the cathedral—sparkling in the sunshine—tourists fed the pigeons and even at this early hour, there were addicts on the steps, forming huddled, squalid groups of dirty clothes. A lot of them were very young—still adolescents. The two Carabinieri in uniform, walking with their hands behind their backs, took no notice of them; but then, later, the same Carabinieri approached a small man. The man started shouting at the top of his voice and maintaining that he was not a pickpocket. A small boy darted through the crowd and headed for the entrance into the subway. He escaped without being caught.

"Photograph?"

They had their photograph taken—Signora Magagna standing between the two men, smiling and holding their arms. She insisted upon paying and gave the photograph to Trotti. "A souvenir of Milan," she said. "In the hope that you'll come and visit us more often."

Pisanelli got out of the car in the via Mazzini.

The woman wore a miniskirt of yellow, high heels and platform soles. A large yellow handbag that she held in front of her. A peroxide blonde. She walked beside Pisanelli who crossed the Piazza. She looked about her nervously. When she saw Trotti, she stopped, turned and headed towards the entrance to the Metropolitana on the far side of the square.

Like a faithful dog, Pisanelli changed direction and followed her.

At the top of the stairway she stopped.

Beneath his feet, Trotti could feel the rumble of the underground trains.

Lia Guerra handed something to Pisanelli and then watched him carefully as he made his way through the crowds across the square. With one hand she held the handrail, and watched Trotti, heedless of the flow of people coming out of the Metropolitana entrance.

As he approached, Trotti saw that Pisanelli was grinning foolishly.

"Get that girl, Magagna."

Pisanelli caught Trotti by the arm and said, "No." At the same time, on the via dell'Arcivescovado side of the piazza, the girl moved away from the handrail and ran down the stairs into the subway.

"There are questions she's got to answer, for God's sake." He tried to shake off Pisanelli's hold, but the grip was strong. "She knows what happened." He turned to Magagna. "What are you waiting for? Stop her, Magagna, stop her."

Calmly, Pisanelli said, "She's suffered enough. Let her go."

"But she can tell me what . . . Pisanelli, let go of my arm."

"Commissario, the girl's told me everything. She's gone—it's better that way." He released his grip.

"Damn you, Pisanelli."

"You see, she holds you responsible for Maltese's death and anyway, you've got the key—she's seen that and she knows she's safe." Pisanelli glanced at Magagna and his wife. For Signora Magagna, a grin and an apologetic shrug. "She said that she would have given you the key anyway, Commissario, once she heard that Dell'Orto was dead. There was no need to scare Marco into contacting her. She says that Marco's a human being but because he's a homosexual, you treat him like dirt. For her own sake, she had to give you the key—for her own safety and that's why she took the train down this morning and went to the hospital. But now she wants you to leave her alone—let her get on with her life." Pisanelli paused and turned to look across the Piazza Duomo. "She says that . . ." There was a dreaminess in his voice. "She says she wants to leave the country—go to a clinic in Switzerland and throw the drug habit. She says it'd never been her intention to become a junkie—and that with Maltese, things were getting better. Things would have got better—but because of you, Commissario, he's now dead. That's what she says and now she's going to inherit her uncle's money, she can afford a proper cure in Switzerland."

"She should have told me the truth."

Pisanelli shook his head and at that moment, with the sunlight on his face and his high forehead, he had the appearance of a martyr saint in a Renaissance painting.

"Leave her alone, Commissario. Lia has already suffered enough."

63: Telecamera

MAGAGNA WAS CARRYING a gun and as he passed through the metallic archway, the metal detector started to bleep.

It took Trotti nearly an hour to make his way into the basement.

The Banco Milanese felt like a building under siege and at various strategic points both inside and outside, uniformed guards stood with submachine guns cradled in their arms.

"The last place you'd think Maltese would want to leave anything," Magagna said. "Who would ever have dreamed that he would have a numbered safe in the heart of the lion's den?"

Trotti smiled. "It belonged to Dell'Orto's wife—to the fat Genoveffa." He added, "Maltese probably got Guerra to come in her wig and leave the stuff here."

The Safes Manager looked at Magagna's identity and then insisted upon phoning through to Narcotici. Even then he was not satisfied, and it took another phone call and twenty minutes to get a warrant sent from the Questura. Only then did the man's thin, humorless face break into an anemic smile. "You understand that we can't be too careful."

"Particularly now," Magagna said and the manager scowled.

They were taken down two flights of stairs. Red carpet on a highly polished marble floor. Nudes sculpted in bronze on stone pedestals. The basement was brightly lit and a guard knelt down and put keys into a series of locks. The iron grills opened and they stepped into an enclosed chamber.

Another door—riveted steel with embedded dials. The manager turned two of the dials and there was a short beeping sound. He waited for it to cease, then adjusted the two remaining dials. He raised the handle and slowly the vast steel door swung inwards.

"Gentlemen, please enter."

Overhead, the telecameras revolved ceaselessly.

64: SIFAR

TROTTI BEGAN TO read Maltese's notes. The thin paper smelt of soap.

> At the time of the Italian Miracle, the Army and the Carabinieri were seeing spies and subversives everywhere. As a result of the increased wealth of the working classes and the fear of a communist infiltration, there developed among the military an obsession with information gathering, an obsession that was fostered, no doubt, by the increase of interest that the Americans in general and the CIA in particular were showing in the Mediterranean basin. For Italian counter-espionage electronic eavesdropping became a way of life. There is even reason to believe that the President of the Republic, Antonio Segni, was being monitored by a hidden microphone in his private study.
>
> Following an article that appeared in Popolo d'Italia—at that time, a highly respected newspaper—a couple of generals were thrown out of SIFAR, the Italian counter-espionage organization, in 1966. One of them, General

Saldini, had been using the spy network of SIFAR to build up his own collection of files.

Faced with the prospect of premature retirement, General Saldini decided to take with him—as a leaving present to himself—all the files he had put together over the previous years. Some dealt with dangerous subversives, but most concerned the major figures in the world of Italian politics and finance.

Italy is a country ruled not by politics but by parties— political parties jockeying for power. This state of affairs, the result no doubt of proportional representation and a deep-rooted fear of the communists, explains why Italy remains—politically at least—a third-world country. But for the man who seeks power through manipulation, power through the parties is a godsend.

Through the freemason network, Valerio Luino came to know about the secret files and he immediately understood that such information in his hands would be a useful source of power. General Saldini, on the other hand, was determined to get his revenge on the politicians who had made use of the press to oust him from the army. Luino, at this time little more than a provincial architect, set about making a marriage of convenience between himself and the general. Understandably, it was not particularly difficult for Luino to recruit Saldini into the P-Beta Lodge, which at this time Luino was in the process of restructuring.

With the information that General Saldini had given him as a dowry, Luino could have created a financial fortune. Files on generals who plotted against the Republic, on politicians who had taken bribes, on industrialists who had paid bribes, on political parties that had facilitated the interests of the capitalists, on members of the Anti-Mafia enquiry that were in the pay of the Mafia—with this kind of knowledge—a data bank for blackmail— Luino could have amassed a fortune comparable to that of Agnelli and Fiat.

But wealth for its own sake has never interested Luino. Wealth is merely a means to an end. For Luino, the true end is power.

He simply persuaded the compromised politicians and captains of finance to join his freemason lodge. Thus to the information from Saldini, he was able to add the information that the new recruits brought with them. And in a very short period, the P-Beta Lodge, which originally had been created to recruit among the ruling classes, was transformed into a personal secret society. The members included some of the most powerful and the most influential men in the land. Luino could now count among his allies and fellow freemasons of P-Beta, several ministers and at least eight army generals.

P-Beta had always been the most exclusive of the lodges of the Grande Oriente. Indeed it owed its name— Propaganda Beta—to the fact that it was second on the general list of over 450 lodges in Italy. It had always embraced—with vows of the greatest of secrecy—those men who had positions of authority within the public domain. This explains why Dell'Orto—at that time considered one of the best investigating judges in Northern Italy—was himself a member. In the past, important figures such as Crispi and Zanardelli had been enrolled in the lodge. However, since the time of Mussolini, it had fallen on hard times, and if Luino was sent to P-Beta in the first place, it was simply because all the other lodges in Italy were closed to him.

For the provincial architect carried with him a past that made the name Luino an anathema to most self-respecting freemasons.

During the period which followed the invasion of Italy in 1943 and the creation of Mussolini's mock Republic at Salò on Lake Garda, the young Luino had collaborated with the fascists. And for most freemasons, fascism and Mussolini have always been considered as the great enemy of freemasonry. No mason can forget that in 1926, the

Duce sent Gran Maestro Domizio Torrigiani into internal exile.

In 1943, although not yet eighteen, Luino was making a name for himself. He led the Repubblichini—and even certain German SS columns—in a bitter fight with the partisans in the Po valley. But as General Alexander's armies pushed their way north, Luino realized that the fortunes of war were fast changing. After the war, in Rome, he was to maintain that he had collaborated with the GAP partisans and other communist formations. Although several leading ex-partisans were to give their support to Luino's claims, he failed to shake off the accusations of collaboration. Like most Italians, but with greater cunning, Luino had known how to end up on the winning side. What was harder was rewriting his own history.

For several years after the war Luino disappeared from circulation. With the money that he had managed to put aside during the last years of the war, he was able to buy himself an education. Foreseeing the boom in housing, he went to Parma University, where in six years, he managed to obtain a degree in architecture. Then in 1951, he went to Rome.

There he approached the politicians of the ruling Christian Democrat party. Fear was a thing of the past, the communists had been beaten in the elections of 1948, and Italy was in the process of rebuilding. By gravitating toward the center of power, Luino soon came to see that there was a new class of businessmen in Italy and that, because of the inefficiency of the Italian state, these men were now referring their problems to the politicians. Along with their problems, these men also brought limitless sources of wealth.

The lesson was not lost on Luino. He saw that political power and wealth went together. He suddenly took up an interest in the Church and started to become a practicing Christian. He sought the favor of several powerful prelates and through them found an introduction into the ruling Christian Democrats. The same prelates, however, would no doubt have been upset to learn that in 1960 Luino took his vows in the Lodge of Gian Domenico Romagnosi of the Grande Oriente d'Italia. He was initiated and assumed the grade of "fratello."

And it was as a "fratello" that he was to spend the next few years. He worked with a small consultancy firm in Rome, while at the same time he was trying to build up a circle of contacts. Luino soon found that whenever he tried to move up the hierarchy of the Lodge, his path was automatically blocked. His fascist past had not been forgiven.

Luino returned to Lombardy, where he remained a humble "fratello" at the bottom of the ladder.

Within the Romagnosi Lodge, there were many old-school masons who could not forgive the past of the Venetian upstart. "He has managed to work his way in. He will, however, remain an apprentice," one member is supposed to have said. Luino tried to cajole, he tried to buy his way up the masonic cursus honorum, but his attempts were all doomed to failure. But by 1965 he had masonic friends upon whom he knew he could count. One of these friends was Tantassi, a Social Democrat and an influential member of parliament. Luino managed to convince Tantassi that he was a victim of a conspiracy—and Tantassi went to see the Gran Maestro himself, the head of all Italian masons, to plead Luino's case. A physically insignificant man, the Gran Maestro taught physics in Ravenna. Alone among freemasons he had the power to transfer members from one lodge to another. And so, in February 1966, Luino suddenly disappeared from the Romagnosi Lodge and a few weeks later he was promoted to the rank of Maestro—a leap of two grades—in a completely different lodge.

No sooner had Luino joined P-Beta than he was recruiting new faces to the Lodge. It was his avowed intention to restore P-Beta to all its ancient glory. Between 1966 and 1967, he enrolled over one hundred new members. "If he continues like this," the Gran Maestro (who was the de facto Maestro Venerabile of the secret P-Beta lodge) declared, "soon he'll be recruiting the Pope."

The following year, Luino recruited the ex-general Saldini. Undoubtedly powerful, Luino now sought to improve his personal situation.

From 1972 onwards, he embarked upon a series of actions that were intended to make him more acceptable to the old stalwarts of Italian freemasonry. He changed his name to Baldassare, he married a young student more than twenty years his junior, the niece of one of his major critics within P-Beta, Judge Dell'Orto. More important, she was the daughter of the city architect. And so Luino— or Baldassare as he now called himself—managed to obtain a teaching post within the Department of Urbanistica at the university. It gave him new opportunities in consultancy work—well-paid jobs for Arab and African governments, wanting to build airports and hospitals. The job—with its four teaching hours a week—suited him ideally. It gave him respectability—and it gave him the free time to look after his masonic affairs. At the same time, he deliberately tried to disassociate his public persona of academic and respected architect from his activities as Venerabile Maestro of what was fast becoming one of the most powerful lodges in Italy.

65: Apron

SIGNORA MAGAGNA WAS in the kitchen preparing the midday meal.

Pisanelli had picked up a magazine.

"Well?"

Trotti looked up.

"Can I have a look?" Magagna sat forward on the chair. He held out his hand.

"I haven't finished yet."

The dossier was on the settee beside Trotti. Twenty or so typewritten pages that had been stapled together.

"What does Maltese say?"

Trotti shrugged and continued to read:

By his marriage to the niece of Dell'Orto, Luino had achieved two major goals. On the one hand, thanks to his father-in-law's position as city architect, he found a back entrance to the communist run administration of the city; on the other, he silenced—for the time being, at least—Dell'Orto's criticism of him within P-Beta.

During the mid-Seventies, Luino was able to recruit 850 new members to his Lodge. Luca Pergola, a local banker and a man of considerable ambition, recounts how he took his vows of loyalty in 1979.

"I went to a small office in the Upim building in Corso

Cavour. After knocking three times, I was let in by the Venerable Master himself. He was wearing a silk apron and white gloves. With him were two other men, one of whom I recognized as a general of the Carabinieri. My jacket was removed and I was told to roll the cuffs of my trousers up to mid-calf. Then I knelt down. The Venerable Master placed the tip of his sword on my shoulder while muttering something in a foreign language. I then went round a make-shift altar three times holding a Bible in one hand and taking my oath in a loud voice: 'In the presence of the Great Architect of the Universe, and in the name of my dearest and closest friends, I solemnly swear on my honor and conscience, that I shall never reveal the secrets of my masonic initiation, that I shall respect the honor of all my brothers, that I shall succor, comfort and defend them, even at the cost of my own life, and should I at any time or for any reason fail to keep this most sacred of oaths, may I become the object of contempt for the Order and for all humanity.' After having taken the oath, I was embraced three times by each brother present. I was then given an apron and a pair of white gloves wrapped in cellophane. Before leaving the apartment, I was asked to make a gift. No sum was mentioned and I left a check for five hundred thousand lire. I later discovered, much to my chagrin, that other new members sometimes would leave as little as twenty thousand lire in cash."

Because of the massive recruitment, Luino came under attack from the old traditionalists still within P-Beta. Luino was accused of not respecting Masonic rites. At the instigation of Dell'Orto, the Gran Maestro allowed himself to get involved in the squabbling.

The battle between Luino and the Gran Maestro for the control of P-Beta was long and bloody. The Gran Maestro tried to dissolve the Lodge, but as a consequence, all the members—with the exception of the traditionalists—stuck with Luino and the Gran Maestro *had to acknowledge the existence of a lodge with Luino at its head. Then, in 1974, at a masonic meeting in Bologna, a move was adopted by the "brothers" present for the dissolution of P-Beta. At this point a "fratello" rose to his feet and started accusing the Gran Maestro himself—the man at the head of all Italian lodges—of having received certain sums from an American aircraft company. He also accused the head of the Italian masonic movement of taking bribes from various political parties. Bitter infighting ensued, followed by the break for lunch. After lunch, the accusations against the Gran Maestro were withdrawn. At the same time, the vow for the abolition of P-Beta was suspended indefinitely.*

Dell'Orto would not forgive such a travesty of the masonic code.

66: Jacket

"You phoned me in the middle of the night."

He shrugged. "I hadn't spoken to you for nearly twenty years."

"And that's why you had to threaten me?"

"It was for his sake."

No longer the woman's voice. Now Douglas Ramoverde spoke with his slight lisp. The same lisp that Trotti had heard on the telephone.

"The judge?"

"I don't know if you can understand, Commissario, but in his way, he felt ashamed for what he did."

Trotti frowned. "When?"

"Of course he was a mason and as soon as I could get to a telephone without being seen, I phoned him." He held out his hands. "I had helped kill my father-in-law."

"Dell'Orto helped you twenty years ago?"

Douglas Ramoverde nodded. He was fatter than Trotti remembered him, with a heavy jowl. But there was nothing feminine about his face. The skin was very pale. "My son should have left Italy—and if he'd had any sense, he would have cleared out after he helped Novara. I told him he was risking his life—but he knew that anyway. There are relatives in America, relatives in Argentina, but he wanted to be with the girl. He thought he could help her." Douglas Ramoverde raised the shoulders of his tweed jacket and sat back on the settee, crossing his legs. "It was obvious that Bastia—or whoever was behind Bastia—was going to have him killed. And that's what happened. Giovanni was shot dead—murdered professionally. And it just so happened that you were there with him. But it could have been in Milan, it could have been in Borgo Genovese. Instead it was on Lake Garda."

"Where he went in the hope of meeting me."

"You were always very sharp, Commissario."

"How many years do you think you're going to spend in jail, Signor Ramoverde?" Trotti asked and he noticed that Magagna smiled.

"An old woman?"

"Old women can go to jail. Some die there."

Ramoverde shrugged and stroked one of the cats. The back of his hand was devoid of hairs.

"What did your son want to see me for?"

"Dell'Orto knew you were going up to the lake and for some time Giovanni had been saying that he wanted to contact you."

Trotti frowned. "You discussed these things with your son?"

"Of course I did."

"Then you saw your son regularly?"

"You could say that." Ramoverde raised a hand. "After all, he was living here."

"And not in Milan—not in viale Lodi?"

"Sometimes he would go up to Milan to see the girl—to take her some money or to see if she needed help. Of course, he wanted to stay with her, but he realized it was dangerous to live in Milan."

"And he lived here?—here in the Villa Laura?"

Ramoverde nodded. "Would you gentlemen care for something to drink? Some coffee perhaps?"

"With grappa, if that's possible."

Magagna took out a cigarette and was about to light it.

"Please."

Magagna looked up.

"My cats don't like smoke, you know." Ramoverde turned away and called for the girl, who promptly appeared.

"Coffee for the gentlemen."

She nodded in silence and disappeared into the kitchen. One of the cats followed her at a distance.

"Traveling between here and Milan was a risk," Ramoverde said. "I lent him some of my best dresses."

Trotti smiled.

Magagna moved away from the wall—he had been standing close to the painting of General Diaz. "Which would explain the razor and the shaving cream. Clothes weren't a problem—but stubble was. Stubble on his face and on his legs."

"Personally, I always wear long dresses." Ramoverde smiled. "It's shaving the backs of my hands that's a nuisance. That and having to change my clothes whenever there's somebody at the front door. Fortunately, Sandra keeps most visitors away—she's a bright girl. Orazio's granddaughter."

Magagna continued, "It would also explain why he pissed down the sink."

"I beg your pardon," Douglas Ramoverde said primly.

"He wouldn't have dressed up as a woman each time he had wanted to go and piss—and so he wouldn't have used the lavatory on the landing."

Trotti took a sweet from his pocket and was about to unwrap it. He had second thoughts and returned it to the pocket. "I know how Dell'Orto knew about my intention to go to Gardesana."

Ramoverde nodded.

"But how did Bastia or the men that Bastia sent—how did they know?"

"Through Dell'Orto."

"He told Baldassare?"

"Don't be stupid, Commissario. The old judge phoned Lia Guerra from the hotel. He wanted to tell her about Uras . . ."

"About Uras?"

"The Sardinians had taken part in the Banca San Matteo robbery. They realized that they had been used; that's why they contacted Dell'Orto. They realized that it was more than just a robbery and they wanted to make some money."

"By blackmailing?"

"They felt they'd been cheated and they told Dell'Orto they were in possession of some money stolen at the Banca San Matteo. But Dell'Orto was in a hurry. So he phoned Lia Guerra at the shop in Senigallia." Douglas Ramoverde looked down at his shoes. "That is the only explanation we could find."

Magagna said, "What explanation?"

Trotti turned to face him. "At the Ambassador the reception takes down the number of all out-going phone calls. And that enabled Baldassare to locate Lia Guerra. He found out she was at the shop—and through her, he got to Maltese."

"Because of that phone call—he was in a hurry, he wanted to speak to my son, tell him about the Sardinians—Dell'Orto believed that my son's blood was on his hands. And so—" He shrugged. "And so he decided he didn't want to live anymore."

"Dell'Orto would have saved me a lot of time and effort if he had told me the truth."

"The judge was a good man. A very good man and he had a strict code of ethics. He was a mason—but he was also a judge. And he believed in the Republic—for him it was something sacred." Ramoverde paused. "He always spoke well of you."

"He should have told me about the freemasons."

"You are not devious enough, Commissario. Those are his words. Very fond of you—very fond indeed. He said that you were honest and you were the only person in Lombardy for whom he felt genuine respect. And because you were honest, he said that you would never get very far. As for P-Beta, it wasn't something that he wanted you involved with." He raised his hand. "It was Gianni's idea to bring you the Sardinians' money. Gianni wanted to show how Baldassare was behind the shooting at the Banca San Matteo. And he would produce the two witnesses of Uras and Suergiu."

"The judge should have told me the truth if he respected me. I thought we were friends—after all, he came to see me. But he told me lies—nothing but lies."

"He was your friend, Trotti—he liked you like a son. You and your wife. But there was something that he couldn't bring himself to admit—not to you." Ramoverde sighed and was about to say something more but the girl returned with the coffee. She gave small cups to Trotti and to Magagna; she gave a large cup to Douglas Ramoverde.

"Since his wife's death, his behavior had become erratic. He turned in on himself, went over his past. There were times when he would phone me here from Arezzo and for forty-five minutes he would go into the details of my trial. It still obsessed him, he still wondered whether he should have behaved as he did. But I know that if I were to have phoned him last week or last month—twenty years on—asking him for his help, he would have behaved no differently." Ramoverde stopped. A sad smile. "A good man—but Dell'Orto was getting old. There were other times he would call me to tell me about a holiday he'd spent with Genoveffa—his wife—on the Adriatic. Or a trip he'd made to Syria. He'd started to live in the past—it helped him to accept his loneliness. That and his determination to destroy Baldassare, whom he'd never forgiven for debasing P-Beta."

"He could have told me the truth. Why didn't he? Or come to that, why didn't you? Why has everybody lied? Even the Guerra girl."

Ramoverde raised his cup. "As for Lia Guerra, I don't think she likes you, Commissario. She still feels that you're responsible for what happened to her. Even if she can now see her past as a terrorist objectively, that doesn't mean she loves the police and the Carabinieri. You will always remain a fascist in her eyes."

Trotti was silent.

"She didn't want my son to contact you. She never trusted you—and she holds you responsible—directly or indirectly—for my son's death."

"Where did she hide when she left viale Lodi?"

Ramoverde shrugged.

Another silence while Trotti nibbled at the edge of his lip. "But why lie? Why did the old man invent the tale of a letter? Not only a waste of time, Ramoverde, but it also put my life in danger."

"I don't think your life has ever been in danger, Commissario."

"Why did Dell'Orto refuse to tell me the truth? Maltese wanted to see me—but Dell'Orto couldn't bring himself to tell me the truth."

"My son wanted to talk about Baldassare—and how Baldassare had been to New York to see Scalfari. How Baldassare had seen Scalfari in jail, how they had patched up their disagreements and how they had decided to work together. And my son wanted to tell you about the shooting at the Banca San Matteo. And how Baldassare was behind it. But, you see, for Dell'Orto to talk to you about all that . . ." He shrugged. "It would have meant explaining things."

"Things?"

Ramoverde drank more coffee, then put the cup down. "Grappa, you said, Commissario?" A gesture. "I'm afraid there's no alcohol in the house."

"Two spoonfuls of sugar will suffice."

"The same sweet tooth?"

"Dell'Orto sent me on a wild goose chase looking for some dead woman. He lied to me. He was my friend and he lied to me."

"He lied, Commissario. Because what had happened here—in this villa—had become a point of honor for him. He had acted out of friendship—or if you wish, he had helped a "fratello" . . . in those days, I was a freemason, too. But Dell'Orto was a man of law, a man of the Republic and he knew that he had made use of his position for my sake. It was something that he had accepted; but it still hurt him. Because it made him realize . . ." Again Ramoverde shrugged. "It made him realize that in fact there wasn't really any difference between him and Baldassare. Of course, he had behaved selflessly—what he did he did for my sake. But the fact remained that he had sacrificed his idea of Republican justice for his idea of masonic aid." He watched Trotti spoon sugar into the cup and then drink the coffee. "Above all else, he did not want you to know that. Not you, Commissario—because you were somebody like him. Somebody special—somebody with the same values. That's why he killed himself."

Trotti put the cup down and stood up. "Are you trying to

tell me that Dell'Orto died because he didn't want me to know about his past?"

"He was going to die anyway." Ramoverde's eyes followed Trotti as he started to pace up and down the marble of the hall, the coffee cup in his hand. "He was going to die anyway—and he didn't want to live. He felt that he had sent my son to his death. Or rather, had taken him in the hired car to meet his appointment with death. I tried to dissuade him. I told him that my son knew what risks he was taking—it was my son's idea to give you the stolen money and even if Dell'Orto hadn't known about your trip to the Lake, Giovanni would have found another way of meeting you. Meeting you in private, and talking to you confidentially. But the old Judge didn't want to listen. He talked about Belluno and he talked about the past and he talked about you, Commissario. And he talked about Genoveffa. And by the time I left him, I realized that he wanted to be with his wife again."

He shrugged. "A last pill, a last cup of good coffee—the best coffee in the city—and then die in the sunshine, knowing that he would soon be with his wife—you know, there are worse ways for an old man to die."

"Like in prison, Signor Ramoverde."

"I wonder if she weighs a hundred kilos in heaven."

67: Sampierdarena

It was my first love.

She was more than ten years older than me and at first I just looked at her from a distance, admiring her. It was not until Christmas—Christmas 1959—that I realized that my feelings were reciprocated.

Looking back, it all seems so strange—childish, even. And that is how it ought to have ended—a first love, something intense and magical for a few months and then, inevitably, we would have grown tired of each other. But that never happened. Instead we both talked of marriage. Indeed, Eva was talking of marriage when she was killed.

She was running the bath—it must have been past midnight and I was sitting on the bathroom stool. I can still remember its cork surface. Sitting with my back to the door and Eva quietly getting undressed to take her bath. We were not bothered by the thought that we might be disturbed. For several weeks now she had been putting something into his evening drink—not just to

*put him to sleep at night but to make him less arduous during
the day as well. Lately he had become more aggressive. There were
times when he would fly off the handle even with me—and I was
his favorite. Mama and Papa worried about him, worried about
the change in grandfather's behavior. I never told them about the
little pills we bought from the herbalist in Castelveltro.*

*We were chatting, Eva and I, making plans, talking of
marriage—a twenty-eight-year-old woman who admitted to
already having an abortion, and a seventeen-year-old spoiled
brat. I think we were both rather proud of ourselves—she in having fooled the Nonno into thinking that she felt tender emotion
for him, and me because I had managed to convince Papa that
an adventure with Eva was the only way he could ever save the
three villas from her hands. Of course, Eva had no intention of
marrying old Ismaele—and she was not particularly interested
in his will. If she put on airs, it was all a ploy. The more she
appeared to be counting on my grandfather's will, the more
Mama and Papa played into our hands. It was all tremendous
fun. And so we sat in the bathroom, young, happy, laughing and
in love. And that night, we didn't even make love—it was the
wrong time of the month. Just talking and happy to be together.
We were really in love—what had started out as a game for me
had become something quite, quite different. And then suddenly
the Nonno came bursting in. He struck me immediately and he
must have used the onyx paperweight because when I gathered
my senses he was bent over the bathtub, foaming at the mouth
and holding her down. He was swearing at her, calling her a
whore and a bitch and other words in his Pugliese dialect. He did
not hear me get to my feet and he took no notice of me when I
tried to pull him away. I tugged at his arm. He was an old man
but there was the strength of the devil in him. The strength of
the cuckold.*

I picked up the paperweight and I struck him.

*I did not kill him but the sight—the sight of him lying like a
landed fish, his eyes open and the mixture of blood and mucus
that poured from his mouth and nose—terrified me.*

Later a witness was to say that she had heard a scream.

Perhaps it was mine. I do not kn0w if I screamed—I cannot remember. But I recall staring down at him, not knowing what to do. I did not even think of the girl. Then I came to my senses at last. I remember feeling ashamed that I had wetted myself and my trousers were damp. Quite suddenly I found myself thinking clearly and I left them both. Perhaps she was dead already or perhaps I could have saved her. If I had pulled her from the water and given her respiration, perhaps she might have regained consciousness. Instead of trying to help her, I rushed from the bathroom, went down the stairs and climbed through the window.

Papa was asleep in the car. Goodness knows what he must have thought when I awoke him and he saw me covered in blood. It was at that moment I must have left stains on the front seat. Of course, Papa knew what to do. He calmed me down, told me to explain what had happened and he accompanied me back to the Villa.

Medically and legally speaking, it was Papa who killed Nonno Ismaele. He felt there was no choice. He hit him once— very hard with the onyx and then dragged the corpse halfway down the stairs. It was horrid and I watched with amazement as Papa worked so methodically. Of course, he had studied as a doctor and he must have seen corpses before in the hospital. But for me—it was all terrifyingly impressive.

He then cleaned up the bathroom, wiping away the sill and all the other places where I might have left my fingerprints. He spent over an hour wiping everything with the meticulous attention of a Charterhouse monk. Fortunately, when Eva had let me into the house, I had accompanied her immediately upstairs and apart from the bathroom, there were few places where I had left my prints. As it happened, several were found—but as a regular visitor to the Villa Laura, it was only normal that my fingerprints should be there, along with Mama's and Papa's. Then with the same, clinical detachment, Papa smeared blood on the walls of Eva's bedroom. To make it look like rape, he said.

Before we left, I took a last look at Eva.

She lay in the bath and her battered face was pale. The bath water was cold by now, and red with blood. She looked like a child.

Papa turned off the current at the fuse box and then we crept out of the back window.

We drove to Voghera where I was to catch the train. Papa parked in the dark outside the station. He wanted to buy the ticket for me but in the end, I did. The front of my face was not even bruised—and the lump on the side of my skull went down long before the police ever came to see us. There was a long wait for the train and during that time I sat in the car, Papa made his phone call. It was already past three o'clock in the morning, but fortunately no one ever saw him at Voghera station—or at least, no one recognized him.

It is possible that if Dell'Orto had had more time to think, he would have come up with a different plan. Possible but not certain. The point is that both Papa and Dell'Orto agreed that for me to be safe, for me to be above all suspicion, there would have to be another possible culprit. Papa would never have accepted that I should confess the truth to the police. And so, with the active support of Dell'Orto, Papa agreed to become the scapegoat. He acted out of love and I don't think it ever occurred to him that perhaps he would not be found guilty. Many years later he told me that he acted out of self-interest. He said that if ever the truth had come out and it had been discovered that not only had he been aware of the relationship between me and Eva, but that he had even gone so far as to encourage—organize, even—our meetings, then his reputation would have been ruined definitively. Admit that he had pimped for his son, admit that he had allowed his son to carry on with a maid so that the family fortune should never end up in her hands?

But I know Papa and I know that his only concern was for my well-being. In his cold, detached way he has always loved me. And I have always loved him, though I sometimes wish that I had never inherited the recklessness that was in his blood.

And so I returned to San Remo.

At Genoa Sampierdarena I had to change trains. It was there that I broke down and started to weep. To weep like a child while I hid in the dark, empty compartment.

I reached San Remo just before dawn.

68: Garda

FROM MILAN TO Brescia the train was crowded and although they had first-class tickets, it was impossible to talk, impossible to sleep. Pioppi looked out of the window at the monotonous countryside while Magagna read the paper.

They got off at Desenzano and took a taxi to the port.

A cool breeze came down from the mountains and blew the length of the lake—a cool, fresh wind that ruffled through Pioppi's hair and for the first time since leaving the Policlinico she smiled. Trotti took her by the arm and they went aboard the *Giuseppe Verdi.*

Later there was a short blast of the horn, and the boat pulled out across the water and headed towards the open lake. The sky was cloudless but the lakeside soon grew misty in the afternoon haze. Pioppi went to the aft rail and stared at the green water as it was churned by the propellers. Trotti noticed out of the corner of his eye that one of the officers glanced at her from time to time.

Later when Trotti turned to look, he saw that the man was in conversation with Pioppi. She was smiling and he was pointing towards the faint outline of the Pre-Alps.

Magagna sat down beside Trotti and lit a cigarette.

"Why do you smoke those things? They're expensive and they're bad for you. When I smoked, I used to smoke Nazionali."

Magagna laughed.

"It's not funny."

"I gave up eating sweets when I was a kid." In the same breath, Magagna went on, "I still don't understand who killed him."

"Him?"

"Maltese."

"You read the notes he wrote."

Magagna shook his head. "I had a look at them while you were having lunch in Milan, Commissario. But not at length. There wasn't time—you were in a hurry to get to the Villa Laura."

"I didn't stop you from looking at the dossier."

Magagna let the smoke escape from his mouth; the grey wisps were carried away by the breeze. "He was working on the P-Beta, wasn't he?"

"Maltese?" Trotti nodded. "It was probably Dell'Orto who put him in touch with Novara. With his knowledge of the Banco Milanese's dealings in South America, he was the man Novara needed. But that wasn't what either Dell'Orto or Maltese were really interested in. Dell'Orto had an old score to settle with Baldassare and he thought that Maltese was the right man." He paused, turned to glance at Pioppi. "Maltese owed the judge a favor—and anyway there wasn't anything else for him to do. He was out of work—he'd been out of work for nearly two years. But with the information from Dell'Orto he had the beginnings of a book—a book that he hoped he'd be able to sell to the Germans or the Americans."

"Then why the Night of the Tazebao? It brought him out in the open."

"Out of friendship for Dell'Orto, probably. Or perhaps he

didn't care—or perhaps he felt that he had enough information to get on with."

"And that's why Pergola got shot."

Trotti laughed then. "Good." Still smiling, he turned and looked out over the lake. They were approaching the Veneto coastline. Like toy soldiers standing to attention, standing shoulder to shoulder, there were rows of cypress trees. Sirmione and the castle formed a misty horizon further south.

"You're jeering, Commissario."

"Not at all. But you've realized that robbery was never a motive."

"A hundred million lire is a lot of money. It would keep you in Charms . . ."

"And you in Murattis—it would even pay for your hospital bills." Trotti frowned. "Cigarette smoking makes you aggressive."

For a few instants Magagna was silent, sulking. Then he said, "I thought you said you wanted me to come with you to your Villa Ondina for the weekend."

"I said I wanted somebody to keep my daughter company."

"And that's why you've invited my wife and me?"

"You've been invited for Pioppi's sake."

"If you want, Commissario Trotti, I can get off at Sirmione or Garda and get a coach back to Milan."

Trotti held out his hand. "Here, give me a cigarette."

Silently, Magagna took the packet from his pocket and handed it to Trotti. Trotti extracted a cigarette, snapped off the yellow filter. "Now give me a light."

Magagna did as he was told.

"First time I've smoked since I saw that corpse in the river." He turned and gave Magagna a wide grin. "You know that I wish you'd never left the Questura for Narcotici in Milan."

"I didn't want to leave."

"Pisanelli might be coming too."

"What?"

"I told Pisanelli that if he and the psychiatric student wanted to get away from the city for a few days they would be welcome . . . and that there were plenty of dusty bottles in the cellar waiting for him to come and open." Trotti laughed. "I could see his eyes light up."

"You're almost human."

"Almost." Again Trotti smiled and inhaled on the cigarette. "I prefer the black tobacco of Italian cigarettes."

Magagna shrugged. "Tell me about Pergola."

"There's nothing to say. Or very little. He must have at one time told Dell'Orto of his disenchantment with the P-Beta and that's why Dell'Orto sent Maltese to see him. It was about the time—a week before, I think—of the Tazebao. That's why Maltese gave him his name as Ramoverde. And wittingly or unwittingly, Pergola told him about P- Beta—told him things that he should not have revealed."

"You don't like Pergola, do you, Commissario?"

"Pergola is a courageous man. He came to see me and he knew that the bullets in his leg had been a warning. A warning from the mafia that calls itself a masonic lodge. He knew that Novara had been killed in Paris and that Maltese was murdered here on the lake. But despite that, he had the courage to come and see me—in the Questura—and tell me what he knew. I can admire that."

"But you don't like him."

Trotti removed the cigarette from his mouth. "It's not a policeman's job to like or dislike."

"You never answer my questions."

"What d'you want me to say?" Before Magagna could speak, Trotti continued, "The robbery at the Banca San Matteo was just a way of veiling the threat. Pergola realized that—and so did the Sardinians."

"Sardinians?"

"Uras and Suergiu—the two men who beat me up. They thought I was the journalist who was going to pay them for their confessions. They were in Gardesana and they saw Maltese get killed. That's why they followed me—they wanted the money that Maltese was going to give them for their confessions."

"What confessions?"

"They took part in the robbery at the Banca San Matteo—but

when they got only a fraction of the money they'd been promised, they realized they'd been cheated. And they realized that they'd been used. They were working with professional killers—the same gun used on Pergola killed Maltese—and almost killed me."

"We don't want to lose you, Commissario."

Trotti dropped the cigarette stub to the deck and ground it out.

"They knew Dell'Orto and they contacted him." Trotti shook his head. "This was all in Maltese's papers."

The *Giuseppe Verdi* hooted and slowly approached the small port of Sirmione.

"They knew that there was something odd about the shooting and they thought they could make some money. Dell'Orto told Maltese and I can only assume that in addition to paying for the stolen money he must have offered them extra cash. And they probably thought that cash was coming from me."

"But how did they know that Maltese was driving up to the lake to meet you?"

"Dell'Orto."

Magagna shook his head.

"Dell'Orto told them. And they saw me with him and then they saw him get killed. They were probably in one of the parked cars along the quayside. And so they felt cheated—and they hoped to retrieve their five hundred thousand lire."

"And give you a few bruises."

"And a broken tooth." He ran his tongue along the jagged edge of the tooth. "But they've paid for all that."

"Paid—or were made to pay."

"It was a mafia killing." Trotti smiled. "You know, Spadano phoned me this morning to say I could pick up the Opel."

"You could drive a car that's had two corpses in the trunk?"

Trotti shrugged. "They didn't deserve to die—but to the southern way of thinking, they'd betrayed their word. Omertà. Instead of cutting out their tongues, the killers chopped their hands off. Grisly."

"And not very easy."

"You can understand Dell'Orto. He believed in freemasonry.

When he was a young man, it was an alternative to fascism—
something in the place of fascist philosophy. Something better
in the place of fascism. And then to see Baldassare—an upstart,
not a doctor or a lawyer but somebody who had probably bought
all his architectural diplomas—to see a man like that taking the
P-Beta and transforming it into his own power-base, transforming it into a means of holding some of the best men of this nation
to ransom . . . it shocked and disgusted him. And making use
of the mafia, making use of hired killers to do his dirty work—
that is what Dell'Orto was fighting against. It's what he'd been
fighting ever since the Gran Maestro had put Baldassare into
the P-Beta. Dell'Orto knew that when Maltese was murdered,
he was defeated. He knew that there was nothing he could do
about Baldassare or the P-Beta."

"He could have told you the truth."

"You remember Gracchi, Magagna?"

Magagna ran his finger along the line of his mustache.
"Guerra's old boyfriend? The middle-class terrorist."

"Middle-class terrorist perhaps, but I remember when we
caught him—I think you were with me. We caught him and he
started ranting and raving, and accusing us of being in the pay
of the fascist state—all that revolutionary stuff. And he seemed
to believe it. I found him pathetic. If he'd been my own son, I
think I would have slapped him and told him to grow up. But
there was something he said—about violence being a trap and
that we're all caught up in it. I couldn't help thinking about Gracchi when I was reading through Maltese's notes—his notes on
P-Beta and what it had done. How, with his friends, Baldassare
had encouraged terrorism, the bombs on the *Italicus*, and the
whole philosophy of the strategy of tension."

"You're not suggesting that P-Beta has been responsible for
the years of violence?"

"P-Beta may not have been the sole cause—but it has its share
of responsibility. Forty years ago, Baldassare sought power by
dressing up in a black shirt and leading SS columns to the partisans in the Po valley. He learned his lesson. Power in Italy now
resides elsewhere. Not in Parliament, not in a democracy but in

the submerged state—and perhaps Gracchi wasn't so far off the mark when he accused us of being accomplices." Trotti gave a thin smile. "Unwitting accomplices—but accomplices all the same."

"What are you going to do?"

"Do?"

"Baldassare directly or indirectly was behind the death of Maltese—what d'you intend to do?" A shrug of the broad shoulders. "A dangerous and powerful man . . . and you slap him around, accuse him of playing with your daughter and her emotions."

Trotti said, "Pioppi wanted to bring her urbanistica books with her."

"What are you going to do, Commissario?"

He said nothing.

"You're scared?"

"You don't understand, Magagna. Baldassare uses the mafia—but he's not a mafioso. He's not going to have me thrown into the Po just because I tipped his books on to the floor. In his way, I doubt if he could care less—and he's not going to send some psychopath to do knife-work on my skin." He shook his head. "Baldassare is not worried about his self-esteem. What he is concerned with is his power—and he knows that there's nothing that I can do. What can I do? Even if it were possible to prove that he was behind the death of Maltese and the murder of the two Sardinians, what could I hope for? When most of the judges in this country are his collaborators? When they belong to the same secret society, the same P-Beta . . . or to another secret lodge just like it?"

"Then Maltese died in vain?"

"Everybody dies in vain if there is still the chance of staying alive, of eating food and breathing the air. Of course Maltese failed. He's dead and he'll never see this lake again—he'll never see Garda as you and I and Pioppi are seeing it now—beautiful and timeless."

For a moment Trotti said nothing. Then he took out the packet of sweets. "But that doesn't mean that Baldassare is untouchable."

"Then you plan something?"

Trotti snorted. "Not much that I can do. If Dell'Orto was helpless, what do you expect from me?"

"Then what happens, Commissario?"

"There are other people and they're going to be jealous of his power. Eventually he'll have to face up to people who will want him removed. Look at Bastia—Bastia at the Banco Milanese who thought that he was untouchable—who thought that he could sell Scalfari to the American police. But the Night of the Tazebao changed all that—and Bastia was scared, very scared. Who could he turn to for help? There is just one man—the boss of P-Beta. And so Bastia went running to Baldassare, begging him to patch things up between him and Scalfari in his American jail." Trotti stopped. "You should read what Maltese has to say."

"What does Maltese have to say, Commissario?"

"Bastia's days are numbered. He worked his way to the head of one of the country's most respected banks—and he's brought it to the edge of collapse. There will be a day of reckoning—and that is inevitable. Perhaps he'll just quietly disappear—or perhaps he'll be shot to death—like Novara—in a Paris street. Or perhaps his body will be found hanging in London. But the day of reckoning will come because he overreached himself."

"And Baldassare?"

"He will go. Perhaps not now and certainly not because of me. Magagna, don't count on the Pubblica Sicurezza or the Carabinieri or the Finanza to reach Baldassare because we never will. A university professor above all suspicion?—and with so many friends in high places? Don't count on this puppet Republic ever turning round and doing something about the puppeteer. But there are countries other than Italy, thank God. And if the Americans can arrest Scalfari perhaps in time they can arrest Baldassare. He'll get more powerful and the Americans won't like that. Or perhaps the French. Or perhaps the Swiss." Trotti glanced again at his daughter. Then he said, "In time, Baldassare will go. Just as with the mafia, he'll be killed or he'll be edged out. He'll disappear because ultimately he's no more than a symptom—an ulcer on the surface of the Republic. But the disease will remain. The disease will remain because it is in us, it is part of us. We are the disease, Magagna, and the disease is Italy."

69: *Giuseppe Verdi*

DUSK HAD BEGUN to fall by the time the *Giuseppe Verdi* sailed round the promontory at Bogliaco and the village of Gardesana came into sight. Olive trees, red tiles, the remaining lemon groves and, rising out of the mist at evening, the village church.

Pioppi had come to sit with them. She now sat with her hands on the rail and her chin propped between her fingers. She was smiling to herself. Trotti was beside her and his body almost touched hers, though she had her back to him.

Magagna had been silent for some time. Then he leaned forward and said, "And Guerra?"

"What about her?"

"There's still something I don't understand." He nudged at the teardrop frames.

"I like the way you think I know all the answers." Trotti laughed. His temper was improving as he got closer to the village.

"Maltese . . . why did he stay with her?"

"It was her uncle who sent Maltese to her. Dell'Orto was trying to help her and he must have sent her money from time to time—including the fifty thousand lire bills that so impressed your friend Marco."

"A faggot."

"Milan hasn't made you very tolerant, Magagna."

"He lied to you a lot. Dell'Orto. For somebody who respected you, he didn't object to leading you up the garden path."

Trotti said nothing for a while. Then when he spoke, his voice was soft. "Yes, I think he did respect me. And he didn't want me to know about his behavior over the Ramoverde affair. It was something that he felt ashamed of. Because even then, twenty years ago, he had lied to me. And that would explain why even after Maltese had been killed, he couldn't bring himself to tell me the truth." He raised his hand and touched the small of Pioppi's curved back. She turned and gave him a brief smile. "He felt that he personally couldn't tell me anything without revealing his involvement in the Ramoverde affair. He had wanted Maltese to tell me about P-Beta and the shooting at the Banca San Matteo—because he hoped that I'd be able to do something. He didn't know that the Banca San Matteo dossier had been taken from out of my hands." Trotti smiled. "Dell'Orto had a blind kind of faith in me."

"What could you have done?"

"What can I do now? Nothing—there's nothing I can do about Baldassare and there's nothing I can do about the P-Beta."

The boat cut through the water that was now as smooth as glass in the failing evening light.

On the far side of the water, high above Malcesine, Monte Baldo caught the last rays of sunlight, and the runnels along the mountain's flank were intricate and clear.

In Gardesana, men and women were walking along the Lungolago. There were children playing. And Trotti noticed, standing near the small harbor, the black uniform of two Carabinieri. The *Giuseppe Verdi* let out a mournful hoot as it moved towards the quay. An officer, standing on the deck only a couple of meters away from Pioppi, threw the rope to the Capitano, who caught it and looped it round a bollard. Both men spoke in dialect and Trotti saw the Capitano laugh.

The *Giuseppe Verdi* bumped against the old tires and then a gangway was heaved into place.

Trotti got to his feet and he was helping his daughter towards the gangplank. The Capitano caught sight of Trotti.

Trotti shouted, "Ciao, il marinaio!"

The Capitano replied, "Ciao, il Questurino!" and flashed

his false teeth. He started moving up the gangplank and took hold of Pioppi. He lifted her bodily—although she was several centimeters taller than him—and carried her on to dry land.

Trotti and Magagna came down the plank on to the jetty.

There was shouting.

Gardesana smelled of orange blossom and Trotti smiled happily.

More shouting and he saw Guerino, a cloth over his shoulder and a tray in his hand, hurrying across the road towards him. He was grinning and in his Roman accent, he called out, "Telephone, Commissario, telephone."

Magagna turned.

"Hurry, Commissario—and I think it's Agnese."

Trotti started to run towards the Bar Centomiglia.

"It's your wife, I think."

"Where's she phoning from? Is she phoning from America?"

"America?" Guerino threw up his hand in a gesture of mock exasperation and then he slapped Trotti on the shoulder. "From Malpensa, you mean. She's at the airport and she wants you to get a taxi for her."

The juke box had been turned on and, in the gathering dusk, the neon light seemed to illuminate the entire wall. Bobby Solo and Fausto Leali.

Trotti entered the familiar bar. The smell of coffee. He headed towards the telephone booth. He was smiling.

The rear propeller of the *Giuseppe Verdi* began churning the water and the hull swung away from the land.

Other Titles in the Soho Crime Series